THE PEOPLE WHO REPORT MORE STRESS

ALSO BY ALEJANDRO VARELA

The Town of Babylon

THE PEOPLE WHO REPORT MORE STRESS

STORIES

ALEJANDRO VARELA

ASTRA HOUSE ∧ NEW YORK

For information about permission to reproduce selections from this book, please
contact permissions@astrahouse.com.

Various stories from this collection first appeared in the following publications:
"An Other Man" in *The Rumpus*; "She and Her Kid and Me and Mine" in
Blunderbuss Magazine; "Carlitos in Charge" in *Harper's Magazine*; "The People
Who Report More Stress" in *Boston Magazine*; "The Great Potato Famine" in
Split Lip Magazine as "Taxi! (Spring)"; and "The Six Times of Alan" in *The
Hopkins Review*.

This is a work of fiction. Names, characters, places, and incidents are products of
the author's imagination or are used fictitiously. Any resemblance to actual
events, locales, or persons, living or dead, is entirely coincidental.

Astra House
A Division of Astra Publishing House
astrahouse.com
Printed in the United States of America

Library of Congress Cataloging-in-Publication Data

Names: Varela, Alejandro, 1979– author.
Title: The people who report more stress : stories / by Alejandro Varela.
Description: First edition. | New York : Astra House, [2023] | Summary:
"The People Who Report More Stress is a collection of connected stories
examining issues of parenting, systemic and interpersonal racism, and
class conflict in gentrified Brooklyn"—Provided by publisher.
Identifiers: LCCN 2022045372 (print) | LCCN 2022045373 (ebook) |
ISBN 9781662601071 (hardcover) | ISBN 9781662601088 (ebook)
Subjects: LCGFT: Short stories.
Classification: LCC PS3622.A7413 P46 2023 (print) |
LCC PS3622.A7413 (ebook) | DDC 813/.6—dc23/eng/20220928
LC record available at https://lccn.loc.gov/2022045372
LC ebook record available at https://lccn.loc.gov/2022045373

First edition
10 9 8 7 6 5 4 3 2 1

Design by Richard Oriolo
The text is set in Adobe Jenson Pro Regular.
The titles are set in Helvetica Neue LT Std.

I dedicate this book to all the people who stay focused on the upstream causes and solutions;

To everyone who retreats to their psyches because they've been excluded from the conversation;
To the people who wouldn't dare bring their dogs to a children's playground in a city defined by inequities;
To my parents—Maria, Ernesto, Miriam;
And, as always, to Matias

In memory of Gene—what a wonderful guy he was;
And Rosario, a warrior.

CONTENTS

THE PEOPLE WHO REPORT MORE STRESS

AN OTHER MAN

IT'S LATE JULY, AND YOU'RE sitting on a stoop covered in faint cracks. The scorching brownstone beneath your thighs is crossing slowly into unbearable when, all of a sudden, the postcard across the street—a sylvan park, a profusion of inquisitive dogs and distracted owners, toddling children and rigid adults—reveals a group of Frisbee-playing twenty-somethings. What begins as a harmless, anthropologic scan of skinny legs, knee-length denim, and Victorian mustaches descends into an obsessive survey of mounds, mesas, and bulges—more often than not, they catch the flying disc. Your husband, who burns easily, is sitting in the sliver of shade beside you. He is unaware of the panorama, immersed instead in the science-fiction novel he downloaded onto his phone. His pale white feet rest over his sandals' brown leather straps; knobby toes grope purely decorative buckles. He's been wearing these sandals since you met him. He orders a new pair every few years. These are his fourth.

"The heat makes it worse," he says, while balancing Octavia Butler on his superhero thighs. "The exposed skin roaming around always does this to you." His voice is free of judgment, almost bereft of it, but its certainty dredges up a gnarled tire of your own shame.

"How can we be so different from each other?" you wonder before saying aloud.

"If this is going to gnaw at you, then just do it," he says and places his hand on your lap, less a lover and more a coach; both are a turn-on. "I'm not worried about us. I'm only worried you'll beat yourself up afterward."

These are words you would never say to him. You can't imagine a deathbed scenario where you could be so magnanimous.

"What if you end up wanting to do it, too?"

"I won't."

You believe him, but you fear going up in a hot air balloon full of imperceptible tears. On the other hand, it's just sex.

"Once we have kids, this'll all get more complicated, logistically speaking," he says. "Might as well do it now."

"I'll give it some thought," you say.

You begin by downloading online dating applications. First, one. Then, two. You draw the line after three. Before you can even ponder your decision, faces appear. They fill your phone's screen, in grid formation. A few of the squares are recognizable: acquaintances predominantly, a few neighbors, and possibly a poorly lit coworker. You resist an urge to say hello, fearing you'll impinge on Internet etiquette or that your greetings might be misconstrued. You worry that the people who recognize you will think you're cheating. You panic, disable your profiles, and disappear. You do this three times. A few days pass, and you re-enable everything.

You try to be innovative with your greetings ("What do you think: one- or two-state solution?") and pleasant with your rejections ("I appreciate you reaching out, but I don't sense compatibility"). You chat and endure the eternal pauses. You are hamstrung by the reliance on punctuation as a conduit for emotions—a misplaced semicolon can rapidly alter the mood; exclamation points are ubiquitous and no longer connote the urgency they did pre-Internet. You're awkward about addressing sexually transmissible infections: you had crabs when you were nineteen, but sharing that feels like an unreasonable standard of honesty. What about HPV? Does that require an announcement? *Likes*, *barks*, and graphic images appear as if from nowhere. A few conversations escalate, but you don't commit to meeting anyone.

You get ignored too.

One man says he likes his men fiery and that you have a Ricky Martin vibe. Another, younger than you, says he's not into your people: "no offense." Before you can contemplate whether the Digital Age is, in some ways, undoing progress, you secretly marvel at his honesty. You swipe away. You block. You disable and delete, again. You uninstall. You give up. You try watching porn. Every day is a new day. And after a few new days, you try again—there are no limits to downloading and reinstalling.

Tweaking your profiles becomes a compulsion. You overvalue yourself. You undervalue yourself. You add a year to your age because numbers that end in 5 or 0 look commanding. You subtract two because numbers that end in 5 or 0 begin to look too neat to be believed. You aim for humorous and self-effacing. You don't post naked pictures for fear of destroying a career in politics that is nowhere on your horizon. Before long, you start sending tasteful, faceless nudes to appease the men who are interested. One night, after your husband has gone to bed, after you've convinced yourself that anonymity is a devolution, after your second homemade martini, you send explicit and easily identifiable images to a "banker with a swimmer's build." You accept that you are not cut out for elected office. You'd rather be an agitator anyway, though you have no history of agitating. You never meet the banker.

You're drawn to charming profiles with hints of self-awareness and intelligence. Salt-and-pepper hair, average bodies, and dorky demeanors are especially appealing. You prefer subtlety and clothed images. You equate explicit images with a depravity that you quickly intellectualize as internalized homophobia, which, you remind yourself, is just misogyny by another name, one more of capitalism's divide-and-conquer tactics. You wonder if it's possible to transform this reasoning into a palatable campaign slogan.

You continue searching, but the guilt rarely subsides. Not only does this digital cruising feel like cheating, you also have an unfair advantage. You are, after all, playing with house money. There are men on these apps looking for love; you already have that. Come to think of it, the similarities between the men on your screen to whom you are most drawn and your husband are impossible to ignore. You put the phone down and go for a run. At mile four, you decide to give up on white men altogether because of the intrinsic power dynamics— some things are undone during sex; others are magnified.

Sidestepping white men proves an onerous task on a distance-based application in a hyper-gentrified neighborhood.

You focus on men who are direct about their proclivities and desires—but not too direct. You are especially curious about anyone who identifies as radical, a fairy, or an anarchist—you are keenly aware of the distances you are trying to bridge.

Some men list sex without condoms as a precondition. You mull it over. But every public health message of the last twenty-five years flashes through your mind, and you just can't, even if they are regularly tested for infections, even if their viral loads are undetectable, even if the science is on everyone's side, even if their beauty feels like a prophylaxis. You desist and remain bothered by the implications.

You contemplate calling your therapist, but it's been a while. Besides, he's the last person with whom you'd want to dissect your sex life.

"Describe your type," you say to your husband while pointing to your phone. "Maybe he's on here." It's almost noon on a cloudy Saturday of a nothing-special weekend in August. You're both in your underwear, draped over the couch and each other. Your husband shrugs with one shoulder and one cheekbone, but you insist, and he begins listing attributes. He clumsily concocts you, and a proud smile takes over his face. Before you can slide his boxer-briefs down to his knees and swallow his cock, he looks up at the window: "Do you think we should re-pot the basil plant?"

Afterward, he naps. He always naps.

Your search continues. The phone regularly emits dings and whistles, but your husband doesn't hear them, or pretends not to.

Doesn't he know that a hint of jealousy might signal an end to your extramarital desires? Doesn't he know that his territoriality would turn you on? Doesn't he know that a middle-child's craving for attention is an almost subcellular penury that requires an entire reimagining of society's economic structure? The answer is yes. You've told him this, many times before, but he's terrible at roleplaying. He simply cannot act out what he does not feel. You can say, without embellishment, that you married the most self-assured person you have ever known. No one is less afraid to raise his hand in a crowded auditorium, send back an overcooked steak, or share his spouse. And never in a mean-spirited manner. Always matter of fact.

You've been with him for most of your adult years. Plenty of time to observe and overthink. And you've surmised that your disparities in temperament, self-efficacy, and propensity for obsession are likely a function of your trajectories and positions in society's hierarchy—as a researcher in a field of the social sciences, you feel equipped to draw these types of conclusions. He's white; you're brown. He was raised in a home with more staff than family members; you've been conditioned to eat rice and beans for months at a time if the circumstances should so dictate. In moments of stress, everything in you travels with the speed and tidiness of lava on the descent; in him is a durable glass beaker with a finely calibrated release valve.

And yet, your love isn't only measured in distances. You're both gay men with degrees. You read the same things. You can have a conversation without straining in either direction. All the leveling that's happened naturally over the years has made you a Venn diagram with a beautiful, comforting, and egg-shaped overlap. And that may be the best you'll ever be. Anything else would be inauthentic.

Or maybe you can't work race and class into everything, hard as you try. It's quite possible you just come from a long line of libidinous Lotharios; whereas his chaste chromosomes line up neatly, barely touching. Who's to say?

You keep to your conjugal schedule—Wednesday nights and Saturday afternoons. And when your husband leaves the room or nods off, your hunting resumes in earnest.

Cruising was once anxiety inducing and soul shaking—docks, crowded streets, empty streets, public restrooms, changing rooms at The GAP, interstate rest stops. It was a fevered, and often crapulous, pursuit for the cup of Christ, more exciting for the journey than the stemware. The online version is less personal, while somehow more invasive. And frenetic. At every single moment, you know if there are cis, trans, or gender-nonconforming bears, cubs, hungry otters, silver foxes, discreet jocks, and leather geeks within a five-hundred-foot radius. The wealth of options is arousing and disorienting.

Noteworthy leads are thwarted by incompatible schedules. They disappear; you do too. This is more difficult than you imagined. A kid, a candy store, bins that are out of reach. It's been nearly a month since this all began, and most everyone fits into one of three undesirable categories: no, distracted, or possibly perfect. Perfect, as you well know, is the enemy. Under no circumstances do you want to fall in love. You want to play out fantasies while avoiding antibiotics, antiretrovirals, and body lice. Nothing more. The target is increasingly smaller, but you keep giving it your all. Life imitates carnival game.

The problem might not be the game, you realize, but instead, the player. You begin to feel old in a virtual space where your age isn't far from the median. It's not only the culture—you could fill a bathtub with all the acronyms and pop references you don't know. It's the cadence too. This is a carousel that never slows to a point where you can board gracefully.

It's difficult to recall the feeling of truly meeting someone in person. The Internet traffics more men than a gay bar, but you don't recall so consistently leaving a gay bar alone. Maybe you did. That was a long time ago.

On a warm, sunlit evening when your husband works late, you find your way to a happy hour in the East Village. You approach with the trepidation of a tourist who doesn't understand all the signs and who is embarrassed to speak a language he studied only briefly in his youth. As cliché as it sounds, you still feel like the boy who'd tell his parents he was sleeping over a friend's place but who instead snuck into the city with a fake ID. Throw a backward baseball cap on, squint a little into the mirror, and you're not far off from that seventeen-year-old—your brown skin has brought you some grief over the years, but at least it refuses to crack. And yet, in this room, you are mid-career. Apart from the worn survivors nestled at one end of the bar, everyone else is in his late twenties or, worse, his early twenties. Near the other end of the bar, a group of coworkers or friends are celebrating a 30th birthday. A waste of time and energy, you think. Thirty means nothing. The overall vibe in the bar is more quirky than shiny. You nonetheless fear several types of discrimination at once. Intersections, you think.

You wait six minutes for a drink. You hate this. The bar is far from crowded. How could the bartender not have taken your order yet? Drinking establishments would do well to implement an equitable system of numbered tickets, like deli counters—both are meat markets, you think, before smiling at your own observation. To make matters worse, everyone the bartender is serving instead of you is white, a few of whom certainly arrived after you. This is why you prefer to stay home; this is why you splurge at the liquor store. Everything is being confirmed. The seconds race. The cortisol courses through your channels. You're already drafting a letter to the owner and rehearsing the call you'll make to the local community board if the letter goes unanswered, when, suddenly, he looks your way.

His hair is a pink faux-hawk; skin, blond. The straps on his tank top are dental floss; his mustache is a car wash. He has a bull ring in his nose and tattoos everywhere—unicorns, Roman numerals, quotes, a subway car. He makes it all work. He looks familiar. Very familiar. "Hi, honey, what can I get you?"

"Slightly dirty gin martini, straight up, three olives, a step up from well."

As he fills a smudged glass with imperfect cylinders of ice, you realize you've clapped eyes on this post-impressionistic figure before—the online matrix. By this point, you've seen the faces of several hundred queer, gay, or bisexual men in New York City, and the torsos, cocks, and asses of dozens more. Come to think of it, it's been days of double-takes and second glances.

"Here you are, darling." He sets the drink down on a small napkin without spilling a drop. His artistry is evident but understated.

"How much do I owe you?"

"Nothing. It's been taken care of."

"Really? Thank you," you say, feeling somewhat foolish for having assumed the worst of a working-class stiff who's living off of tipped minimum wage and probably wasn't thinking about skin color or socially constructed racial categories when he ignored you repeatedly only moments before. His lurch from villain to saint is swift.

"Don't thank me. Thank daddy over there." The bartender raises his chin toward a man too far down the bar for you to see clearly enough in the dim, red-filtered lighting. He has gray hair and a loose-fitting, short-sleeve button-down shirt, probably linen, either light green or blue. He's white or orange. You try to refuse the drink, but the bartender walks away before you can open your mouth. You indulge in the moment and raise your glass in gratitude, spilling a fifth of the martini in the process. Maybe no one noticed.

Your free drink begins to feel like a tether. Whenever you browse the room, you make unintended eye contact with your benefactor. You fear you might lead him on—this sweet, or lecherous, old man. You pull out your phone and look down. Seven of the people on your screen are within seven feet of you. None have pinged you. This isn't deflating, but neither is it insignificant. You cease browsing online for the sentient beings who are chatting, laughing, and releasing pheromones in the immediate vicinity. You listen instead to the music: Lisa Lisa and Cult Jam, Sylvester, Blondie. Gay bar jukeboxes today are indistinguishable from gay bar jukeboxes fifteen years ago, and possibly twenty-five. It's comforting to still feel like part of the club. A stakeholder. You finish your drink, savor the olives, and go to the bathroom.

When you return, your patron has taken your seat. You change course and head for the door, but he spins around on his stool with great ease. "Why the rush?"

"I'm late to meet my husband," you say, even though your dinner reservations aren't for another hour, and the restaurant is only a few blocks away.

"I guess all the gorgeous ones are taken," he says with the grin of a man who doesn't lose.

Up close, he's objectively attractive. Broad-shouldered. Late-fifties, not the vague early seventies you'd suspected at a distance. He's more than fit; possibly, strapping. He's Omar Sharif in hue and smolder. His large watch, a lattice of silver and gold wrapped around his wrist, is endearingly anachronistic. You wonder if sexy and avun-cular are mutually exclusive. You've always been attracted to older men, even if you don't have daddy issues—in fact, your dad is great and you get along quite well, and except for those complicated late-teen years, you always have. You believe older men can appreciate beauty in ways that contemporaries cannot. To be clear, you're into men who are older than you, not necessarily old men. This man is somewhere in between.

"What are you going to eat?"

"Cuban," you pull out of thin air.

"Oh. Where?"

"I didn't pick the place. I'd have to look." Another lie.

"I ask because, at some point or another, I've eaten at every Cuban restaurant in the city," he says with a subtle accent. Then he smiles, revealing neat, white teeth, like piano keys. They're real, you assume.

"Which is your favorite?" This—asking for authentic food rec-ommendations—is something you do. The circumstances don't need to change your ways.

"Well, I haven't been for some time, but it's across town, on Christopher," he says.

You feign ignorance. A familiar prejudice creeps up, and you're forced to remind yourself that New York Cubans aren't Miami

Cubans capable of tipping national elections unfavorably. Besides, this man might not be Cuban.

"I don't want to keep you," he says and leans forward, resting his hand on his knee. It's a virile hand, attached to a brawny forearm—this man could race up a tree faster than you. You feel simultaneously safe and inadequate. You stare for longer than you should. "I live upstairs," he continues, like a highly specialized surgeon. "How late are you?"

His eyes double in size, leeching the remaining light from an already drab room. He rises onto his sporty black loafers—he's not quite an inch shorter than you. You two are slow-dancing in a tenebrous and foggy hallucination, like Maria and Tony in *West Side Story*. You feel pretty. You haven't been in this situation since the second Bush's first term, and you're amazed at how familiar it is and at how quickly your blood is flowing. Your time-tested abilities to be evasive and witty have abandoned you. You purse your lips slightly, slide your tongue across your teeth, and squint. A faint tremble appears. You struggle to remember your husband. Beautiful man, but he's not a character in this vignette. You make your peace with that. "I'm not late at all," you say. You didn't have to say that.

"And whose acquaintance do I have the pleasure of making?" he asks.

"Ricky," you respond although it's not your name.

An extended hand materializes. "Mucho gusto, Ricky. Me llamo Guy," he says. You don't believe him, but you also don't care.

He leads the way out of the bar, up a brick stoop, then two doors, then two flights. As you climb, it crosses your mind to text your location to someone, just in case you're never seen again, but you can't decide to whom, and you're not sincerely afraid.

His apartment is long, white, and narrow for fourteen steps, then bursting bookshelves, floor to ceiling. Everywhere else: postmodern stacks—more books, some magazines—including a few skyscrapers on the glossy cherry wood floor. His living room is a fire hazard, but it's spotless and the chaos is perfectly curated. One pile is waist high and appears to be all astronomy books. Atop another is a self-help guide, unimaginatively titled, *Self-Help*. You begin to judge him and wonder if this is reason enough for you to leave. You glance at your phone.

From behind, his chin finds its way onto your shoulder. A delectable bouquet of cologne and deodorant feeds your senses in ways that a semicolon never could. His lips graze your ear with precision and heat—you wonder what he does for a living. He picks up the book you were only just eyeing. "She's very good. Have you read her work?" Side to side, your head turns, slowly caressing the prickliness of his shadow against your cheek. "If you're into short stories . . ." he says and taps the book against the air, before returning it to its rightful place. You feel stupid but grateful you erred toward silence moments earlier.

"Have you seen Venus?" he whispers directly into your ear, making every hair on your body stand. "She reappeared last week. If it were night, I would show you."

It takes a moment for you to realize that this isn't a figurative conversation. "Even with all of the city's lights?" you respond.

"That," he says, and points to an enormous black telescope by the farthest window, "is very powerful. You should come by one evening."

His lips devour your neck, and his hands travel assuredly across the rest. You bite down on your tongue to quell an unspecified chattering: Is this regret or possibility? Are you afraid or excited? When he pulls away and disappears, you look back briefly at the long hallway that led you here.

You're on an imperfectly painted bench in Tompkins Square Park, combing your hair with your tears and your fingers. You need to pull yourself together. A disconsolate brown man in an unabashedly gentrified neighborhood is the beginning of a below-the-fold news item. You take a deep breath, look out at the orange sky, and scan the park. It's busy, harmlessly peculiar, and casually segregated: New York City. You're staring at a postcard. You're always staring at a postcard, it seems.

What have you done? How could you have ruined something so beautiful? How will you ever look at your husband's face again? At your own? What would your mother say? This was what she'd feared all along. She'd seen your *lifestyle* as a condition, a relic of biblical times, an eccentricity that proved the downfall of grand civilizations— the Egyptians, the Greeks, the Romans, the 1980s. It took years for her to seem truly comfortable with your relationship, and now, here you are callously queering it up. Your ability to find a middle ground between your desires and your husband's apathy suddenly feels like a wasted compromise. You have typecast yourself.

A long, slanted shadow appears at your feet. At first, you don't look up because you assume it's a request for money or a request for directions that's ultimately a prelude to a request for money. The shadow remains.

His T-shirt is cut off at the shoulders; his shorts are frayed just above the knees. He's an urban castaway. His skin is of a hue similar to yours, but tauter and with more sheen. Youth, you realize, is relative. You're dripping snot, but embarrassment doesn't occur to you. He hands you a napkin from inside the paper bag where he's stored the falafel sandwich that he interrupted to come see about you. There's a small smear of tzatziki on his otherwise bare chin.

"Thank you," you say after blowing your nose.

"Why is such a cute guy crying on such a beautiful day?" he asks.

"I'm married," you respond with unwarranted force and hold up the hand with the finger that has the matted silver band you bought at an antique shop that had a glass cocktail shaker in its window.

"So what?" he says playfully before scanning you as conspicuously as anyone ever has.

Well if this isn't the kicker. If all you had to do was put away your phone, you might have done so weeks ago. You're still upset, but now irony or coincidence or both are hoisting you onto their shoulders. The world is much clearer up here, even if the line between cause and cure is muddled.

"An odd day, that's all," you tell your scene-stealing Puck as you rise to your feet—he's not quite an inch taller than you.

Your thigh vibrates. It's your husband. This is either his second call or his third text. You're fifteen minutes late. The restaurant is less than a block away. "Thanks for your concern, but I'm okay," you say, spreading the remaining tears with the back of one hand while the other surreptitiously silences the kind, loyal, uncomplicated interruption in your pocket.

"You sure?" The Nuyorican texture in this stranger's voice reminds you of what the neighborhood used to be like. His deep brown eyes are . . . truly something. Wow. Is this the meaning of puppy-dog eyes? You're not a pet person, so you honestly don't know.

"Yes, yes. Thank you," you say while forcing a smile.

"Can I have something before you go?" he asks. You're so entranced by his eyes you never see his lips move. "Your phone number," he continues, as he digs into his pockets. Triceps, marvelous. Everyone, it seems, has been at the gym for the last decade.

This encounter is intriguing but also unsettling. It shouldn't be this easy, you think. He's too forward. What if he's a cop? Or high? You fear he'll mount a campaign that won't allow you to leave the park quietly or, worse, will follow you all the way to your husband if you resist—there's endless gumption in those twenty-something cheekbones.

"Fine," you say, and pull out your phone. In your hands, it rings again. "Sorry, I really have to run. Another time."

You scan the faded bench for your belongings, but there's nothing there. Your eyes dart anxiously around the perimeter for a bag or jacket. This was all a ruse, you realize. He distracted you while his accomplices stole your things: New York 101. And you failed. You feel like a fool and also afraid. The odd sensation of being trapped in a wide-open space takes hold, until you remember that you left home with nothing. You also remember why you were here in the first place. You walk away.

At the precipice of Avenue A, he calls out to you, "L'Agrado!"

His high-top canvas shoes are wedged into the park's waist-high perimeter; the vertical bars frame his brawny, contoured legs—soccer or genetics. He's a foot off the ground, one hand gripping the wrought-iron railing. Now, he's Mercutio and Romeo, and the park's magic has trapped him. He's not going to follow. You were wrong about him. "It's my handle," he calls out. "Look for me. Anywhere!"

You nod and cross the street. You know Agrado. You know her well. She's the sex worker-turned-personal assistant in Almodovar's *Todo Sobre Mi Madre*, possibly your favorite of his films. Certainly, one of his greatest protagonists. This guy has just endeared himself to you in ways he couldn't possibly imagine. You're walking quickly, but that doesn't prevent you from perusing one of the three dating apps on your phone. There he is: "L'Agrado, 27 y/o. Bottom, powerful. Queer. Anarcho-syndicalist. Poet. Latinx. ¡Independencia pa' Puerto Rico o muerte! I am a shame-free zone. No bullshit hang-ups, please. #fuckwhitesupremacy."

You reach the restaurant and catch your reflection in its windows. You've looked better. The indisputable man of your life is in there somewhere, sipping slowly at his gin and tonic—his summer theme. An exhilarating fear flits through you. What if this is the onset of the undoing? Or, worse, the midpoint? Again, you remind yourself: it's just sex.

Before you open the door, you pivot eastward: a corridor of multicolored awnings, a laconic stream of glistening humans, an interstitial field of fleeting yellow cabs. In the distance, amongst the park's green giants, is the man. Just another. One of many. He is perched on the gate, looking at his phone. Waiting.

SHE AND HER
KID AND ME
AND MINE

"ARE YOU SURE?" SHE ASKS as we trot down the tree-lined street, barely able to keep up with our kids.

"No problem at all. I prefer him to be entertained with someone his age than drive me crazy," I respond before committing to a tight-lipped smile. "Besides, I don't have to pick up my youngest from daycare until later."

"Oh, perfect."

We approach my apartment building—a prewar, five-story brownstone tucked seamlessly between other prewar, five-story brown-stones. The block is a set of antique encyclopedias, and she lives only a few shelves away. I hoped she was walking us to my place to acquaint herself with where I live, and from where she'd have to pick up her son later. But she makes no mention of leaving and, instead, is now waiting for me to dig keys out of my pocket.

I'm to blame. We were fine outside, in the public playground, surrounded by a wrought-iron fence, on rubber turf. But then I went and got cold and peckish, so I gave my Julio an it's-almost-time nod, which led him, an intrepid four-year-old, to ask his pre-K buddy, another intrepid four-year-old, over to our place. All of which was still fine because it was a semiprivate interaction that I was tracking from across the jungle gym, but the conversation soon spilled over, engulfing more participants: "Daddy, I never have a play date! Please, a play date!" The emphasis on "never" was exaggerated and infuriating.

It's not that this other parent is a particularly unpleasant person, but if I can avoid an hour of awkward interaction and, in the process, secure some time for myself, I will.

"How long have you lived here," she asks, as we follow our children up the stairs.

"Approaching twenty years," I say, suddenly very aware of the strident creaking of each step. Embarrassed, in a way.

"Oh, wow. I'm sure the neighborhood has improved a fair bit. I can't imagine . . ." Her singsong voice trails off, but her eyebrows lift the whole of her long face.

If she were one of my students, I would ask her to define *improved*. I would ask her who benefited from the improvements, and who didn't. I would ask if there is a human cost to gentrification. I would ask her where the displacement and suffering end up. I'd ask her about all the isms. But she's not one of my students, and I speak public health all week long, and sometimes I just want to speak plain English. "Yeah, it's a very different neighborhood," I say, "some good things, some not-so-good things."

Before unlocking the deadbolt, I apologize for whatever mess may be inside. "We have a friend staying with us for a few days. He's not the neatest guy in the world," I say. Our friend left a few days ago.

She nods her empathy, all the while helping her son out of his coat and shoes. She tucks them into the mess of layers already in the hallway outside of the apartment. She pulls a phone from her bag. "Bobby, we have one hour before we have to go home," she says. "I'm going to set a timer."

Bobby doesn't betray whatever he might feel about his mother's declaration. Instead, he shows himself inside and begins to peruse our bookshelves, running his small hand along the spines. His fingers pause briefly on *Anal Pleasure & Health: A Guide for Men and Women*, which sits next to Larry Kramer's *Faggots*. My chest seizes, but before I can even consider what his mother might be thinking, Bobby moves on to the shelf of knickknacks.

I don't mind Bobby. He's high energy, like my son. Together, they're two fugitive electrons escaped from a Ken Kesey novel. They talk over each other, run into each other at full speed, cry and scream within an inch of each others' faces, never balking, only escalating, the threat of disaster ever upon us. I also like Bobby because his name does nothing to my limbic system. With all the Thors, Lakes, and Birches toddling around town, I am grateful for a solid, working-class Irish name. In my Catholic youth, he would have been Bobby for short. But this Bobby's mom and this Bobby's dad certainly didn't name their kid Robert. Not a chance. They're part of this new wave of parents who think nicknames are proper names. Bobby was Bobby in the placenta and on his birth certificate.

"Did you hear that, Julio?" I shout toward my son as he and his friend take off down the hallway. "One hour. I don't want to hear any crying or screaming. I'm setting a timer too."

Timers. Christ.

Don't get me wrong. I'm grateful for any tools or techniques that facilitate the trauma-free domestication of our small, wild humans, but the gulf between my childhood and my children's is vast and vertigo inducing. My parents used to set timers with the backs of their hands. Sometimes, the timers were made of leather. But those were different times, I've heard people say. I assume they meant different income brackets.

"Julio. Where is that from?" she asks as she makes her way to the couch.

Are you serious? I wonder. It's in a Simon & Garfunkel song that she's undoubtedly heard a thousand times.

"I ask because I have a coworker named Julio; he's from Puerto Rico."

"It's my grandfather's name on my mother's side, Salvadorian, as well as my father's side, Colombian—Would you like something to drink?" I don't feel like having the Spanish colonialism conversation. I lock the front door and walk toward the kitchen. "I have water, milk, beer, or whisky."

Alice's or Betsy's or Carolyn's eyebrows perk up a bit, and she grins. I never forget a face, but I have no idea what her name is, and by this point, we've known each other for too long—months—for me to ask. She'll be Alice. And I can tell Alice is a whisky drinker. Something about the preserved streak of gray in her reddish, Bonnie Raitt hair tells me she enjoys sitting at a bar by herself from time to time.

I stand in the archway between the living room and kitchen, a half-empty bottle of spirits in my hand. At least this, I think to myself. No ulterior motives. No suspicion. I could offer her absinthe and a speedball, and she wouldn't wonder if I was trying to seduce her. This is, as far as I can tell, the only magic in the much-ballyhooed relationship between gay men and straight women. "I shouldn't," she replies. "I have to make dinner and get some work done tonight. Just water, please."

"Remind me, what do you do?" I ask on my way to the faucet. I know she's a lawyer, something to do with human rights, but I ask anyway because I sense she's about to ask me what I do for a living, even though I've told her several times before. I get tired of having to repeat myself. It gives away the upper hand.

"I'm a lawyer," she says.

I hand her the water. "Right, of course. International . . ."

"We're suing the current administration over its use of drones."

"Interesting," I say. I mean it. It does interest me.

She digs into her large purse decorated in gold-plated touches and again pulls out her phone. The milliseconds on the timer are racing, but it hasn't been even ten minutes. "And you're in public administration—"

"Health. Public health," I say. "I research the effects of basic income and wages on societal health. I teach graduate students."

"Fascinating." She doesn't pretend to remember. "And do they all go work at the health department afterward?"

"Several do, but some work in hospitals, some in grassroots non-profits, some in unions. A few pursue doctorates. A couple end up at Best Buy."

Just then, Bobby's voice pierces the small-talk balloon tied around our necks. "Mommy!" His elephant stomps follow, loud, then louder, until the leader of the pack reaches us. "Julio hit me. Will you tell his mom?"

Alice looks at me and goes down on one knee toward Bobby, whose left nostril is exhibiting either last or next week's cold. "Honey, we talked about this. Julio has two daddies." Alice looks up again, but not nervously, more self-important. Poor thing, I think.

"Where is his mommy?" Bobby presses, like a four-year-old. A brief but unmistakable silence follows. It occurs to me that I rarely have to witness or participate in this type of conversation. My small, insulated world takes place about forty years in the future, and I'm jarred by the unexpected time travel.

"Bobby!" Alice reroutes the subject. "You must have done something to get Julio so upset."

As if on cue, my little wombat skulks into the room with a guilty but also aggrieved turbulence in his eyes and brow. We adopted Julio, and he looks nothing like me, not his hair, not his teeth, not his marshmallow face, but he is me, almost more so than I am. "Why did you hit Bobby?" I ask.

Julio's face goes blank, and he offers nothing, until my jaw tightens up. "He said he didn't want to play with me anymore."

"C'mon, is that a good reason to hit someone?" I ask.

Alice again looks up at me. But now her eyes are wide and barely white, as if her brain can no longer contain its thoughts and her pupils have become the primary egress. I'm not certain of what she is trying to communicate, but I suspect she doesn't approve of my rhetorical question. She probably wants to tell me there is never a good reason to hit anyone. If that is, in fact, what she is thinking, I hope she doesn't say it because I completely disagree. I mean, don't get me wrong, I hate physical violence—I can't sit through more than a few minutes of a Scorsese film—but there are degrees and root causes to everything. And sometimes, bringing someone to the brink of violence and then feigning displeasure when they commit the act is a bit, well, artful. Like when Andy Cohen eggs on the Real Housewives. But I don't want to be the one to explain this. Not right now. This is not the kind of conversation one pre-K parent, male and brown, should have with another, female and white, and definitely not in a place without cameras and audio recording. You see, Alice strikes me as the kind of person who clutches her purse. The kind of person who makes me feel like I'm doing something wrong when all I'm doing is commuting. The kind who catalyzes increases in my cortisol levels and makes me rehearse soliloquies that I want to deliver in a full-throated kinda way as I walk briskly beside and past her on my way home. But I can't say these things to Alice because she also strikes me as a good person. Someone who uses words like community and peace and diversity—probably cares about them too—and who would surely lecture me for not understanding what it's like to be a woman in this world. She's someone who probably knows the exact disparity in wages between men and women, down to the cent. Someone who knows intimately the feeling of walking into a room, elevator, or bar full of men, where expectations and judgment hang in the air, like pollen at the height of spring. Someone who has experienced violence in ways big and small that I'll never know firsthand.

No, I don't want to have those conversations with Bobby's mom, not in my living room, and maybe never. Not because she's wrong, but because there'd be no wiggle room to discuss solidarity and no space to strategize how we should wrest power from white men, who seem to walk away from all of our situations unscathed, their stress indicators unchanged, whistling even. To further complicate matters, we are both married to white men.

She returns her gaze to her son. I ask mine to apologize; she asks hers to reciprocate. Their high-pitched sorrys drag out, long and inauthentic, but still an evolution. The kids waste no time barreling back toward my son's bedroom.

"I'll take you up on that whisky," Alice says, tying her long, loose curls into a ponytail.

I notice, for the first time, that she has piercings in her ears. Many. At least five pieces of jewelry run along the ridge of each ear. How have I never noticed that before? Maybe I have. Maybe these are the details one forgets as they age. Or maybe she's never before worn her hair up around me.

"Neat or on the rocks?" I ask.

"Neat," she calls out.

"You know, I have the ingredients for a Manhattan, if you prefer."

Alice meets me in the kitchen. She's wearing slacks that are equally businesslike and chic—flowing material, loose then tapered, an imperfect gray, like spent charcoal. She is very emotive with her eyebrows, and here, again, they tell me that she's pleased. "Yeah, sure. What a treat."

I fill the glasses with ice and water to chill them and grab the other ingredients from the pantry. It occurs to me then that I haven't offered anything to the children. "Would Bobby want some mac and cheese? Julio never turns the stuff down."

"That would be great. Can I help?"

I hand her a pot. She fills it up with water and hands it back to me. It's heavier than I expect, and I fumble for a second, accidentally grazing her hand in the process. "Sorry," I say almost involuntarily. Immediately, I regret being so deferential. She doesn't respond, but instead scans the box of pasta. She's wearing a gold band, but no engagement ring. I'm relieved. Literate women who wear engagement rings destabilize all my notions of feminism. I'm grateful this tradition seems to be falling by the wayside. I cover the pot on the stove. The splatters of tomato sauce on the white enamel are egregious all of a sudden. If she sees them, she'll deduce those stains have been there since at least the previous night's dinner because I was at work this morning. She'll think we're slobs. Truth is the stains have been there since Sunday. It's Tuesday.

I shake the drinks. She turns to the three small plants resting on the window shelf. She gently rubs the leaf of one and brings those fingers to her nose. "You should trim this basil. It'll flourish," she says.

I've been meaning to, but I don't tell her that. I just thank her for the suggestion. Then it crosses my mind that if she ever comes back to our place again and sees how much the basil has grown, she'll feel pretty good about herself, as if she saved the linchpin in our urban herb garden. She'll tell her husband or another mother that our home is missing a woman's touch. In her mind, this, along with the untidy living room, and splattered red sauce, constitutes an unloving environment for a child. All at once, I feel overwhelmed by the need to tell her that I've had that basil plant for three years. Doing so will communicate that I must know what I'm doing because a basil plant doesn't grow easily indoors in the window of a Brooklyn apartment. I'm certain of this because this is my fourth such plant. But I don't want to announce the hardy plant's age in a way that will make me sound defensive. Maybe something like, *Wow, I can't believe how long that thing has survived.* Then she'll ask, *How long?* But instead, I wait too long, and she tells me that she likes our apartment.

"Thank you," I respond.

"Small New York City apartments are the best," she says.

That's the best backhanded compliment I've heard in a while. Our apartment is small, but more so because her place is twice as big. She and her husband bought their home before they moved into the neighborhood. They're about the same age as my husband and me, and neither practices a particularly lucrative profession. Her husband does some sort of eco-friendly design work, mostly consulting, I think. That's what he told me when we visited their place for Bobby's birthday at the beginning of the school year. The husband was perfectly friendly, but also tense in a way that made me tense. Whenever I left the center of the party to grab a beer or use the restroom, he'd follow. It crossed my mind that he was attracted to me. If we'd been in a gay bar, I'd have been certain of it. But last fall, I think he was just uncomfortable. I was the only non-white parent at the party—and maybe the only one ever to set foot in their home—apart from the Japanese mom who was there for all of twenty minutes before leaving her white husband at the party with both of their kids. I wished I'd done the same, but my husband and I have this rule about both of us being present in situations where queer families are underrepresented. We both try to be there. That's the rule. Come to think of it, the Japanese mom probably had a similar arrangement with her husband, with respect to multiracial families, and my husband and I were her exit strategy. Whatever the reason, Alice's husband kept following me around their tremendous apartment and asking if I needed anything. It was a stressful dynamic that led me to drink more, until the stress was submerged and the fear that everyone at the party thought I was too much of a lush to be parenting—never mind same-sex parenting—floated to the top. And yet, from the truncated conversation with Alice's husband that day, I was able to retain that they received financial help from their parents to buy their massive place—too big, in my opinion. This is, in part, why I don't care for Alice very much. It rankles me dearly to meet so many white people who use their inheritances and no-interest loans to buy homes in previously Black and brown neighborhoods, while (probably) secretly questioning—or allowing their parents and drunk uncles to—the spending habits of poor Black and brown people, as if slavery and Jim Crow and wage-law chicanery and redlining aren't still lurking, as if poor white people don't also buy wide-screen TV sets and phones and sneakers.

The water boils, and Alice accommodates the colander inside of the sink. I put on an insulated glove because the pot has gotten too hot, including the handle. Whenever I do this, I'm reminded that I've never seen my mother or my aunts prepare for heat in this way. Their tolerance is frightening. I don't know if it's a Latin American thing or a woman thing or an age thing. A part of me thinks magical realism is to blame.

"Phil and I haven't been to the movies in ages," says Alice, apropos of nothing I can decipher, leaving me to wonder if I zoned out mid-conversation. "When was the last time for you?" she asks, backing away from the rising steam.

Phil! Of course! That is certainly his name. Of course. If she hadn't said it just now, his name would have remained forever captive in an inaccessible fold of my gray matter. Phil's face, however, is clear and present. This is a special ability I have: I never forget a face. It's even crossed my mind to find someone who does this type of research: facility with facial recognition. But what use would I be? And to whom? Besides, it should be said, I am inclined to remember a man's face more clearly than a woman's. For example, I could give a sketch artist a pretty confident description of Phil—sandy brown hair, beleaguered chin, hapless jowls, scar above his left eye—but Alice's would be broader. Even now, with my back to her, I'm hard-pressed. Red hair; rounded, long face; green, maybe blue, eyes. That's the best I can do. But I'd know her if I saw her. That's for sure.

I can't quite isolate it, but I'm starting to feel as if there's a strain of misogyny in my analysis of Alice. Why should she, after all, carry the brunt of my distrust for one couple or generation or entire racial category? I take a swig of my Manhattan and try to engage meaningfully. "Hmm . . . The last movie we saw . . . It was the most recent *Star Wars*. On our birthdays, we usually take the day off work, catch a movie, and have a nice lunch."

"Gosh. That's great. You guys have better relationships than we do."

Now, apart from the party at Alice and Peter's place a few months ago, a couple of school meetings, and all the half-hearted smiles in the hallways during drop-off, this is the first time that Alice and I have ever truly socialized, so I'm not sure what she means by *you guys*. I assume she means gays. And maybe she meant just that, *you gays*, but the Manhattan went to her head and tongue, and she slipped.

"My brother and his husband are the same way," she continues matter-of-factly. "They enjoy each other and do romantic things like that. How long have you two been together?"

I have no problem answering these types of questions, but since I don't know where this conversation is headed, I'm feeling like I don't have control, and so I pause a moment.

She doesn't wait for my response: "Phil and I just celebrated our twelfth."

"Twenty years! Next month, it'll be twenty years," I half-shout.

My enthusiasm was unexpected; her eyebrows tell me so.

"Wow. That's great," she says.

I mix in the powdered cheese. We call the kids to eat and float behind them, like boxing coaches, offering water and milk, and reminding them to chew carefully and to wipe their faces before getting up. I'm grateful for Bobby's healthy appetite because Julio mimics everything he sees, and if Bobby had eaten one shell of macaroni, Julio would have too. They clean their plates. Again, they race off.

"Five more minutes," Alice calls out to Bobby after his footsteps have disappeared.

"Did you hear that?" I bellow toward Julio, but nothing is returned.

Alice offers to wash the dishes, but I point to the dishwasher and make up something about how filling it is one of my favorite things to do. I tack on a passing, joke-y reference to OCD. But then I wonder if she or someone she knows has OCD. It's no joke. I regret saying it.

"Would you like another drink?" I ask almost instinctually. In this way, I am exactly like my mother, who doesn't like people but is an irreproachable host.

"Oh, no, I really shouldn't."

I motion toward her empty glass. She picks it up quickly, and the dregs of Manhattan fly onto the jute rug and dissolve. She hands the glass to me without mentioning the minor faux pas and proceeds to scan our coffee table. A collection of short stories by Raymond Carver rests atop a stack of books. My husband rescued it from a box on a nearby stoop over the weekend. I wish Julia Alvarez's *In the Time of Butterflies* or anything by Paul Beatty was visible instead of stacked perfectly beneath Carver's *Cathedral*. She asks me if I've read Adichie's most recent novel. I haven't. I don't know if I want to. She says she can lend me her copy. I don't want to commit to anything. I smile and attempt a head sway that ends up looking like a drunken bobble. I hope she sees, *No, thank you*, without me having to say it. The moment passes.

"I better start gathering—Bobby!" she calls out, interrupting herself. It's only been forty minutes. "It may not be pretty when we try to leave. He can get . . . Well, let's just say, loud."

"Julio is the same."

"This was fun," she announces on her way to the door. "Let's do it again."

I don't know that I would have classified this as fun, but it certainly wasn't what I'd feared. "Sure," I say. But all I can think is that I've been worried Julio is having most of his play dates with white children. This is a cause for concern because his ideas of self, of normal, and of beauty are forming, and it matters who surrounds him now, lest he spend a lifetime undoing. It's difficult enough finding children's books and TV shows that reflect our real world.

"Great. I work a flex-schedule on Tuesdays," Alice tells me as she pulls up the calendar app on her phone. "We can start in the playground and move to one of our places if the weather turns." She sits on a short stool in the hallway and zips up her leather boots, nice equestrian-style boots, a stiff and imposing black leather.

I wasn't prepared for these problems. I'd spent years comforted that, if we ever had children, they would grow up around a diversity of races and ethnicities, but now, playgrounds once full of Black and brown children are almost exclusively white. And most of the remaining non-white families are at least one generation away from *flex-schedules*. "Cool," I say, feeling like a traitor.

"Bobby!" Alice calls out again. We hear nothing in response. I know they're hiding. She smiles at me, but I can see the frost spreading across her face. Something has changed. Something is coming. And then: "Robert Walden Hayes!" The boom in her voice is that of an angry sitcom mother. Her eyes dart nervously around the room.

Walden? Hayes? Robert? Bobby Hayes had the ring of a scrappy 1950s high school football player or a fallen member of the IRA, but Robert Walden Hayes is a future president of the United States, and possibly related to a previous one. Her family's ambitions fill the room. I already miss the vibe we had moments ago.

Alice is on one foot, leaning, a forward slash inside the doorframe. She unzips the boot she'd only just zipped up. "Please don't," I say. "I'll go grab him."

Truth is, I enjoy getting other people's kids to leave my house. It's easy, and I'm good at it. I aim for their fears. I take on a low whisper and a deep stare and tell them their parent is leaving without them. Even for a child who is hell-bent on staying, this is an alarming declaration. This works well with Bobby, who bolts for the front door.

Alice and I exchange pleasantries while our kids squeeze in a few more seconds of imaginary play. Then, it's all over.

From one flight below, Alice calls out to me.

"Yes?" I responded.

"Are you going to the PTA meeting tomorrow?"

I walk back into the hallway. Julio follows and squeezes into a space too small between the railing and me. He resumes waving at Bobby. "I hadn't planned on it," I say.

"You should. We could use more dads."

"I'll see if one of us can," I respond.

"Okay. Great."

"Bye, Bobby!" Julio screams, frantic and high-pitched, as if his life were in grave danger. It makes me want to squeeze his arm, but I restrain myself and tell him to keep his voice down because we share the building with our neighbors. He makes no sign that he's heard me. Then he runs inside and hurls himself onto the couch, like an errant cannonball.

MIDTOWN-WEST
SIDE STORY

VILMA AND HER THREE CHILDREN were in a station wagon, parked illegally on 56th between 7th and 8th Avenues—closer to 7th—waiting for Jorge to finish making the sale. It was June and dark. Eduardo was the only one of the kids still awake. Earlier in the week, he'd convinced Vilma to buy him the new Madonna album—another soundtrack. Vilma hadn't needed much convincing. She was the type of mother who enjoyed pop music and pleasing her children. They were on their third consecutive listening when Vilma let out a yelp that caused Eduardo to jump. A short, dark silhouette was peering through her window: Dad.

At times, it seemed that Vilma's love was a Venn diagram of equally sized and nearly concentric circles: one, affection; the other, exasperation. She rolled her eyes and the window down. Jorge craned his head into the car as if he were something four-legged and gentle in search of nourishment.

Jorge had already come by twice that night, the first of which was a couple of hours earlier, before the sun had disappeared behind the Art Deco horizon. Vilma had been cleaning out the coffee stains from the cup holder when the three children saw him approach. "¡Mami, ahí viene Papi!"

"¿Dónde?"

"There!"

Vilma reached over to unlock the passenger-side door.

"¿Se están portando bien?" Jorge asked the children as he stepped inside of the metallic gray trapezoid.

"Yeah, except for Eduardo. He keeps cheating," responded Inés, holding a worn white paper napkin that was graffitied in blue ink: an early evening's worth of Tic-Tac-Toe games.

"La niña tiene que ir al baño," said Vilma.

"Me too!" Marcelo called out from the back seat.

"Me three!" Eduardo yelled before laughing, as if he'd just discovered the potential of language.

Jorge encouraged Vilma to also go to the bathroom, knowing well that she wouldn't. His wife detested public restrooms and drawing attention to herself. A clandestine trip through the lobby of a hotel where she wasn't a guest would be dreadful.

"Just get out of the car and stretch your legs, Mom," Eduardo suggested.

"¡Estoy bien!"

Vilma didn't like to be coddled, especially when she was hungry, and certainly not when she was pregnant. And she was pregnant, almost six months, even if, seated, there was no sign of it. The first three pregnancies had stretched her face, swelled her fingers and toes, and endowed her with the sort of large, albeit painful, breasts that she'd never dreamed for herself. She'd been miserable throughout. This time, the weight gain was primarily in her belly. Vilma's face remained thin, her skin clear and glistening from the humidity, her hair a thick black thatch somewhere between pompadour and pixie. She was a young mother, and she looked like a young mother.

Jorge's face, too, retained the charm and softness it'd had before life had become about survival. The rest of his body, however, was undergoing a premature decay. After years of balancing trays well above his head and hauling fifteen- and twenty-pound bags of clothes between Park and 7th, he'd developed a radiating pain in his back and shoulders, an electricity that had become, rather perversely, one of the few reliable things in his life.

Vilma swatted the crumbs from her children's shirts, grooming that transformed into a ritual of aggression when her children were about to be seen by the world. All of it accompanied by grumbling: How disheveled they looked. How embarrassing. What will people think? Vilma took a brush to Inés's hair, tying back every loose strand, glossy and perfectly black, as if a brand-new vinyl record had been stretched from a racetrack into a straightaway. Tears budded in the child's eyes, but they remained as still as the rest of her.

"Don't be wild. No running or screaming! Quiet all the way to the bathroom," were Vilma's parting words.

"Quiet," repeated Inés.

"How quiet?" Eduardo responded cheekily.

"Like you don't exist," Vilma said. "Three little ghosts."

"Dale la mano a tu hermana," Jorge demanded of Marcelo, the protector—pudgy, reticent, and the eldest by only a few years. Eduardo, thin, excitable, and with an eye for mischief, was already hopping up and down, lapping up the freedom of open air. Inés, only seven, was the most confident and obedient of the trio. She held her hand up for Marcelo to grasp.

The three walked quickly and unevenly toward the hotel, managing, in their way, to exude fearlessness and trepidation at once. Vilma couldn't bear to look, conflicted by the clash of instincts: to protect them and to protect herself.

Jorge's thoughts were elsewhere and traveling at a different speed. He scanned the car doors to make sure they were locked. Then he pulled a long receipt from his wallet. On one side, he'd written a list of names and prices.

"No, the Bill Blass suits are 175," Vilma said, as she slipped her hand between Jorge's back and the cracked upholstery. It was a forceful yet comforting touch.

"What about the Hickey-Freemans?"

"Ask for 225, but you can go as low as 200. Those pieces are from last season. The new ones come on Sunday."

Jorge scribbled furiously onto the thin, crinkly paper, while simultaneously mouthing Vilma's instructions to himself. "¿Y los Oscar de la Renta?"

"Más. 300."

"Do you want to go up to the room instead?" he asked. "Ramiro and Cristina don't trust my advice when it comes to clothes. They prefer you."

Vilma shook her head. Ramiro and Cristina, two flight attendants on a layover, were notoriously indecisive, and she had little patience for it that night. "I feel disgusting. I don't want to be around anyone."

"Okay. But before I go up, eat something. A gyro from the deli across the street? El Griego."

"Without tomatoes," she said, her face now changed by the smallest of smiles. "Please."

The second time that Jorge came down to the car was more than an hour later and only briefly to drop off munitions. He'd brought with him two Styrofoam containers filled with well-appointed burgers—pickles, tomatoes, lettuce, red onions, thick french fries. He'd also handed off the night's entertainment: a brand-new deck of Spanish cards—oros, espadas, copas, bastos. "Here. ¡Rápido!" He emptied the ketchup packets from his pockets, as if he were bailing water from a sinking ship. "The bellman wasn't there just now; I want to get back before he does," he explained. At this hour, the hotel's lobby was sparse, leaving Jorge without the cover of a crowd. An intrepid employee was capable of anything. Jorge and Vilma were well acquainted with the American array of *How can I help you?* glares.

"Ramiro and Cristina are making their final decisions. Should be done soon. Tonight's going to be big. Adios," Jorge whispered before cutting through a small line of sidewalk traffic and into the newly settled darkness.

For the remainder of the evening, the children did their best to play in the cramped space. Inés held her cards with one hand and used the other to prevent the pick-up pile from sliding behind the belt buckles—the place where crumbs, G.I. Joe limbs, and My Little Pony heads vanished. Over the course of a few hours, Vilma had only to ask them to stop fighting three times. *Mami, Eduardo's cheating!* had been the catalyst on each occasion. There was little to separate this evening from any of the others.

After Marcelo and Inés dozed off, Eduardo climbed the two hard-vinyl hills into the front. Madonna had been singing for well over an hour, in part because Vilma repeatedly interrupted.

Stop > Rewind > Stop > Play > Stop > Rewind a bit more > Stop > Play > top > Fast forward a smidge > Stop > Play.

Even as a young girl in San Salvador, Vilma had been a devoted fan of American and British music—the Beatles, Stones, Doors—even if she hadn't always sung the correct lyrics or known what she was singing. Minor errors here and there. And who cared? No one else knew what she was singing anyway. But now she was preoccupied with speaking the language perfectly. She utilized her children and Top 40 radio. Who better to assist her than those very creatures who ridiculed—sometimes in front of other adults—her grammar and pronunciation? They were unwitting ESL instructors at the peak of their training, steeped in the esoteric rules of this most arbitrary of Western languages—Who or whom? Had or had had? Use to or used to?

"'Soon-er or la-ter you are go-ing to be mine.'" Vilma repeated the syllables while jotting the Sondheim lyrics onto a receipt for the antiacid she'd bought that morning.

"No, Mom. It's 'you're,' a contraction."

"But that is informal for writing."

"Everyone learns contractions in school, but we're never supposed to use them in our homework. Later, it's okay to use them when you're older."

"Who told you that?"

"Sister Donna."

Vilma erased with care as she flatened the crinkly paper across the dashboard. "Okay. 'You're.'"

"And it's not 'going to be mine.' It's 'gonna be mine.'"

"That is just bad English."

"It's a song."

"It does not matter. If she sings 'going to,' it would not change the song."

"Yeah, but if she sang 'you are' and 'going to,' it would be harder to sing that line."

"Okay. How about the next one? 'Ba-by it's time that you face it. I al-ways get my man.'"

"Almost. It's past tense: 'faced.'"

"Why? She is telling him to do something now, not in the past. It should be *face*."

"That's true. I don't know why."

"I wonder, could it be a mistake?" Vilma asked.

"Maybe."

"¡Ayyyy!" she screamed. The dark silhouette appeared behind the glass. It took a moment for Vilma to recognize Jorge. "Don't do that! You scared me!" she said, as he leaned into the car to kiss her.

"Dad!"

"Shhh!"

"But Mom yelled too!"

"Don't be fresh."

"¿Cómo te fue?" Vilma asked.

Jorge tipped his head a few degrees to one side before exhaling with force. Then he dug his hand inside the car to pop the trunk.

Eduardo regarded the narrow eyes, accordion brow, and vanishing lips of his father's face. It hadn't gone well. He hadn't sold enough.

"Dos blusas," Jorge said. "¡Miércoles!"

Two blouses after nearly three hours. An evening of finagling and hoping, only for it to end with a mercurial coda. Their clients' sudden change of mind would alter the mood of the family for an entire week, possibly two.

The children would be wise to remain quiet. Better not to be the source of any problems on the way home. Definitely not the night to suggest a slice of pizza. Or to request a bathroom stop. Their father, although typically a tired sort of affable, could ignite after a night like this one—a werewolf for whom financial precarity was a full moon. Two cans of Löwenbräu while zoning out on short skirts and fútbol highlights was what Jorge needed, but only after one of Vilma's pep talks. The one that began with "Don't worry." The one that was sprinkled with quick and hopeful math. The one that ended with "¡Sí puedes! We can do this, mi amor!" and kissing his face all over, which then typically led to one of the children saying something like "Eww. Get a room!" which, in turn, elicited a chuckle from Jorge.

But first they had to survive the trip home.

Eduardo woke the others. They would take turns eyeing the road and squeezing their father's arm if the car drifted toward the highway median or if another car swerved too close: their contribution to the family business.

From a map, Vilma and Jorge had chosen the all-white suburban town where they lived—a quaint, three-bedroom house in a gated retirement community that had been advertised in the back of a newspaper. They'd wanted to escape the bustle and crime of the city, but not so far they couldn't commute back to serve food and sell clothes. Evening trips to Manhattan happened four or five times per week. The kids would be home from school by three-thirty. Dinner was on the table by four. In the car by five, and in the city by six. Sometimes Jorge couldn't get out of his dinner shift in time to join the traveling bazaar, leaving Vilma with no choice but to entrust the children to Jorge's cousin in Queens, something she preferred not to do. Úrsula smoked cigarettes—*¡Todo el santo día!* Then she'd empty a bottle of air freshener, somehow creating an odor more intolerable than the cigarettes. There was also Tía Beti, a family friend who the kids loved because of her lax dietary restrictions—Twinkies, marshmallows, colorful cereal, chocolate milk—which Vilma suspected were the roots of Marcelo's tinted molar and Eduardo's stomachaches. But Beti had a thing for bourbon, which always left Vilma uneasy. When neither Úrsula nor Beti were available, Vilma sold the clothes by herself and left the kids in the car alone.

The very business of fencing designer clothes had begun a decade earlier, at the restaurant where Jorge worked—an upmarket French place, tucked obscurely at the base of a skyscraper—where it wasn't uncommon for a few weathered paparazzi to be parked outside, drinking coffee and smoking, doing their best to fade into the drab grandeur of Midtown, east of 5th Avenue. The restaurant's profile brought out the moneyed set, the glamorous ones, and the pretenders. And because airline employees in the 1980s and 1990s retained the sheen of celebrity they'd had in the 1950s and 1960s, when air travel was for the well off, uniformed pilots and flight attendants dined there as well. It became a usual haunt for the flight crews of British Airways, KLM, EgyptAir, Alitalia, and Aeroméxico.

Despite being the only short server with a thick accent at the restaurant, Jorge maintained the air of someone who might have done more if he'd had more opportunities. He was gregarious and confident beyond what his colleagues and customers expected. His charm, along with the Park Avenue menu prices, made the restaurant work lucrative enough for down payments (home, car, vacuum cleaner, stove), but somehow insufficient to keep up with the month-to-month that followed. So when Aníbal, a thirty-five-year-old busboy from Colombia, introduced him to a fellow compatriot, who worked as a distributor of high-end clothing, Jorge seized the opportunity.

"I'll get you the best designers. Wholesale prices. You mark it up a little, but still less than what they pay in the stores. Even the rich ones won't pass up a discount," explained the twenty-something purveyor, who everyone called El Flaco. Although thin, his presence, too, was outsized. He had a frenetic energy, accompanied by a perpetual shrug and the artful gesticulations of a haggler. He wore a coiffed, handlebar mustache and a drop-silver earring in the shape of a padlock in his right ear.

"Why not sell it yourself?" Jorge asked.

"The guy who gave me a start sensed that I'd be good at this. I sense that in you. Plus, the volume is too much—You in or out?"

El Flaco extended his hand toward the endless rows of clothing racks and circular stands that filled the green-carpet basement in Hoboken.

"Where does it all comes from?" Jorge had promised Vilma he wouldn't get involved if the clothes were stolen.

"Some I buy from another distributor. And some, well, just shows up on my doorstep, leftovers—In or out?"

Jorge bought a dozen to start—six dresses, three skirt suits, three pantsuits—which he sold easily to coworkers, friends, and their one friendly neighbor—a retired postal worker who needed a suit for his granddaughter's college graduation. The next dozen he sold to some of the restaurant's regulars, whom Jorge would size up surreptitiously during their meals, while taking orders, dropping off appetizers and main courses, carefully interjecting the names of designers into their small talk, always attentive to the clothes his customers were wearing. The coup de grace typically came during the pie a la mode or the crème brulee, when he would let the table or the most fashion-conscious member of the group know that he could help them find alternatives to the city's prices.

A stopover in New York for a flight crew might only be twenty-four hours, sometimes twelve, seldom long enough to sightsee and shop. Jorge provided an effortless solution to a problem they didn't even know they had. The pilots and flight attendants could gallivant about the city and have the latest fashions brought to their hotel rooms on their own schedules.

The 1980s were an orgy of deregulation for the Gordon Gekkos, but Ronald Reagan wasn't entirely wrong: some of the spoils made it to the bottom. It was less a trickle than the thump, scrape, and cacophonous clanks of clothing racks falling off of trucks.

In the first ten years of trafficking designer clothes, Vilma and Jorge came to know several distributors and owed each of them a substantial sum of money, which they paid off just in time to put the next season's fashion lines on credit. The scheme proved exhausting, whether business was brisk or stale. When the clothes sold quickly, the previous twenty years of their lives were somehow validated; when they didn't, the tension and regret took over. Every night ended with the same lament: "Dios mío, what are we doing?"

During one desperate month, when all their phone calls sounded like cash registers ringing and Vilma had tired of innovating rice, beans, plantains, and dented cans of vegetables as a main course, she approached another mother in the school parking lot.

"Excuse me. I am the mother of Marcelo," she said. "Simon is your son, yes?" A tall, slender woman with large eyeglasses nodded. "I just wanted to say I've seen you a few times," Vilma continued, as she wrapped and unwrapped a section of her purse strap around her index finger, "and you have great style."

Simon's mother placed one hand against her chest and the other on her hip. She wore a flowing—neck to ankle—beige, cotton dress. The rest of her was the red of fire trucks: wide vinyl belt, cinched tight around her size-three waist; large, plastic jewelry that wrapped her wrist and neck; slip-on flats; lips. "Thank you," she replied. "In this town, it doesn't seem to matter much, but I really do like dressing up. I always say, 'You look as good as you feel.' And dressing up makes me feel good."

Vilma smiled. "My husband and I run a small boutique out of our home. If you ever want to come by to take—"

"I'd love to!"

For several years, Vilma's youthful face had been a liability at the school. The other mothers believed she was the babysitter, and no one wanted to interact with the babysitter, especially the beautiful one. Vilma approached Simon's mother because of her clearly constructed appearance but also because she was the only other non-white mother she'd spotted around the school's entrance during drop off and pick-up. They had never before spoken to one another, and yet, Vilma somehow feared approaching a Black mother less than she did the white mothers. In part, the white women were always in a circle that intimidated Vilma; in part, she cared less about the impression she left on a Black mother.

Word of the clothes spread. And for a couple of months, whenever the children were at school, all the mothers came by the house, where suits, dresses, skirts, and blouses sheathed in thin plastic hung, like headless bodies, in every closet and behind every door in the house. It would continue this way until the summers came, or a check bounced, or someone wanted their money back.

"We can do this," Vilma whispered into Jorge's ear at night, when all of children were asleep and the lights off.

"We can do this," she said after a windfall.

"We can do this," she said when everything seemed to be falling apart.

On a balmy Saturday afternoon in October that could have been summer or fall, the itinerant brood found itself parked near their usual corner at 7th and 56th. Packs of tourists outnumbered everyone else. A breeze perfumed with the exhausts of restaurant kitchens and old cars blew through Midtown. Across from the sprawling, modern hotel where most of their clients stayed was an older, smaller, and more regal one with one fewer star. Norma was there for one night. Norma was a flight attendant with a shopping addiction that always proved a certain enough bet for Jorge to work an abridged lunch shift, trade out his dinner, and remain in the car with the kids, while Vilma handled the sale.

"I've been wearing the same things for years," Norma said, as she fanned out her pleated, navy blue skirt, as if to corroborate a sartorial hardship. The look across Vilma's face toggled between subtle tolerance and ersatz enthusiasm; she had, after all, five months earlier, sold Norma several new dresses and suits, including the skirt that was now twirling around the modest, green-curtained hotel room. "Help me pick something out for tonight. I trust your taste." Vilma took that as a cue and extended the sleeves of a bold chartreuse blouse that she'd set on the bed.

"I wanted to see *City of Angels*, but the man at the embassy got us tickets for *The Piano Lesson*. Have you seen it?"

Vilma hadn't heard of either.

"Let's see. Do I want this orange Nicole Miller pant suit, or this burgundy Adriana Papell? Norma seemed to be asking herself. "The Miller is perfect for a play, no? The Papell is more for a musical."

"They both look great. But the Tahari was also beautiful on you. Maybe as much as the Ellen Tracy." Vilma was suave in her assessments, choosing well the moments and appropriate doses of fawning. "With your figure, you can pull off anything."

Norma, while petite in stature, was an enormous boon to the family business. Earlier that year, she'd also become an invaluable liaison, introducing Jorge to friends who were interested in buying wholesale from him for their own operation in Mexico. For months, she'd been taking home suitcases full of designer clothes and returning with thick envelopes. Her spree that afternoon—three dresses, three pantsuits, two blouses, and two skirts—along with the most recent cash payment from her compatriots, would be enough for Jorge and Vilma to turn the phone back on, pay that month's mortgage, pay one clothing distributor, and the previous three month's Catholic school tuition.

"Maybe I should try them all on again, just to be certain," Norma announced just as Vilma had begun to fold everything.

Meanwhile, Jorge sat with the children in the new Dodge, a mud-brown, wainscoted minivan. The gray station wagon, which the children had named Eeyore, had broken down a final time on the expressway the month before, leaving the family to hitchhike home in shifts. Jorge had been relieved and not a little proud to have gotten a few hundred dollars for the scraps of Eeyore.

Inés and Eduardo were growing restless: proclamations of guilt and innocence being bandied about in the back seat. Carmen, the newest addition, was still too small to be demanding in the ways that her older brother and sister were, and she could be pacified in ways that they couldn't. Marcelo wasn't there. As of his eleventh birthday, he was old enough to stay home without supervision. Since then, he'd resisted all efforts to participate in the family business. No more hotel lobbies for him. No more specter of a bellman's gaze. No more holding anyone's hand.

"Can we go to the park, Dad? Please!" asked Inés, her hair pulled back in a tense, impeccable ponytail that Vilma had styled, knowing well that Jorge wouldn't.

"La policía nos va a multar."

"But we can go without you," said Eduardo, who wore a Garbage Pail Kids T-shirt that betrayed his pleas for independence.

"A tu madre no le gusta que anden por acá solos."

"Don't worry. We won't tell her."

"No."

"Come on, Dad. It's nice out. Kids are supposed to play in parks."

Inés's wryness caused Jorge to laugh. "Okay. Pero dale la mano a tu hermana," he said to Eduardo, who didn't mind one bit his new role of protective, older brother.

"¡Y cuidado con los carros!"

"Don't worry, we won't cross through Columbus Circle," Eduardo responded. "We'll take 7th all the way."

"Si alguien les pregunta—"

"We know, *Our dad just went to the bathroom. He'll be right back*," said Inés as she fastened the Velcro on her shoes.

"Media hora."

"Forty-five minutes?" insisted Eduardo, before examining his plastic Casio watch—a gift for his first Communion.

"Okay."

Jorge glanced up briefly from Carmen and caught Eduardo and Inés, in their neon colors, shin-high socks, and plastic accessories, before they crossed 56th, hand in hand, and made their way along 7th toward Central Park. A few strands of Inés's hair had come loose and now hung by her cheek. He didn't care.

Eduardo and Inés had just returned, ice cream congealed in the webbing of their fingers, when Vilma appeared in the distance.

Jorge handed Carmen to Inés. "¡No le digan nada a tu mamá!"

"Not a word," Eduardo responded. "Promise."

"Close the window!" Jorge shouted to Eduardo before stepping out of the car.

"But it's hot in here!" Eduardo shouted back after the door had slammed shut.

Carrying two large brown-paper department store shopping bags, no longer bursting with clothes, but heavy enough to mark her palms, Vilma waddled across 7th.

Jorge grabbed the bags as soon as he reached her. "¿Y? ¿Cuánto?" he asked.

Vilma's lips spread before coming apart. She signaled with her chin toward her purse. They kissed with an expectant, albeit fleeting, passion and took the bags to the trunk. The children were already on the sidewalk, waiting for Vilma, who set her purse down through the passenger window that Eduardo hadn't closed. She lifted Carmen from Inés's arms. "Bebé," she cooed at the pink ball of marshmallow flesh suited in pastel yellow. "Are you hungry?" she asked the others. The *Sí*'s came in unison. "Chinatown?" The *Yay*'s followed. She took a tissue from her pocket and told Eduardo to clean the unseemly evidence of ice cream from the corners of his mouth. Then she tucked the wayward hairs behind Inés's ear.

It was then that a deep voice pierced the family's perimeter: "Miss, your sweater!"

Vilma turned quickly to find two men approaching the car, both carrying soft leather briefcases. One man wore a black, pinstriped suit; the second, a solid gray. Vilma pulled up the tail of her sweater, a knee-length purple and green Lagerfeld cardigan that she'd inherited after months of not being able to sell it. Its powers of concealment had made it ideal postpartum apparel.

"Mom, yeah, there's yellow paint on your back," said Eduardo.

Inés inched her nose toward the sweater: "I think it's mustard."

One of the men searched his pockets for a napkin. The other pulled a silk handkerchief from inside his jacket. But Vilma resisted. "Thank you, but we have—"

"It's running down your back. Here," insisted one of the men, while the other turned away, distracted and impatient. Both had long hair gelled back, like European bankers or traveling fútbol players.

Vilma relented and passed the baby back to Inés. During the exchange, a third man materialized, this one in jeans and a T-shirt. Before Vilma could do anything, he'd reached through the car window and grabbed her purse.

"Mom!" Inés yelled.

Jorge, who was accommodating the bags into a junk-filled trunk, looked up to find the men running in opposite directions. The one with the purse ran east.

"Stop!" yelled Jorge, as he began chasing. Bystanders turned and craned, but there was little they could do as the men sped past. Jorge followed the one who'd turned south onto 7th. "Thief!" he shouted. But his accent transformed it into "Teeth!"

"Teeth! Teeth! Teeth!"

Jorge continued yelling as they crossed 55th and then 54th, but nothing slowed the man, who remained half a block ahead and kept a vigorous stride. An athlete, Jorge thought. Jorge, however, couldn't recall a time when he'd run this fast for this long. Certainly it was during the Sunday soccer games when he first arrived in this country, when he'd had nothing else to do with his free time but spend it in Flushing Meadows Park with all of the other kitchen staff. "Please! My daughter's medicine is in there!" he pleaded at 53rd— there was no medicine.

The sidewalks were loosely thronged, but by the time anyone realized what was happening, Jorge had already sprinted past, making it difficult for an intervention. That's what he theorized later when Vilma complained about "esos gringos estúpidos."

"Please give it back!" Jorge called out breathlessly. And at the corner of 7th Avenue and 52nd Street, the runner with a black purse under his arm did just that. He threw it down and kept running.

Sweat dripped from Jorge's temples. His back and shoulder pain had vanished. Crouched on the sidewalk, too fatigued to stand, he watched the thief weave through traffic and disappear with a bounty bigger than any they'd had in months. Jorge was paying a tax for his own carelessness, he thought. He wrapped the purse's leather strap around his wrist as many times as he could. Then he rested his head on his knee, incapable of engaging with the curious onlookers. The gum-stained pavement was mesmerizing—a pox on the city's streets. When his breathing had resumed its usual cadence, he pulled open the purse's flap. A corner of Manilla jutted out of the unzipped cavity; inside of the envelope was a stack of bills. Jorge dug his hand further inside the purse and pulled out Vilma's wallet, also intact.

Jorge looked up to the sky before pressing his hand onto his knee to give himself a lift. His white undershirt clung to his sweat-coated chest and back. A man in an Islanders jersey and a Mets cap asked if he was okay. Jorge nodded. "Thank you," he said.

Vilma was sitting in the car, her hand splayed across her brow, before she caught sight of him. Inés and Eduardo were crying when he slid the back door open—fear, of course, but guilt too, for having left the window open. When they began to cheer, Jorge held a finger to his lips and pointed to Carmen, who was asleep in her car seat, resting in the console between the driver and passenger.

The children wanted to hear the whole story, over and over, from the moment Dad had started running, until he'd gotten back to the car. He had created too much of a scene, Jorge explained. The thief had no choice but to drop Mom's purse. Yes, it was scary. No, no one got involved. Who knows what would have happened if the man had turned around. Vilma grew exasperated and barked at Jorge and the children to stop reliving it. Once was enough.

They abandoned the trip to Chinatown. Pizza at one of the strip malls along the interstate would suffice.

Jorge, still shaken up and not a little bit fatigued, drove slowly along 56th. Between 6th and 5th Avenues, he saw the three men, mid-block, huddled beneath the awning of a shoe repair shop. They'd be stupid to try something again so soon, he thought. He scanned the sidewalks for a police officer, but then remembered the trunk full of clothes and the envelope in Vilma's purse. When the light turned green, he pulled away.

Everything changed after that. The whole world, it seemed, had been mugged. A perfect storm—Iraq, Kuwait, Reagan, Bush I, Thatcher, Salinas, Columbus, Cortés, capitalism—caused a devaluation of the peso. All of Mexico was suffering, including its airlines. Flights to Rome and Frankfurt were eliminated, as were entire flight crews. There were fewer layovers, calls, and hotel visits. Vilma began looking for full-time work.

One day, Norma, the airline attendant, showed up at the restaurant. Her hair was a blonde pouf from another era; on one side of her neck rested a bow of red gossamer. She embraced Jorge and asked about Vilma and the kids. Everyone was fine, he explained. He asked her if she wanted a table or a place at the bar. That's not why she'd come by, but she didn't want to explain there. Could they go for a short walk?

One of the two men in Mexico who were buying wholesale from Jorge and Vilma was found in the trunk of his car with his hands tied behind his back and a bullet in his head. The other man had been carjacked along with the merchandise they'd been trying to sell. No one had seen him since. There would be no more envelopes.

Norma was apologetic and offered to track down the families of the men. They might honor their debts. Jorge offered his condolences and made something up about her friends not having owed that much. Norma's hands, which had been resting on her hips, dropped to her sides. She pulled a bag of chocolates from her purse. "Para tus niños," she explained.

What would Vilma say? She had warned Jorge—not only with her eyes, but very clearly with her words—about doing business with Norma's friends. She'd been worried all along about their money disappearing. But this wasn't his fault, Jorge thought. He couldn't have predicted a recession.

On his way back to the restaurant, he calculated the number of Sundays he'd have to work to recoup what he'd lost to the dead men: five months' worth. The other servers in the restaurant—tall, young, and aspiring to be something else—would be happy to have their weekends free, Jorge suspected. But it would take time for Vilma to forgive him.

CARLITOS IN CHARGE

I WAS IN MIDTOWN, SITTING by a dry fountain, making a list of all the men I'd slept with since my last checkup—doctor's orders. Afterward, I would head downtown and wait for Quimby at the bar, alongside the early drinkers. I'd just left the United Nations after a Friday-morning session—likely my last. The agenda had included resolutions about a worldwide ban on plastic bags, condemnation of a Slobodan Milosevic statue, sanctions on Israel, and a truth and reconciliation commission in El Salvador. Except for the proclamation opposing the war criminal's marble replica, everything was thwarted by the United States and a small contingent of its allies. None of this should have surprised me. Some version of these outcomes had been repeating weekly since World War II.

I'd been working at the United Nations for a little over a year, and in that short time I'd had sex with the South Korean ambassador, the spokesman for the Swedish Mission, an Irish delegate, a Russian interpreter, an Iraqi translator, the assistant to the deputy ambassador from El Salvador, an Armenian envoy, the chief of staff for the Ukrainian prime minister, the vice presidents of Suriname and the Gambia, a cultural attaché from Poland, the special assistant to the special assistant to the Saudi ambassador, the nephew of the ruling party's general secretary of Laos, a distant cousin of Castro, a film director from Mauritania, countless low-level staffers, a few guides, a half-dozen tourists, and Brad.

William Mycroft Quimby. The other students called him Billy. To me, he was Quimby (sometimes Quim)—the PhD student who led my section of Comparative Government 245 ("Cuba Isn't Finland, but Neither Is Finland Cuba"). Quimby was a smart guy who came across as even smarter because his English was high-register and thickly accented. And he was authentically Irish, unlike the third-generation Catholics I'd grown up with, whose ethnic pride consisted of tattoos of shamrocks and pots of gold along their necks and ankles. In phenotypical ways, he reminded me of my friends' dads back home. He had dark hair (also thick) and a knotted face. Quimby was an academic, but he could have been a middleweight boxer, a boxer who gave me attention I wasn't accustomed to. He also had a gorgeous, uncircumcised cock (it, too, thick) that made me want to know him better, but we drew the line at office hours.

I hadn't seen Quimby for almost twenty years when I ran into him at (W)hole Glory one Friday about fifteen months ago. The red-bulb lighting made it difficult to be certain, but when he walked past the first time, I knew I knew him. The second time, I knew it was from college. The third time, a rush of blood inspirited me. "Quim!" I shouted. He stared at me momentarily, then a moment longer. "Wednesday afternoons," I said. "Your basement office . . . 'NAFTA, Schmafta, Can you hear the world's Lafta?' . . ."

"Charles in Charge? Is that you? Holy shit. I barely recognized you with that mustache. How in the heck are you?"

Before I could respond, Quimby set his pint down onto the small table and joined me. "It's been ages," he said with a glassy stare. "What a truly magnificent surprise, Charles in Charge. Fine as ever, you are."

Carlitos is my given name. "Carlitos Doritos," the other kids used to call me—one more undesirable way in which I stood out. In middle school, I began demanding that my family address me as Alex P. Keaton, but my dad kept mispronouncing it Alice, which my siblings seized upon, so I settled on Charles in Charge. This was the title of a sitcom that starred Scott Baio as a young heartthrob who nannies three children while going to school and juggling a prolific love life. I was drawn to the show because of Charles's (Baio's) relationship with his best friend Buddy (Willie Ames), a one-dimensional, albeit oddly sagacious, buffoon. Their camaraderie and affection were genuine and subtle in ways that none of their other acting ever was. The slapstick humor struck me as either repressed or coded desire. Frankly, I didn't understand how the show made it onto network television.

"Carlitos?" Sister Susan, my sixth-grade teacher, called out. But instead of "Present," I responded, "Charles in Charge!"

"Is that Mexican?" she asked, peering up from the attendance sheet.

"No," I said, "it's syndicated."

"Are you visiting?"

"I live in Brooklyn. Near one of the bridges," Quimby explained, looking even more like the dads of my youth than he had twenty years earlier. "I work for the Irish Mission to the UN," he continued. "I'm seeing someone. He's French. Divides his time between here and Paris—filmmaker. How about you?"

"I'm also in Brooklyn. I work at the Health Department. I'm single."

I explained to Quimby that after college I'd taken a stab at an acting career—some theater, a few clown parties, and a couple of television commercials. In fact, one toilet paper ad paid for all of graduate school. I studied public health, specifically the effects of hierarchies: Does pecking order predict health outcomes? (Well, yes.)

"Fascinating," he said, and reached across the table to squeeze my forearm.

Quimby and I exchanged numbers and had sex once, for old time's sake, a few weeks later. Afterward, he asked me if I was looking for a new job. "The UN relies heavily on health data. You could find work rather easily," he explained.

I wasn't unhappy at the Health Department, but I found the idea of the UN intriguing and romantic, like Juliette Binoche and Naveen Andrews in *The English Patient*, so I followed up.

My official position was Health Researcher (Category IV) for the United Nations Human Rights Council (UN HRC). In brief, I was a summarizer tasked with taking complicated research and reducing it to talking points—bulleted lists, fourteen-point font. Vis-à-vis the HRC, most of the nearly two hundred member states wanted me to build a bulwark of data against my own country. Anything to get the United States to come to its senses was the popular sentiment throughout the UN.

At first, I felt strange about working for the world and not my country, like the orphan athletes who carry the nondescript flag at the opening ceremony of the Olympics. But Quimby explained that we had no choice. "Convincing the US to do no harm is the full-time job of many, many people," he said. "What did you think happened here?"

The truth was I hadn't given it much thought. Also true: it didn't matter. My questionable influence peddling didn't influence shit. In a short period of time, I learned that the United States was immune to easily interpretable, common-sense data on everything—pollution, tuberculosis, birth control, abortion, breastfeeding, war, rape, white phosphorous, blue phosphorous, red phosphorous, lithium, PTSD, GMOs, slavery, winged migration, lions, tigers, polar bears, grizzly bears, panda bears, capital punishment, corporal punishment, spanking, poverty, drug decriminalization, incarceration, labor unions, cooperative business structures, racist mascots, climate change, Puerto Rico, Yemen, Syria, Flint, Michigan, women, children, wheelchairs, factory farms, bees, whales, sharks, daylight saving, roman numerals, centimeters, condoms, coal, cockfighting, horse betting, dog racing, doping, wealth redistribution, mass transit, the IMF, CIA, IDF, MI5, MI6, TNT, snap bracelets, Pez dispensers, Banksy. It didn't matter what it was. If the Human Rights Council (or Cuba) advocated one way, the United States went the other.

I kept at it anyway. This was, after all, what I was paid to do. And a few times, human rights did line up with US interests. AIDS initiatives, for example, were well funded as long as they didn't include mention of sex work, harm reduction, or anal sex. Also popular: eagles and pharmaceuticals.

Charles in Charge, take this report to the top was my primary directive. "The top" meant the penthouse floor, where the United States set up its operations. No other member state had its own floor, but the United States had threatened to leave many times during the George W. Bush years, and since it gave more money to the UN than any other state—although it gave less in proportion to its GDP than most wealthy nations and several of the poor ones—the international community, in an effort to placate, offered the United States the most prime of its already circumscribed real estate. Never mind that the United States was 146th in terms of population density, 83rd in peacekeeper contributions, and that what it did contribute was always late, less than what they'd promised, and came with a bad attitude.

The penthouse elevator, a refurbished contraption with 1970s maroon carpeting and a bright, LED control panel, made only two stops (top and bottom), slowly. On the way up, the trip lasted six minutes; the reverse was four—something about gravity, I was told. The silver lining to all of this elevator travel was that most of the sex I had in the first six months retained an air of privacy. The remainder transpired in the middle stall of the nineteenth-floor bathroom, not far from the Hall of U Thant busts.

I wasn't alone in slipping skins at the nexus of global diplomacy. The UN functioned essentially as a sex club with simultaneous translation. And although everyone kept a shroud of decorum about it, it was frequent, widespread, and usually peaked after voting days. The musty aroma didn't supplant the fetor of failure and futility that hung in the air and along the corridors, like inert gases or the ghosts of the League of Nations. But it certainly helped.

Betwixt the sex, I worked. On Mondays, I gathered and synthesized the relevant research pertaining to a Friday vote. Tuesdays, I delivered the one-pager to the penthouse. Wednesdays, I dropped off a shorter version with larger font. On Thursdays, but sometimes Friday mornings, I received a "We don't understand" memo, occasionally with a list of questions. Often, however, the sheet was blank but for the header ("God Bless America") and footer ("God Bless America").

In a place where the United States had so much power, hope was naïve.

"This is the netherworld between possibility and delusion, but we continue to give it our all," said my supervisor, a soft-spoken Tamil and former resistance fighter who wore pantsuits, shiny scarves, and flats. Jaya rarely interfered in my work, only occasionally suggesting that I add one more bullet point or that I indent my sub-lists. She also never left her office and always brought her lunch from home. If there was a warrior in her, it lay in repose beneath a passive, perfunctory veneer. The Sri Lankan government appointed her to the Human Rights Council during a temporary ceasefire, as a form of exile, Quimby explained. "She hasn't a passport—not an uncommon predicament here."

Each morning, upon entering the main building, my first stop was the second floor, where all of us were required to leave our phones in personalized lead boxes that fit seamlessly into a floor-to-ceiling wall unit composed of thousands of cubbies. The unintended side effect of being phone-less was that cruising happened the old-fashioned way. No dating apps or text messages or semicolons. Just eye contact. Corridors and bathrooms in the UN were how all streets and bathrooms used to be—namely, gay and closeted. The dalliances were too. Discretion, after all, wasn't only the mode at the UN; it was the guiding principle, for both policy-making and fornication. Over time, I inferred that divulging anything might be grounds for termination.

"Yes, it's wise to be circumspect," Quimby said, after another day of deflating No votes and a few pints. "On the other hand," he added, with raised eyebrows and a subtle hunch of his back, "some people have found innovative ways to use these encounters to their benefit."

"Do you mean blackmail?"

Quimby scanned the main room of (W)hole Glory for anyone who might be "earwigging," as he put it. "Not blackmail," he said, leaning in close, "but yes, blackmail."

In addition to being a warren of workplace inappropriateness, the UN also served as an asylum of sorts for people facing all manner of discrimination in their home countries. Discrimination that could easily be weaponized here too.

Quimby must have seen straight through my eyes into the place where the gears had begun to turn, because immediately he switched into a severe tone. "Take heed, Charles in Charge. Once you're caught in the web, it is near impossible to become unstuck."

I nodded.

Quimby drank half of his beer in one go. Then he patted down the drops that had spilled onto his shirt. "Richard's in town," he said. "You wanna come back to ours for a roll in the hay?"

"Another time," I said. I had had a quickie with a Senegalese tourist before leaving work.

It was common knowledge that Saudi Arabia wanted to maintain the practice of beheadings. And since the king and his princes had been, for years, disbursing low-interest gold ingots to the world's most unsuccessful businessmen, no one on the Security Council, neither permanent nor temporary members (except for Venezuela, Vietnam, and Uruguay), was eager to support an upcoming resolution calling for a worldwide ban.

"You will have to give this report more oomph," said Jaya and halfheartedly curled her fingers into a fist that resembled that of a gambler and not of a freedom fighter.

Apart from the usual mix of statistics and boilerplate pith, I included evidence of how the practice of beheadings was applied discriminatorily in the few countries in the world where it remained common practice. I also appended proof of their barbarity—testimonies of loved ones, pictures, verses from the Bible, and a copy of *Braveheart*.

Somewhat surprisingly, no one responded; not even the usual fax from the Americans.

The Saudis, like the Israelis, Egyptians, Russians, and Liechtensteiners, were known for playing rough. Upset them even a little and an onslaught of press releases questioning the very legitimacy of the UN appeared swiftly, which in the case of Israel was uniquely frustrating because the UN had legitimized its existence in the first place. (Periodically, a cartoon drawing of the Israeli ambassador pulling the rug out from under himself circulated the General Assembly.) If I were going to do anything more to give this resolution a chance, I'd need to be cautious.

Quimby lent me his camera—a slender, 007-like device that he kept taped under his desk—which I used to record myself with Mo, the special assistant to the special assistant to Faisal, the Saudi ambassador. Mo was a small fry, physically and figuratively, but he was the closest I ever got to Faisal—the spoiled, third-born son of a very powerful businessman who'd been incapable of putting out the fires his son habitually started back home. (In addition to refuge and asylum, the UN was a rehabilitation camp for those with too much privilege to face consequences.) After arranging the camera on a shelf of the Dag Hammarskjöld library—"the Old Jag-off Hammar library," Quimby called it—I made my way to the halal cafeteria on the thirteenth floor, where Mo tended to have lunch on Wednesdays. From there, it wasn't difficult to lure him into the stacks. The hard part was making sure we stayed in the camera's field of vision. Mo kept whipping me around in overwrought gestures that suggested he wanted desperately to be good at something he hadn't practiced enough.

Ironically, it was Mo's aversion to being decapitated that ultimately led to Saudi Arabia's support for the resolution against beheadings. "I need to show you something," I said to him the day after our gambol in the library.

"Yes, of course. Shall we go back to Jag Hammar?" he asked.

But I pulled us into a nearby office-supply closet instead. When I held up the camera, he began to cry. I was completely unprepared for his reaction. Usually stoic, Mo cried several viscous tears that hung from his chin for a small eternity before free falling toward his wingtips. I felt shitty but didn't know how to recant. *Just kidding* seemed a foolish and insufficient way forward. It didn't matter. Before I could say anything more, he wiped his face with his tie, crossed his arms, and disappeared.

Rumor has it that Faisal rejected Mo's harried request for reconsideration on the resolution and threatened to have him sent home, but instead of folding, Mo threatened back with a video of his own—one he'd been keeping for just such an occasion. Faisal grabbed Mo by his tie and leaned into his face, screaming, spittle flying. "My pet tiger will eat your spleen alive for this," he said. That Friday, Faisal lobbied for an amendment to the day's agenda so that he could speak before the Security Council vote. Saudi Arabia would not oppose the resolution. The surprising reversal led to a brief recess, during which Australia and the United States regrouped with their allies and decided to support the resolution.

"Congratulations," Quimby said at happy hour on the evening of the vote. "Now, lay low. Don't get greedy."

A few days later, I had a romp in the Kofi Annan Memorial Lounge with Robin, the spokesperson for the Swedish Mission. Afterward, he shepherded through the resolution against Iranian sanctions. Next, it was Wojciech, a cultural attaché from Poland, who, after an elevator ride, helped to maneuver a condemnation of the Brazilian president's fascist rhetoric. Then came Joe, the King of Thailand's valet plenipotentiary.

His real name was Apichatpong, but Joe was easier in this country, he told me. At his insistence, we went to his office. The room had no windows, and my repeated attempts at turning on the lights were met with resistance. Eventually, he pulled away and buttoned up his shirt. "I know what you are trying to do," he said, as he re-looped his belt. "That will not work with me. The king cares nothing of what I do. He cares nothing about anything. Try instead to ask me directly for what you need." Joe was a slight man with a shaved head, faint mustache, and rimless eyeglasses. His sincerity embarrassed me. I zipped up my pants and walked toward the door. "Charles in Charge, your way is not sustainable," he called out.

After that, I took a break from sex altogether. I focused instead on writing reports, which proved easy because everyone seemed to be nursing cold sores in those cold months. Herpes, for me, was old hat, but I didn't want to risk co-infection with another strain or a superinfection.

I was on my third gin martini and ninth olive when the stool next to mine crashed onto the floor. I turned to find a contorted figure trying to pick up his mess. It was Brad. Red-eyed, upper-middle-class, youth-adjacent Brad. Drunk but full of vim, vigor, and, as the girthy silhouette in his pants suggested, virility. That night, he fell asleep during sex, and I wasn't able to wake him. The following morning, I fried eggs and bacon and toasted week-old sourdough. It's what I would have made anyway, but since I had a companion, I prepared twice as much. I'd half-expected him to play the role of aloof straight man with amnesia, but he was polite and, generally, quite genial. He was also the first UN coworker I'd ever brought home.

Over several cups of coffee, I learned that Brad was a trust fund kid with an almost undetectable lisp and half an MBA. On the surface, he reminded me of all the guys in college who'd never given me the time of day. His father had been a vice president at IBM in its heyday, and his grandfather had been a well-known confidante of Ronald Reagan, as well as Nancy's paramour throughout most of the

Cold War. In fact, Brad appeared in the annual extended-family photographs of several prominent political families. These connections had marked his life—a warm welcome into Exeter and Yale, then Harvard, then out of Harvard, and, finally, into the UN. I'd known him simply as one of the quiet Americans who waited at the penthouse elevator bank to receive my reports. Once, maybe twice, I'd flirted with him, but he'd been unreceptive, and, to my credit, I hadn't insisted. A younger version of myself would have set aside dignity to pursue him—rejections from white men have always come across as institutional or systemic, serving only to invigorate me. But my adult self met his disinterest with my own.

Despite our height and age disparities—three inches and ten years—Brad and I bound to one another like a small magnet to a refrigerator door. It happened quickly too. I can't quite articulate how or why, but a week after the eggs and bacon, his toothbrush and retainer appeared in my medicine cabinet.

As an unspoken rule, Brad and I didn't acknowledge each other at work, but whenever I delivered a report to the Americans, he made sure to be waiting. The elevator doors would open, he'd pop his head inside, and we'd embrace until the beeping commenced. Those few, wet kisses constituted all of the contact we had outside of my apartment. At his request, we also avoided arriving or leaving the UN at the same time, and we never discussed work. I preferred it that way. Better was to make dinner with him, interrupt dinner preparations to have sex, continue dinner-making, eat while watching reruns of *Designing Women*—a show he'd never heard of, which led to an awkward moment in the third week, when we were both reminded of our difference in age—and have sex again. Through it all, there was no mention of trade relations or species on the verge of extinction or tsunami relief or the official song of the World Cup. Our interactions were of the most basic variety: eat, fuck, sitcoms. And I questioned none of it, including our eventual shift into the middle place between lust and love. No man's land was an unfamiliar, classless, colorblind waiting room so comfortable that I didn't care what was next.

Until the sixth week. That's when I noticed reticence. Reticence in the kitchen. Reticence on the couch. Reticence in the elevator.

"Do you want to call it quits?" I asked.

"What? No! Why?"

"Oh. Well, you've been distant or uneasy lately."

"I'm sorry," he said, and folded himself onto the couch like an origami giraffe, leaving nary an opening between us. "It's work. Just work stuff. Nothing to do with you. I promise." Then he kissed my neck and unbuttoned my shirt. Afterward, both of us were famished but neither wanted to cook. We ordered dinner from the new pan-everywhere vegan restaurant that he'd been wanting to visit, and before going to bed I acquiesced to a rerun of *Modern Family*, which he'd been advocating for all week.

The following night, his typical, upbeat confidence was again adagio. I wasn't as worried as I'd been when I'd thought his mood had something to do with me, but I wanted him back to the way he was nonetheless.

"Do you want to talk about it?—The thing at work, I mean."

"Not really."

"Might make you feel better."

Up to then, we'd done well by our rule of never discussing work, which should not have been easy, since our livelihoods were in some way tied to most current events as well as all of history. But after a bit more prodding, Brad opened up. "You see, the deputy rep is putting a lot of pressure on me to secure opposition for an upcoming resolution. And it's more difficult than I expected. To complicate matters, a colleague let it slip that I'm on some sort of probation. Apparently, I've been underperforming."

"Is it because of me—Us?"

"No, no. I don't think so. I've just been trying to do too much. I was hoping to move from communications into something legislative. But now I have to get my act together. Without this job, it's back to Bunkport for me."

"Which resolution is it? The one that's giving you trouble."

"The, uh—The one calling for a truth and reconciliation commission to investigate war crimes in El Salvador."

"I know it well."

He nodded.

"You know, my family is from El Salvador."

He nodded again, and I suddenly felt trapped. Between what or who, I wasn't sure. I began to nibble the inside of my lip.

"It's more complicated than you think," he said. "This may surprise you, but we plan to get behind the resolution. The problem is that China signaled support for the T&R commission first, and we can't go on record agreeing with China about a human-rights issue. That would set a bad precedent."

Maybe I'd been working at the UN too long, but in that moment, his reasoning made perfect sense.

During dinner, Brad remained quiet. He spent more time dragging his spaghetti around the plate than eating. Afterward, he loaded the dishwasher and washed the pots and lids that didn't fit— something he did often and that felt anomalous to who he was and where he came from. I mean, white men certainly wash dishes, but not white men who have family homes in Kennebunkport and who call Kennebunkport "Bunkport." And never pots and lids. When we were done cleaning up, Brad didn't want to watch any television, preferring instead to continue reading a tome of an LBJ biography in bed. I was left feeling like an unwanted guest in my own home, or the child of working-class parents around the first of the month, or a drunk person in a library. Finally, I broke the silence. "Is there something I can do to help?"

Brad set the gigantic book down over his bare abdomen. "I don't want to mix you up in all this."

"So there is something?"

"I don't know. You see, China agreed to support the resolution after El Salvador cut its diplomatic ties with Taiwan. We believe that if El Salvador were, in some way, to re-recognize Taiwan's existence before Friday's vote—even a minor overture—China would recant its support for the resolution, leaving us free to back it."

I sat on the edge of the bed and thought about it for a minute.

"I don't understand. Why the sudden concern for human rights?"

"That's not fair. We are for human rights."

I didn't respond, but Brad must have read my face. "I can see why an outsider would think that," he said.

"I'm not an outsider."

"You know what I mean."

I knew what he meant, but I also thought it was possible that he could mean several things at once.

"Charles in Charge, we care about El Salvador. It's an ally."

"Nothing else?"

"Well"—Brad sat upright—"there's a Central American trade agreement coming up. We plan to ask El Salvador to rename its largest garment-factory city 'USA.' If they agree, the majority of textiles and apparel coming out of the country will read—"

"Let me guess: 'Made in USA.'"

Brad shrugged.

"What's the point? The clothes would still be made in El Salvador."

"People just want to see it on the label. This is something that unites the local-sourcing movement on the left and the nationalistic patriots on the right," he explained. "No one is going to investigate past the label—we're getting ahead of ourselves anyway. What's important is that we support El Salvador's resolution now, so that they come through for us later. A win for retail and for human rights. It's a no-brainer."

Brad had come up onto his knees and was resting irresistibly on his heels, an impish grin across his face. The bedsheet had slid down onto the bed. Apart from the portrait of LBJ covering his johnson, he was naked.

"You overestimate my position and abilities if you think I can get El Salvador to change its stance on Taiwan."

"I don't have any doubts about your abilities," Brad said before Lyndon Baines Johnson went face down onto the bed.

The center-left party in El Salvador had campaigned on promises of de-privatizing water and truth and reconciliation. After winning the election, the new president signed bills that nationalized half of the drinking-water supply, but he was dragging his feet on T&R. In the 1990s, the first UN-sanctioned investigation into the atrocities of the country's civil war lay the preponderance of blame on right-wing paramilitaries and oligarchs. The Salvadorian government at the time was composed of conservative factions who disregarded the findings and never again mentioned truth or reconciliation. Although the left was now in power, it, too, feared what an investigation might uncover, especially with so many former revolutionaries in the government, including the new president. They knew the right would use false equivalency as a winning strategy, and the left would risk losing a power they had only just acquired. A trap door, vis-à-vis Taiwan, would be an appealing option.

"Oh, mate. Getting into bed with the Americans is a terrible idea. They're all cute hoors," Quimby said, something he was wont to say of anyone he considered unsavory. "Besides, T&R has been sought for years by the survivors of the war. If it falls apart now . . ." Quimby raised his pint and his eyebrows.

Politically speaking, Quimby was a mellower version of the young man I recalled from my college days, the one who wrote his dissertation about the Irish struggle for northern independence as a *J'Accuse* of the British monarchy ("Anglican? How about Angli*won't*! Fuck the King, the Queen, and the Entire Chessboard"). Even so, he never passed up an opportunity to openly disdain the descendants of his own countrymen here, whom he accused of desecrating their anti-colonialist histories: "Is there anything more despicable than a New York City cop with an Irish surname?" he'd say whenever we walked past a white police officer.

"And what about your family, Charles in Charge?" Quimby set the empty glass down, revealing a light foam mustache. "Have you thought of them?"

The political congruencies between El Salvador and Ireland had always interested Quimby. In the afterglow of our office-hour romps in college, he'd ask me to recount the few family tales I knew because he said they reminded him of the stories his mother used to tell him. Lore about aunts, uncles, and cousins who'd worn wigs and prosthetic noses, baked codes and coordinates into pupusas, and trained in armed combat in jungles and university basements. People I'd never met, some of whom were still alive and, frankly, needed—if not urgently, then sooner rather than later—truth and reconciliation. Much of the country did. And while I may not have felt much allegiance to these stories and characters, actively betraying them seemed unnecessary.

"Don't view it that way," Brad said on my couch, on the eve of the vote. "Besides, it's a moot point. Thanks to you, we're free to support El Salvador."

Brad had been right about China. Once Taiwan reentered the picture, the Chinese balked.

I was the one who had made sure Taiwan reentered the picture.

Hipólito, El Salvador's assistant to the deputy ambassador, tended to cruise near the Boutros Boutros-Ghali Gallery on the twenty-fourth floor. As a place of art, it was unremarkable—a room full of empty plinths and lesser works by well-known painters that had been found in the rubble of war zones—but at the end of the mustard-colored corridor, there was a single-occupancy restroom that was rarely occupied. The guilt of cheating on Brad left me impotent at first, but after a few minutes, and despite the cold tile, I was able to enjoy myself. When we were done, Hipólito sat bare-assed on the sink, running his knuckly fingers through his hair. "Uff. Eso me hacía falta," he said before exhaling forcefully.

"I also needed that," I replied, as I handed him his pants. "Oh, and just a heads-up, Australia is going to propose an emergency amendment to the resolution, one that requires immediate extradition to the International Criminal Court for anyone found to have aided or abetted war crimes during the civil war. I heard they want to go hard after the current administration so that the right wing wins the next election."

"¿Qué?" Hipólito hopped off the sink, scrambled for his shoes, and ran off.

By lunchtime, the Salvadorians were abuzz. The following morning, the president of El Salvador, who had been scheduled to appear at the UN for Friday's vote, canceled his visit. This signaled to everyone that something was awry. And when the Salvadorian mission announced that the president would be visiting Taiwan instead, everyone assumed the resolution to be dead on arrival.

"You tested positive for gonorrhea. You're asymptomatic, but you're still a carrier," said Dr. Pangilinan over the phone, on the morning of the vote. "Nothing to worry about, just refrain from sex for a week after you've completed your treatment. And please notify all of your sexual partners since your last exam."

I hadn't had gonorrhea since college.

"Down with your draws," said Quimby, who kept a stash of ceftriaxone and azithromycin in his desk. The former was an injection; the latter, pills.

"Shit, Quim, there have been dozens of men since my last checkup, and I don't have any of their phone numbers. I might be responsible for a global epidemic."

"That's nothing. Half the UN died in the 1980s," he said. "But don't fret, everyone here is on PrEP, and they know to keep a drawer full of these." Quimby held up the bottle of Zithro and the empty syringe. "Feel bad for the tourists."

I nodded along, like a poorly trained public-health worker.

"Are you going downstairs for the session? Your vote should be coming up soon."

"No. I'm going to watch from the Ban Ki-moon Room," I said, as I zipped up.

When I arrived at the viewing deck, groups of second-tier aides and elementary-school students were making their way into the plexiglass-encased chamber above the Security Council. Just outside was Jaya, her hand over her chin, softly squeezing her own face. I'd never before seen her away from her office. "This one has slipped from of our hands," she said without looking at me. "There is a populist fool waiting to capitalize on the disillusionment of the Salvadorian people. Our failure today will certainly guarantee him the next election. I fear for El Salvador's history and its future."

"It will happen today. I'm certain of it," I responded.

"Have you not heard the murmurs in the corridors?"

"Gossip. That's all."

Jaya looked at me askance. "We almost had a win," she said. "Almost."

"Worst case, we can prepare for another vote in a few months," I said, hoping to lighten her mood.

"Tell me, Charles in Charge, during your brief tenure here, have you ever witnessed a motion fail and return for a vote? There has not been a landmine resolution since Princess Diana."

"Have some faith, Jaya."

"Faith?" Jaya gave a scornful shake to her head. "Faith is for the unseen. Am I not visible to you?"

I nodded slowly, unsure if she'd used a double negative.

"You know, Charles in Charge, many people come here looking inside of these walls for what they have never been able to find outside of them. You're not the first."

Although I didn't understand what Jaya meant, I continued nodding. She turned, as if to leave, but remained in place with her back to me. "Charles in Charge," she whispered, "a piece of advice: you don't have to do anything if you don't want to, but don't get in the fucking way either." Then she marched back toward her office.

The speaker system in the viewing room created an uncanny effect: everyone was living the experience while simultaneously listening to it over a radio. The agenda listed the vote on El Salvador as the fourth of five items. On the floor now was the second, a resolution opposing a statue of Slobodan Milosevic in Manila, part of the new Filipino president's homage to his heroes. (He'd already erected tributes to Suharto, Mussolini, and Andrew Jackson.) The first vote of the day, a resolution banning plastic bags, failed 8–7. Australia, which had classified it as an environmental MUSE (a Matter of Utmost Security and Exigency), cast the deciding vote against itself. With the United States breathing down its neck, Australia argued that the resolution was poorly written and ultimately inefficient—never mind that Australia had written the text to begin with.

In a rare win, the proclamation against the Milosevic statue passed 10–4, with one abstention, despite protestations from the Filipino envoy. "Spain and the United States made us this way!" he shouted while leveling his shoe against his desk. "And all of the airports here are named after warmongers!" Afterward, there was a fifteen-minute recess.

The third item was sanctions on Israel in response to its Friday massacres of Palestinians in Gaza. But no sooner had gavel hit table than Israel's representative interrupted to argue that the measure didn't clarify if it included today. "Today, after all, is also a Friday," he said. "If the resolution includes today, it is invalid because we have definitive proof that Israeli Defense Forces have not yet fired upon anyone. And it is too early to assume that anything will happen later." Before any other delegates could respond, the US representative offered a motion to table the resolution until the following Friday so that they could have time to gather information about this Friday. Without a single hand going up or down, the functionary announced that the motion had passed 14–1. Everyone, including the Israeli delegation, looked gobsmacked. A slow train of sighs, boos, and tsks gradually circled the hall and entered our enclosed aerie.

Next was El Salvador.

As the chamber reshuffled, I noticed Brad conferring with his delegation, a small coterie of faint pinstripes and one sienna skirt suit, most of whom were seated and balding. Whenever he bent over to speak to them, he pressed his tie against his midsection—the red one with white diagonal stripes that I had picked out that morning. The Americans nodded with bobble-headed fervor. Brad then walked over to the Australian delegation and went through a similar protocol. He shook their hands before walking up the aisle and disappearing a level beneath me.

The United States put forth the motion to support the Salvadorian resolution. Venezuela, Vietnam, Uruguay, Sweden, Burkina Faso, the United Kingdom, and the United States voted in favor, just as we had foreseen. Opposition arose expectedly from China, Russia, France, Guatemala, Poland, Kazakhstan, and Uganda. Australia was the last to cast its vote, and when the ambassador raised his hand, he said, "No." Then he added, "Without prejudice."

"The resolution fails by a vote of eight to seven," announced a short bespectacled woman at the podium. "We will take a short recess and resume the agenda on the hour."

I leaned forward and pressed both hands against the plexiglass. The crowd of people behind me trickled out of the room. Half of them were nonplussed in a traditional English manner; the other half were North American nonplussed; all of them hummed the "Marseillaise." When I thought the room had cleared, the sound of faux throat-clearing entered. "Charles in Charge," he said.

"You—"

"Let me explain."

"I don't understand. The Australians always do what you want them to. How could—"

"They did do what we wanted them to."

"But—you—"

Brad's eyes widened, like those of an underfed lemur. His body, however, was a steel beam on an ancient burial ground. "Be realistic," he said. "Did you think the United States was going to open itself up to being investigated? El Salvador's civil war was essentially of our making."

Brad's point was completely logical. Still, I was angry. "You didn't have to do all of this. You have the power to veto whatever you want."

"Veto too much and you get a reputation."

"Huh?"

"The world's changing. We can't risk another state actor becoming the moral compass. You prefer Russia? China? No one wants that. Playing the game is the only way."

"Game?"

"Don't be coy. Why don't we ask Mo about playing games? Oh, right, he's no longer here. In fact, he's no longer anywhere. He has the distinction of being Saudi Arabia's last *official* beheading." (I'd heard the rumor about Mo's death, but nothing had been confirmed.) "Perspective, Charles in Charge. That's what you need. You're alive. I'm alive. No harm from this. You've lived to fight another day."

My ears went warm. Something, possibly my heart, was expanding in my throat. Somewhere in my chest was my stomach.

"But I—weren't you—I mean . . . We all suck, Brad, but you're the worst."

His gaze turned downward. Above us was a sketch-like painting of Earth, a graph of gilded longitudes and latitudes: an outlined world with no sign of life.

"I guess this means I'm not going to see you later?"

I continued to stare at the empty globe, silent.

"Okay, have it your way. See you around, Charles in Charge."

"Yes, this is hell after all."

I thought I heard him chuckle in response, but I wasn't certain because by that point the sounds of outside had come in through the open door.

Quimby was waiting for me at my desk. He'd come to give his condolences about El Salvador. "Don't get down on yourself. I've been there before," he said. "We all have. You have no idea how much the future of this world is shaped by a few shags."

I nodded.

"But didn't I tell you never to trust the emissary of an empire?"

"You did."

Quimby patted my shoulder. "Lesson learned," he said. "Well, the Puerto Rico resolution is next on the docket. You coming?"

"I don't have high hopes for independence."

"No, of course not. But that's not why we're here."

"Then why are we here?"

"Harm reduction, Charles in Charge."

"Not today. I'm taking the afternoon to myself."

"Suit yourself. (W)hole Glory later?"

"Of course."

THE GREAT
POTATO FAMINE

IT WAS HOT—ATYPICAL OF EARLY March. An op-ed in yesterday's paper had urged Obama to call for a drastic reduction in carbon emissions. These op-eds seemed to appear weekly ever since that Al Gore documentary a few years ago. Yesterday's writer was particularly incensed by "humanity's obliviousness" and "our lack of concern for the planet's imminent immolation." Misplaced anger, in my opinion. People won't confront anything they perceive as far away or out of their control, like heart disease or the world's end, if they can't first meet their own needs, like rent or diapers.

In any case, it was lunch time, and I was trying, without much luck, to catch a cab on 8th Avenue. Fifteen empty, on-duty taxis zoomed past me, but I found it difficult to be upset. It wasn't apathy. It was, as my doctor had said twenty-five minutes earlier, "Probably the flu. Stay home, rest, steam baths for your lungs, ibuprofen if you can't tolerate the fever."

Sixteen. Seventeen. Eighteen. Nineteen.

I distrust cabs—there, I said it—same as they distrust me. I've known the indignity of being denied a taxi from Penn Station after finding a way out of Penn Station. I've felt the injustice of being stranded in the East Village while drunker, more impertinent, and worse tippers, who haven't waited nearly as long, are whisked away. I've been enraged. I've been diminished. But I've found ways to rebound: the subway, more whisky, the middle finger. The ignominy, however, of being denied a ride home in full light—on a day when standing upright bordered on hardship—was in a category all its own.

Let me be clear: I am uncomfortable with the race and class implications of all this. Being denied a cab is hardly the Indian Removal Act of 1830 or a poll tax or the NYPD. But does my mundane, middle-class experience with interpersonal racism not deserve redress because it's a somehow more civilized offshoot of systemic, state-sponsored racism? I didn't, after all, say anything when my younger, white colleague, Connor, who researches the effects of pesticides on human gonad development, was offered tenure before I was. And I kept my mouth shut when the dean of our school called me *José* at the first seven faculty meetings, even after apologizing three of those times and promising not to do it again. And all I did was smile and wave when my neighbor welcomed me to the neighborhood, two years after he, his wife, and kid moved in two doors down, which was eight years after I'd moved there. But at some point, it feels almost like a responsibility to raise a red flag. I mean, if one does everything exactly as they are told to and, by bootstrap, one arrives to the exclusive place that everybody is striving to reach but somehow still isn't allowed inside or, worse, is allowed inside but no one inside engages with this person meaningfully, it seems that said interloper should report this to the line of class jumpers waiting behind him, as a warning of sorts: Don't come any further! It was all a ruse! The ATM is out of service! These are not the droids you're looking for!

No?

In all fairness, I couldn't be certain of what was passing through the minds of the cab drivers who kept driving past me earlier today. As a slightly built Latino with flu-like symptoms and an asymmetrical goatee, I was shaped by worn stereotypes. The effrontery might well have been a vestige from the initial AIDS panic, when everyone trained themselves to stay away from sickly men in Manhattan.

Maybe . . . ?

Except that the cabs earlier today weren't veering away or speeding up with the evasiveness one associates with fear of contagion. There was a more traditional form of discrimination at play, an almost imperceptible acceleration that screamed, *It never, for one second, crossed my mind to stop*—the kind of prejudice that correlates my brown skin with unsavoriness or, worse, frugality.

White men in dark suits, white women in pencil skirts, white tourists wearing white shorts and cameras, old white people, young whites, tightly sculpted, shiny whites, and one racially ambiguous person in business casual: everyone seemed to be getting into a taxi, while I remained, one fatigued arm propped up by another, in a slack, impolitic military salute.

On an emptier street, a taxi would have stopped. I am, after all, better than no fare. In a Black neighborhood, too, I would have caught a ride. In that scenario, I become the white person.

"Save me. Can't catch cab."

My boyfriend appeared amid the throng of lunchers jaywalking toward me, only a few minutes after I'd texted him—his office was just up the street. He wore a linty black fleece jacket, loose-fitting brown canvas pants, and in his beard were flecks of popcorn, the eating of which I must have just interrupted.

He'd barely stepped foot onto the corner, when "I'm sorry" poured out. Typical of him: apologizing for society, as if he'd been at the Constitutional Convention. "I should have gotten one for you at the doctor's office instead of letting you walk me to work," he said.

Although infantilizing, he was right. The protective sphere that accompanies whiteness is undeniable. Don't get me wrong: I love my boyfriend. But when I'm asking for a table at a restaurant, walking through security at the airport, applying for a home loan, in the ER, at the ice cream shop, at Whole Foods, at the gay bar, the post office, or any time I see a cop, I'm much more confident if he's by my side.

"I should have just taken the train," I said.

"The C at this hour? And then the walk home from there? You can barely stand."

The taxi halted at my boyfriend's feet less than ten seconds after he'd flung his arm into the air. I'd expected exactly this, but I was nonetheless amazed. I pressed my fingers onto my cheek bones to relieve sinus pressure, before wondering how complicated it would be to fashion a Molotov cocktail from the hand sanitizer in my pocket.

Getting angry.

Flooding my body with cortisol.

Distracting my immune system.

That's exactly what they want, isn't it?

Who's they?

"Here." My boyfriend pulled a bunched-up plastic bag from his jacket. "In case you get sick on the way home."

I stepped into the yellow car.

"I'll leave work early," he said, before pressing the door shut.

·　·　·

"Where to?" The driver's booming voice startled me. He was a large man reduced to a rectangular reflection: ruddy, translucent cheeks, a bulbous nose with large pores, and thin ash-blond hair that was chin-length and well receded: a composite of Gerard Depardieu and Mr. Potato Head.

"Brooklyn. Over the Manhattan Bridge. Left onto Myrtle."

The driver sighed, murmured something, then craned his neck to stare at me directly, as if to end a conversation that we'd never started. I fixed my eyes on the loose upholstery hanging from the ceiling. The car remained still.

It'd happened a few times before that a driver refused to leave Manhattan; once, even when I was with my boyfriend. This man, however, seemed to be willing me to relinquish the ride of my own volition.

"Jesus freakin' Christ Brooklyn!" he bellowed, when I showed no signs of comprehension. Then he turned on the meter and raised the volume on the talk radio, before pulling away.

This is what you get for leapfrogging someone in the hierarchy, for inverting the power dynamic.

The cab's interior reminded me of my local diner. Inside of me, organs and vessels squirmed. I ran my hand along the chipped, navy blue vinyl and breathed in the worn plastic. Outside, I could see the people—gay veterans, unwed mothers, Muslims, socialists—being seared by the anti-everyone vitriol blaring through the taxi's speakers.

I did my best to tolerate the intolerance, but by the time we reached Canal, I couldn't bear it any longer. "I have a headache," I said, "Could you lower the volume a bit?"

He mumbled to himself something about "his cab" and "his right to listen to whatever he wanted to." He said it loudly, so that I had no choice but to eavesdrop. After an obstreperous belch, which I took as an insult, and some indecipherable grumble that I pretended not to hear, he brought the volume down. I tipped my head onto the frame of the half-opened window and lapped up the minor victory. The warm, exhaust-laden air massaged my scalp and blew out my curls. I recalled *Crash*, the movie that missed the point but won the Oscar anyway. My mind replayed the scene where Matt Dillon rescues Thandie Newton from the burning car, miraculously solving racism in the process. I decided then that if the cab were to explode before I reached home, I wouldn't try to save the driver.

I thought, too, of my father, who once worked as a porter at an apartment building on the Upper West Side, where he hailed thousands of cabs for his tenants. And yet, I have no memory of ever stepping foot inside of one. Not until after college. I don't recall that first time being a traumatic experience. ("Taxi!" And Poof! it appeared.) It was later—the second or third time—that the cab-hailing began to resemble the drink-ordering at crowded Midtown bars where one regularly meets their college buddies, who are all white because *someone* spent college trying to get in with the *right* people, after drawing the conclusion, however subconsciously, that connections were more important than skill, hard work, or racial solidarity. And now, that same human-shaped bundle of ambitious neurons and wayward neurochemicals can't order a drink, can't catch a cab, and doesn't have many friends with whom he can commiserate.

"Where to now?" he shouted.

I had dozed off for a couple of minutes, and we were a few blocks from my home, driving up the commercial strip known colloquially as 'The Great Divide,' where one side is a bleak wall of public housing still recovering from the effects of redlining; the other, an inexorable flood of new money and brownstone renovations propped up by the stock market and generational wealth. All of it teetering on a fulcrum of distrust.

"Take a right at the next light. I'm on the left, just after the scaffolding."

Four construction sites on my block alone. Between them were trees, childcare workers, and cracked pavement—people spend millions on a new home but not a dime to fix the sidewalk. The taxi stopped abruptly, two houses too soon.

"Your credit card machine isn't on," I said.

"You don't have cash?"

By this point, it seemed he was yelling, but because my ears were plugged, the anger was muted.

"No, not on me."

"You got cash at home?" he asked.

"I do," I responded, before I could remind myself that I don't have to respond to every question that's posed to me.

"I'll wait for you here then; leave your ID."

This man was talking to me like the nuns in high school used to.

"But you have a credit card machine."

"It's broken," he said.

The square contraption affixed to the partition between us looked perfectly new.

"What if you drive me to an ATM, and I take out some money?"

"I already stopped the meter. I'm not driving anywhere."

"Is this a prank?"

By way of a response, the driver turned the keys counterclockwise and pulled them from the ignition.

Perhaps his wife had left him recently, I told myself. Perhaps he'd been diagnosed with colon cancer or diverticulitis. Perhaps she'd survived—

No! This is not my problem! I didn't invent Brooklyn or race or the Southern strategy or Manifest Destiny or Spanish colonialism or Christianity. I am merely a passenger.

I felt penned in by the driver's posture and my proclivity toward decorum. Even so, I was besieged by a base desire to tell him off, to let him know that whatever potato famine or religious persecution had inspirited his great grandparents to abandon their leeward-facing, bluff-situated stone cottage and risk their lives on a transatlantic voyage was no longer. That he could probably apply for any number of EU citizenships and return to his ancestral village, where he would be welcomed (arms open, eyes blue) because of its stagnating population growth. That his family line had gone stale here, and because social mobility wasn't what it had been in the 1950s, through no fault of his own (unless he voted for the villainous clowns who'd decimated unions, diluted the minimum wage, and opposed every egalitarian policy of the last fifty years), he had no chance of achieving one sliver of what his parents had wished for him all those years ago when they'd cradled him in the well-appointed room of a fully funded hospital that had since been razed and was now a luxury high-rise. In fact, why was he still here? What exactly was he waiting for? The New World was for us now.

"Fine." I pulled at the door handle. "I'll go get the cash."

"Good. Your ID," he said, and extended his sweaty, tumescent digits through the opening of the divider.

Jumping out of the car and running full sprint was, in retrospect, a silly thing to do. It was also irreversible. Even if I'd had a mid-block change of heart, the driver's stream of invective was already so loud and intractable, I knew I would have been met with an ass whooping and a citizen's arrest. So I kept going.

I ran to the end of the block and turned the corner, against traffic, so that he couldn't follow in his car. In the arched entryway of a vacant storefront, I crouched, out of sight, and pretended to tie my shoes. I was no longer nauseous, but the days-long throbbing in my head, ears, and throat brought on by the flu was now more intense, even if somehow painless. To my right was a dry cleaner with a small vestibule and a large plexiglass barrier—there was no place to hide in there. To my left was the narrow yard of a brownstone, surrounded by a spiked wrought-iron gate that I would never be able to climb.

I heard the siren of a police car.

Everything I'd ever accomplished in my life was suddenly meaningless. I peeled off my thin V-neck sweater and tied it around my shoulders, just as an affluent tourist might. I ran my fingers through my hair and moved speedily, trying my best to appear uninteresting. At the corner, I entered the bodega, the one where I regularly buy overpriced things, and walked straight toward the back. I stood in the narrowest of aisles and pretended to read the labels of jarred tomato sauces, periodically sneaking a look into the multidirectional mirrors that were tucked into the corners of the ceiling. There was a line of helmeted construction workers waiting at the deli counter. The bodega owner, affable and long-armed with a patchy beard, was printing lottery tickets for an elderly man wearing a wool cap.

After a few minutes, I made my way back toward the front of the store. Through a sliver of window that wasn't obstructed by columns of La Croix, I watched a cop car drive by. I panicked and turned toward the ATM console next to the rotting bananas. *I was only going to get money*, I'd tell the police. *This was all a big misunderstanding.* Surely, I could talk my way out of this. A brown public health economist must outrank a white cab driver.

Unable to recall my PIN, I typed four zeroes repeatedly until the machine timed out.

I needed help. The bodega owner had been, for years, a fixture in my life, but I knew only that he was Yemeni and that he arbitrarily set prices—the same six-pack could be eleven dollars one day, fourteen another. I had no idea what his name was or where he lived. It was safe to assume that ten years' worth of Doritos, beer, kombucha, and the occasional breakfast sandwich weren't enough for him to risk trouble with the law.

When the old man had collected his ream of lottery tickets and the construction workers had left with their paper-bagged meals, the owner looked my way. "You need something, buddy?"

Buddy. That's what he usually called me; sometimes, *my friend*. My boyfriend was always *Sir*. I should have minded, but I chose to view his informalities as blips of camaraderie.

"Just waiting for someone," I said. "They'll be here soon."

He nodded and went back to staring at his phone.

After a few minutes, I watched a taxi and two cop cars pull up to the liquor store across the street. Four cops filed out, the cabbie followed closely behind.

An epigenetic urge to leave flooded my insides. If I ran, I could make it home before the cops and the cabbie reemerged. But what if there were cops waiting on my block? I could take a parallel street . . . Cut through my neighbor's yard . . . Climb our fire escape . . . My boyfriend would let me in when he got home from work.

Too late: they shuffled out of the liquor store.

"I need a favor," I half-yelled to the owner.

"Yes, my friend."

I left it vague. I told him that I'd run away from a disagreement with someone who might have called the police. The bodega owner squinted at me and tilted his head, as if he were staring at a painting he didn't quite understand.

"You kill someone?" he asked.

"No! God no! Nothing like that."

"I don't want trouble with police. They never stop harassing me."

I'd become a large cartoon snowball who picks up innocent bystanders as it barrels down a slope. I didn't want this guy to go to jail for me, but I also didn't believe the cops were invested enough in a taxi fare to give him much of a hard time.

"If you let me hide in the back, I'll spend fifty bucks before I leave."

"Two hundred," he said quickly, as if this rate had been established long ago at a council of neighborhood bodega owners.

I acquiesced, and he pointed to a door beside the dairy cooler. From there, I went down a narrow passage that left me behind the beer. It was like being in an alley on a cold night and peering into a brightly lit bar or restaurant.

As I sat their waiting, the adrenaline subsided, and I felt sicker than I'd felt all day. I slid my sweater back on carefully, one limb at a time, then over my head. The cold was coming mostly from within me I realized. The beer cooler itself wasn't chilly, which lined up well with all the years of tepid beers. I quietly crumbled up a large paper bag that lay on the floor and rested it between my head and the brick wall.

Somewhere between thirty seconds and five minutes had passed when I heard the synthetic clanging of the electronic bell. Someone had come through the bodega's front door. I remained as still as I possibly could and closed my eyes. When I opened them briefly, three sets of feet—thick, matted black shoes and dark blue pants bunched at the ankle—appeared. They moved ominously over the tops of loose Corona and Heineken bottles and a smattering of IPAs. I pressed my back against the uneven wall, into the barbed cement, hoping to make myself more unseen. I held my breath and clenched my jaw until I felt lightheaded.

The electronic bell rang again. Almost immediately, the glass case in front of me opened. "They left," said the owner.

"Can I stay here a little longer, please?"

He nodded and turned his palms out, as if to say, *Have it your way.*

I'm still here, shivering, hungry, half-asleep, rubbing my ankles, trying not to imagine that all brown men in the immediate vicinity are being harassed on my account. I contemplated calling my boyfriend, but I feared making noise. I composed a text instead. Then it dawned on me that my phone records could be subpoenaed, so I didn't send it.

How could I have allowed this to happen? What exactly was *this*? Was it the beginning of a long descent? Am I a different person?

I wonder, too, if today's taxi ride was my last. Or maybe the rogue cabbie was of a dying breed, the last gasp before the dawn of a classless, post-racial society. I would now command respect by virtue of being. The kind of person who would step out into the middle of the street and demand cabs to stop.

Or maybe today was an aberration. I'm not, after all, the sort of person who steps out into the middle of the street. I am accommodating, a pleaser, an apologizer, a power bottom with subtendencies, a person who votes far left in the primaries but center in the general. I long ago succumbed to the constructed order of things.

Truth be told, I only take taxis when I travel, when I've had too much to drink, and when I'm sick, none of which happens enough for me to do anything about this. Maybe I just have to suck it up and deal with the C train.

This all makes sense. Humans regularly report behavior change in response to discrimination. I haven't come across research on people who stop hailing cabs, but they do stop seeing doctors whose intentions they don't trust. They stop going to parks where they no longer feel welcome. They stop applying for jobs they don't believe they'll get. Anything, it seems, to avoid unnecessary stress.

ALL THE BULLETS
WERE MADE IN MY
COUNTRY

THERE WAS A PERSON MY sisters and I called Tía. Her name
was Beti, and she wasn't related to us. She was married to Aníbal, a
Colombian man who we called Tío and who also wasn't related to
us. Aníbal and my father worked at the same Manhattan restaurant—a French place where the tables were packed tightly and
the burger platter was legendary, not only for its fries but for
its cornichons.

Beti and Aníbal were a good-looking pair who wore their hair
large and their pants bellbottomed. They comported themselves with
an air of fame, and they were possibly the first cool people in my life.
Beti was from Puerto Rico, and it took some time for Aníbal's relatives and friends to accept her. It wasn't only her Caribbean-ness that
set Beti apart—Aníbal hailed from the interior of Colombia and
held little allegiance to its coast—her dark, freckled skin, wide nose,

and tightly curled hair gave everyone, including Aníbal, license to look down on her. The slights were subtle and usually delivered playfully. Beti said she didn't care, but she'd bring it up from time to time.

"Everybody wants to feel superior," she'd say. "¿Y para qué? We all have nothing."

"¡Tranquila!" Aníbal whooped in response, before joking that it must be her time of the month.

"¡No, idiota! Wake up! This country ruins everything. First, the gringos ruin us there. Then they ruin us here!"

"Then why don't you leave this terrible place, Doctora Seuss?"

"As soon as esos hijos de puta leave my country, I'll leave theirs."

Beti's grim outlook and everyone else's casual racism did nothing to dilute our affection for her. She was the only person who talked to my siblings and I as if we were adults, but who also protected our status as children. Under the auspices of Beti, we were permitted to watch uninterrupted hours of TV and eat whatever we wanted. If our parents tried to intervene, she'd pull a beer from the fridge or a bottle of whisky from the cupboard. "Here, drink this. Let these children be children. Nuestra gente a sufrido suficiente."

Beti, too, had suffered something, but no one ever said what it was. All we knew was that she'd left Puerto Rico in a hurry. "La maestra swam all the way. In one breath," said Aníbal.

"That's right, cabrón, and I'll swim all the way home, too. But first they're going to have to spit me out. Like a fishbone."

Beti often described herself in that way, as if she were proud of causing pain—fishbone, thorn, headache—but that was the opposite of how we saw her.

Whenever the adults huddled around a table to eat, drink, or play cards, Beti retreated to the kitchen to be with us. And when the nights got long and the ire of our parents grew, she would volunteer to tuck us in. To drown out the music playing and the boisterous games happening down the hall, she'd sing us nursery rhymes in her high-pitched voice and tell us a story—usually the same one.

"Do you know what happens to survivors when they die?"

We'd shake our small heads artfully, as if we didn't know what was coming.

"Something, an essence, like love mixed with anger, leaves their bodies. It dissolves through the ceiling," she'd say, pointing toward the cracked paint above. "Then it soars into the heavens, leaving a stream of white light that, for a moment, binds their bodies to the most purple sky you've ever seen, before falling back to Earth, somewhere near New Orleans, near where the French ruined everything.

"Its return is slow at first; then it pours down in sheets of rain and enormous hail. Big, big pieces. There's flooding too. The dirty runoff then travels south along the Mississippi and revives all of the plants in its path before pooling in the Gulf of Mexico, where it shines for days. Days and days. Sailors travel hours away from their shipping routes to see it. Far, far away. The pieces of light eventually grow tired of treading water and begin collecting themselves. They climb onto one another carefully, as if by instruction, getting less bright the tighter they pack. After all the lights have disappeared from the surface of the water, a tall figure, human in size and shape, stands above the water. With each step, it flickers, like a loose bulb. People along the coasts—Mexico, Texas, Haiti, Cuba—claim to see a silhouette on the ocean walking toward them. Big and imposing, but not scary, the image heads west toward Matamoros, where it touches land.

"Rumor has it that this incandescent being patrols the border. People with origins from Baja down to Ushuaia tell stories of how they were able to cross into the United States with her help. They call her L'Ampara. She appears on cloudy nights to lead them through the desert, brightening just enough to blind border security and vigilante militia so that pilgrims may sneak past."

Then, we'd fall asleep.

I don't know when—we stopped visiting them as often after my parents moved us to the suburbs—but Beti eventually left Aníbal, who then moved to Miami because he preferred to be lonely in warm weather. Soon after, Beti went back to Puerto Rico; she could no longer tolerate living on the same land mass as Ronald and Nancy Reagan, I heard my father say to my mother. There was no word from Beti or Aníbal for years, but at some point, my parents began receiving postcards, usually around New Year's and always with the same message: "I'd rather suffer here than there. Visitors welcome. Besos, Beti."

Even as a child, I remember feeling that Beti didn't fit. She was somehow better—smarter, more interesting—than everyone in the room. I got the sense that my mother thought so too. For starters, she spoke English more fluently than any of the other adults. Whenever we spent the night there, my mother would remind us to bring our homework, so that we could ask Beti for help. My mother cared more about Beti than she did about most of the other people that my father met through work. One time, I recall my father referred to Beti as *la negra* during a gathering of friends and neighbors, just as everyone else used to, and my mother slapped his thigh as forcefully as she'd done to me when I'd stuck a pencil inside my sister's ear. And yet, after we left the city, she never invited Beti to Thanksgiving or Christmas dinner. A few years ago, my mother mentioned in passing that Beti had been an alcoholic.

"When?"

"Always," she said.

It was then that I realized that my memories of Beti's demeanor, character primarily by a loopy energy, corroborated my mother's assessment.

But that's a Puerto Rican story; this one is Salvadorian.

· · ·

I cried at the news of my grandmother's death. It was Valentine's Day, and the other travelers at the gate must have thought I'd been dumped. I was halfway to El Salvador, to meet my mother, who'd already been at my grandmother's bedside for a few days. It should have been my father to travel instead of me, but he couldn't pass up his shift at the restaurant—in tips, Valentine's Day was the third most lucrative day of the year.

The voicemail was waiting when I landed in Texas. "Mi mami," my mother said through sobs, "she's dead."

My grandmother had been alive when I boarded the plane in New York. "She's with us still, but I hope your flights aren't delayed," my cousin Adela had messaged. I deduced that my grandmother must have died while I was flying over West Virginia. That's when the turbulence had forced me to chug my bottle-let of red wine and grip the armrests. I recalled eyeing the map on the small screen affixed to the back of the seat in front of me. A small avatar of the very plane I was inside of toddled smack in the middle of West Virginia, a state that had once signaled great potential when it cleaved itself from the Confederacy.

In retrospect, I was lucky my grandmother hadn't downed the plane altogether. To hear my mother tell it, she was always going to put up a fight. "Ni me voy ni me callo," had become her mantra during the morning calls with my mother—*I'm not leaving, and I won't shut up*. Intrepid was the cancer, as far as she was concerned.

I hadn't expected to care. I'd only met my grandmother in person once. But there I was, Gate B22, surrounded by heart-shaped things. Full of secondhand love and, in a way, dumped.

The enduring memory of my first trip to El Salvador is of a mischievous experiment involving matches and perfume as fire accelerant. I destroyed my grandmother's underwear drawer and ruined a suitcase's worth of beauty care products that my mother had gifted her. My spoiled and arrogant yanqui grandchildren, she must have thought.

On that trip, I slept alongside my sisters and mother in a gray room of exposed concrete, inside a two-story house that rested at the bottom of la colina in Santa Tecla, a small suburb of La Libertad. Feral dogs with more bark than meat on their bones sauntered the empty roads on thin dirt-dusted legs. A tin-roofed shop on the corner sold an entrancing array of candy and accepted our coins well before El Salvador officially adopted US currency as its own.

Two hundred kilometers east, in El Mozote, a village near the border with Honduras, a US-trained battalion killed close to nine hundred Evangelical Salvadorians under suspicion of collaborating with rebel forces. By that point, the civil war was being fought almost exclusively in the countryside, far from the capital. I don't recall anyone uttering a word about the war.

What I recall instead is my grandmother preparing breakfast but never eating with us. She remained in the yard, collecting water and flesh from coconuts she'd cracked open with her trusty dagger-shaped rock. After breakfast, she ran errands while my grandfather took the bus into the city's center to attend mass. They returned in time for lunch, through which my grandmother sat quietly, and after which she disappeared again, to one open-air market or another to buy the ingredients she'd forgotten during her morning excursion. In the evenings, my grandfather allowed us to climb him while he read his right-wing newspapers, which he held with the hand of one arm, while the other trembled uselessly at his side, incapable of gripping anything—the result of nerve damage from a bullet that had ripped through his shoulder at a pro-government rally in the early 1960s. Men in uniform had somehow mistaken him for a counterprotestor.

. . .

In the nearly forty years they were apart, my grandmother and my mother spoke every day. Sometimes in the morning before my mother went to work; sometimes during lunch; sometimes in nightgowns after they'd wiped the day away from their faces. Although taciturn, my grandmother was a shale of support and clarity. By comparison, my grandfather was a geyser. My mother labored to tell him things: that she was never coming back; that she was getting married; that my youngest sister was living with her boyfriend. Rather than blurt anything out, my mother always found it easier to end calls earlier or to ask my grandfather to put my grandmother on the line sooner.

To my mother's surprise, her father wasn't upset when she told him I was gay.

"¿Qué?"

"Gay."

"¿Qué?"

"Homosexual."

"Oh."

Then, laughter. Endless laughter, it seemed. Rather than interrupt him, my mother set the phone down and used the time to iron her work blouses, preferring to pay for the extended call than divert the trajectory of her father's emotions. Eventually he composed himself and said, "En el país más rico del mundo tiene que haber una medicina para su condición."

In the richest country in the world, surely there is medicine for his condition.

"He took it well," my mother later explained.

By comparison, my grandmother's response was muted. "Eso no importa, Hija," was all she said before reminding my mother to eat smaller portions.

That doesn't matter, Dear. My grandmother said this in response to almost everything: marital spats, earthquakes, authoritarianism, late-stage cancer. Whether it was the tone or the pith that made her words so persuasive was unclear. But whomever heard her say them understood that she knew well the distinction between problems and pain.

In addition to pragmatic, my grandmother was also dour in expression, wiry of frame, and proletarian at heel. In person and in pictures, she wore her housedresses knee-length and tapered, her hair short (black, then silver), and carried her head as elegantly as an uneven gait allowed—the result of a bullet lodged near her pelvis. In the early 1980s, she'd gone down to the university to stop her only son from joining an anti-government protest. She'd just begun to twist his left ear when the line of soldiers raised their guns.

In fact, three of my four grandparents (across two countries) survived bullets in their lifetimes—in all cases, the bullets had been manufactured in my country. The fourth grandparent, my paternal grandfather, was the only one of the quartet who was killed. He died shortly after the small bit of aerodynamic steel tore through his esophagus. He'd been carrying a crate of eggs and whistling. "Beneath him spread a shade of orange I'd never ever seen," recounted the boy in a Catholic school uniform with chocolate under his fingernails, who'd found my grandfather face down in a pool of yoke and blood. "It looked like the sun had crashed into Bogotá." If my grandfather hadn't recognized his assassin, the eggs would have survived. It was the shock of knowing, more so than the bullet, that caused him to lose his balance. But that's a Colombian story for another time; this one remains Salvadorian.

The second time I saw my grandparents was on a screen, nearly two decades after the first visit, several years after my mother had outed me, and not long before my grandmother died. My mother had asked me to call. "There won't be too many more opportunities," she said. When I hesitated—I truly had no interest in talking to them—she blurted out, "It was her idea—tu abuela."

"¡Hola, primo! ¿Cómo estas?" asked my cousin, Adela—a second cousin—who was tasked with helping my grandparents set up the call. Her face was soft, young, and oblong, like a dinosaur egg turned upside down, not all that dissimilar from most of the faces in my mother's family. Adela was a lawyer who defended union organizers against powerful people who hid behind other more shadowy powerful people. Adela's career was unique in my family. Most relatives of my generation—cousins, second cousins, young aunts, young uncles—were call-center workers who didn't seem to have political opinions one way or another. Adela was unique in one other regard too: she was the only openly gay person I knew of in my family.

"Bien, gracias," I responded, straining to sound like a native speaker.

Adela winked before disappearing from the screen to reveal my grandparents.

They were exactly as I'd remembered them: my grandmother, steely and parsimonious; my grandfather, lumpy and gregarious. In their living rooms, we chatted—me, in my prewar home; they, in their postwar one. A large, ornate crucifix hung prominently in their background, the savior's white face, hands, and midriff dripping red. Behind me was a poster of something abstract and geometric with sharp edges, a Picasso poster I'd bought on vacation, at a museum gift shop in Madrid. Whenever the Internet connection froze, the frame of my laptop screen gave the impression that my grandparents were trapped in a poorly lit photograph. At one point, I asked if they planned to visit. *No, hija, no* had been my grandmother's standard reply to my mother's countless invitations over the years. On that day, however, my grandmother said nothing. She merely swatted the idea away gently, like a winged insect harmless enough to be spared her precision. After a few minutes of stilted conversation, my grandmother put an end to the intergenerational experiment. She thanked me for calling. I lamented how seldom we spoke. "Eso no importa, hijo," she responded, no doubt having sensed my lack of conviction. My grandfather remained silent, waving and crying.

My grandfather completed his first century a couple of years after my grandmother died. Everyone traveled, hoping the special occasion would snap my mother out of her depressive state. During our descent into the capital, the pockets of air tucked between the lush green undulations below caused turbulence that was strangely lyrical. My mother, who hadn't been back since her mother's funeral, gripped the armrests and smiled. The disturbance was a wry welcome from her mother, she explained—a where-have-you-been rebuke. I was too busy waterboarding myself with tiny bottles of liquor to care about anyone's superpowers.

A mix of yanquis and Salvadorians celebrated my grandfather's three-digit age in the courtyard of a military club—the type of venue that only right-leaning and apolitical people had no compunction about renting. Across the courtyard, men dressed in fatigues, consorted in groups of three and four, limbs akimbo, drinks in hand, grins expansive, confident, thoroughly convinced their own words were consequential. Some of the men were old and bloated; others were trim and willfully ignorant. The party guests seemed inured to the surroundings. Except for one.

He stood on the perimeter of the celebration, scowling for most of the night. He was a cousin thrice removed—younger than my grandfather but older than my mother. He had a craggy palimpsest of a face and walked with a distinct hobble. Everyone called him Streets because he knew his way around and because he'd often drink himself into uselessness and collapse on his walk home. He'd spent most of the country's civil war in the countryside training law students and farmers in armed combat. My mother had only ever spoken of him in a way that led me to believe he was dead.

When everyone else grabbed plates and formed a line at the buffet, Streets approached my table and whispered, "You resemble your dead uncle." Then he walked away. When I'd finished eating, he returned and announced, unprompted, that he was still a communist. "But I'm a Trotskyite. Don't confuse me for a Leninist— ¡Hijos de puta!"

Later, as my mother lit the birthday candles, Streets pulled me aside somewhat aggressively by the elbow. "Mira ese—¡Ahí!" he said, pointing to a soldier too old for combat but still in uniform: oversized pants that bunched at the ankle and a dark khaki shirt unbuttoned midway to his chest that revealed a canvas of white hairs and a large gold crucifix. "That's the one. He killed thousands. Bestia repugnante."

What I had until that moment experienced as guilt for cavorting near the enemy, turned to shame and anger. It crossed my mind, ever so briefly, that Streets and I might join forces and do something unexpected, something severe, something to avenge.

"The assassins always live next door, hijo," he said, while jutting his chin toward the soldiers and patting my shoulder.

It was then that the scent of rain saturated the air, bringing with it cool gusts of wind. The gathering of people had barely enough time to line up beneath the terracotta eaves. Streets remained in the deluge, nodding. "Tu abuela," he said faintly, a few times. She was chastising us all for forgetting. I assumed he was referring to my uncle, whose death has always been a well-guarded, inconclusive tale—it was political, it was cancer, it was an accident. Streets dropped his head back, in what appeared to be a combination of gravity and a desire to empty the bottle of beer in his hands. After a lengthy eructation, he added, "Penance and punishment. That's all it ever is." Then he let out a wheezy cackle that caught everyone's attention, before vomiting into a tree pit.

Adela took me to a discotheque after the birthday party. It was on a quiet residential street with few signs of life apart from the tall palms and their feathered fronds. I suspected the dancing was her attempt at cleansing us of our time spent with the enemy. I couldn't be certain of her intentions because Adela, too, remained agnostic about her political views whenever she was around me. Whether this was a postwar precaution or a general mistrust of anything produced in the United States was unclear.

Inside the club, she introduced me to another lawyer, a friend of hers. Because of the thumping music, I wasn't able to decipher whether he practiced employment law or if he was currently unemployed. He was thin, of average height, with large ears, a narrow, aquiline nose with flared nostrils, and a neat mustache. In a hallway, as we waited to use the bathroom, we kissed. "I don't live far from here," he said. I declined the invitation, suddenly fearing intimacy and isolation with a stranger, in a city and country I barely knew. The lawyer and I slipped into the club's bathroom instead, where he remained with his back pressed against the door because of its broken lock, while I lowered myself into a crouch, unwilling to set my knees onto the wet tiles. I hadn't expected such a large cock from such a slight man. He came quickly and offered to reciprocate, but the taste of his ejaculate, the cloying scent of disinfectant in the air, and the murmur of voices beyond the door killed the mood. We danced for a bit a longer, albeit with less urgency, before I made my way alone back to the house my parents had rented in the upscale Colonia Escalón. I found the empty, damp streets pleasant—the humidity of the afternoon had transformed into a warm, breezy night. Still drunk, I ignored the countless warnings I'd received about gang violence: young Salvadorian immigrants and refugees who'd left in no small part because of the United States' intrusion in Salvadorian affairs and who then banded together in the United States because they were unwelcome upon their arrival, before being deported back to El Salvador. It was a sort of triplication of hopelessness. I paid it no mind and counted the trees instead. I'd gotten to twenty-three when Adela drove up beside me and told me to get in.

On the last day of our visit, before boarding a large and imperfectly painted van to the airport, everyone took turns saying goodbye to the centenarian. My grandfather's large frame, easily felt through a pappy and sagging flesh, hugged us all with the same desperation. His left arm vibrated like a tuning fork that had just been whacked. His tears swelled before streaming his bronzed cheeks.

While my sister and I accommodated the luggage into the trunk, my mother beseeched her father to come live with her. "No puedo, hija," he responded, as he steadied his trembling hand against the thin, gold crucifix beneath his shirt. My grandfather had reached a bracket-less age characterized primarily by loneliness. There would only be one way out of his predicament.

The housecleaner my parents had hired to care for my grand-father came out of the house to retrieve him and to blunt the trauma of goodbye. Her name was Blanca, and she remained behind him, like a sentry prepared for anything. Her skin had a youthful doughiness and her lips were boldly red. "Don't worry. He is never alone," she whispered, her hands tucked into the front pouch of a blue apron. "Your mother is still with him." At this, my mother veiled herself behind a handkerchief she'd been using to dab at her brow and sobbed. Blanca continued matter-of-factly, but now in a smaller voice, "He talks to her. In the morning. In the evening. It's odd. I tell him so. All he says in return is, 'Odd is someone disap-pearing suddenly after always being there.'"

· · ·

The day that my grandmother died, I called my mother several times while I waited for my connecting flight. There was no answer, only ringing accompanied by the echo of international calls. I was relieved not to have to offer condolences. All of the things I could think to say didn't seem enough. Or accurate.

A short while later, a sullen voice came over the speaker system. As a result of an unforeseen and fast-approaching storm, all flights were canceled. "And happy Valentine's Day, folks."

The airport began its chaotic transformation into a ruin of unrequited love: abandoned half-eaten heart-shaped boxes and cheap bouquets strewn about everywhere. I sent Adela a message asking her to tell my mother about the delay. Then I found a row of empty seats near an electrical outlet. I sat for a long while doing nothing but staring out of the enormous floor-to-ceiling windows typical of airports. The sky had already commenced its march toward darkness, but the reflective vests and electric torches of the workers stacking luggage and performing semaphore remained visible. I thought of the story that Beti used to tell at bedtime, the one about L'Ampara—a portmanteau: lampara means *lamp* and amparo means *help, shelter, protection*. With each bolt of lightning, the sky's ominous and striking purple was revealed. Soon, hail, larger than I'd ever seen before, began to fall. Followed by the rain.

THE MAN IN 512

THE CO-OP BOARD HADN'T YET approved the new security system because Artie, the treasurer, had been too ill to attend the vote. In the interim, the seven-member board—six retirees and one young tax attorney—agreed to have the current camera system serviced, but the earliest appointment wouldn't be for another two weeks. This delay explained all the signs in the lobby (mirror-comprised) and in the elevator (also mirrored) reminding residents to lock their doors and not to allow strangers to follow them into the building. Coincidentally, it was Artie's apartment that was robbed.

As Mr. and Mrs. Peterson recounted all of this to me, they interrupted themselves a couple of times to reassure me I wasn't in trouble. "We believe you, Manny," they said preemptively. I believed them that they believed me, but their insistence that I wasn't a criminal started to feel as if maybe they weren't entirely certain I wasn't a criminal.

I'm not worried about losing my job with the Petersons. I didn't plan on being here this long to begin with. I took the job to make my uncle feel like a useful intermediary—his ability to facilitate mutually beneficial relationships has always been a source of great pride for him. My uncle knew I needed money for textbooks and meals. Besides, it's not as if I'd been relegated to an Amazon warehouse. It was a cushy job, and the Petersons were good people. "Always big tips and cookies for Christmas," my uncle said when he first told me about the opportunity. It's true, Mrs. Peterson in particular rounds up for everything. She's not from here. She's from Sweden, and she doesn't think anyone gets paid enough in this country. "It's immoral," she said to me when I told her how much my dad makes at the flower shop, where he drives the delivery van. "How can this country expect anyone to make the right decisions or to be well, if they don't protect their workers?"

"I agree with you, Mrs. Peterson."

"How many times, Manny, have I told you? Call me Lisa."

"Right, Mrs.—Lisa."

Our conversations were all the same. The words were different, but the purpose seemed to be about putting someone at ease, me or them.

Before she had kids, Mrs. Peterson worked for the Swedish government. I don't know what she did exactly, but I think it was translation work. Her English is impeccable. There's a stiffness to it, but she speaks it better than my uncle, who's been in this country for almost forty years. Frankly, she might speak it better than I do, and I've been here all my life. The Petersons have been here for only three years. Mr. Peterson is a representative for Sweden at the United Nations. They were only supposed to be in New York for the two years that Sweden was on the Security Council, but the Swedish government asked him to stay longer. And the kids wanted to stay in New York, as did Mrs. Peter—Lisa!

That's what my uncle told me when he explained that the Petersons were looking for a tutor for their kids. "Después de la escuela. Un par de horas no más," he said. Since I was going to BMCC only a few blocks away, a few hours after school seemed like an ideal work schedule.

Before I even knew there was a job, I used to meet my uncle for a hotdog and a Sprite on Wednesdays. We'd sit in the small park on Hudson and Duane. It's not really a park; it's a shortcut with benches and shrubs. It was there that he told me about the job. "They can pay good," he said. "They don't pay rent. They don't pay for their kids' school."

It's true. The Swedish government paid for the Petersons' first two years in New York—a brownstone in Park Slope and private school for the kids—and their current apartment also came by way of a Swedish connection. The owners (the Fridhs) went back to Sweden, sublet their apartment to the Petersons at a discounted price, and have yet to charge them. Mrs. Peterson writes a check every month and puts it under a magnet on the fridge. I've counted thirteen checks. It's become a joke between Mr. and Mrs. Peterson. He'll say to her, *Darling, have you paid the refrigerator yet?* And she'll respond, *Oh, no, I accidentally paid the freezer this month.* Then she'll slide the magnetic clip with the stack of checks down the front of the steel box. They wouldn't be able to afford to live in this country if it hadn't been for the United Nations and, now, the Fridhs. On multiple occasions, I've heard Mr. Peterson say something to this effect. Mrs. Peterson is usually quick to remind him that the uncollected rent is something like a nest egg. "We can use it to take the kids to Cuba or Kenya. Or maybe Vietnam."

The Petersons are friendly enough. So are their kids. Super blond too. Not blond, actually, it's like a white-yellow. Is it platinum? Even their eyebrows. Halvar, Harald, Hjalmar: those are their names. The parents are Lisa and Eric, but their kids are Halvar, Harald, and Hjalmar. Fifteen, ten, and six: those are their ages. Halvar, the aloof one with an undercut and a 1980s-style comb-over, told me once that his parents' generation all have modern-sounding names, but the younger generation of Swedes have all been saddled with old-school ones.

When I'm with the boys—Triple H, I like to call them, although I've never said it aloud—I don't use a textbook or anything really. I just talk to them in Spanish. It's very casual, sporadic. Halvar, the eldest, spends most of his time out with friends—fellow UN kids who rarely come up to the apartment and instead text him or ring the buzzer and wait for Halvar to run down. Except for Omar, who always comes up. Omar, like Halvar, is fifteen and attends the UN school. He's from Djibouti, and his dad is currently on the Security Council for two years, which Omar explained to me upon our first meeting, as if it were essential to my understanding of him. Omar is engaging and charming, even if slightly robotic. Charming for his age, that is. And possibly charming only in comparison to Halvar, who, as I said before, is rather quiet and underwhelming, like a block of unmarinated tofu, thinly sliced. Halvar's dad has been advising Omar's dad because of his previous Council experience. It's like a mentor program, where past temporary members help acclimate newly appointed temporary members. In my time here with the Petersons, I've also learned that only China, France, Russia, United Kingdom, and the United States are permanently seated on the Security Council. Every other country gets two years. I vaguely recall something in high school history class about the League of Nations, the predecessor to the United Nations, but if it weren't for the last ten months of casual conversation and eavesdropping on Omar and Halvar, I would have remained largely ignorant about our system of international governance. For example, El Salvador, my mother's country, has never been elected to the Security Council—Omar told me that. The omission of my ancestral land didn't bother me, but I found it humorous, if a touch unsettling, that two teenagers should, in this regard, have more geopolitical influence in the world than I did. I drew some comfort from the fact that one of the teenagers was Black and from Africa. It made the inequity feel less racist.

Harald, the ten-year-old, plays Minecraft or Roblox in his room from the moment he gets home until his mom comes back from her writing group—Mrs. Peterson is working on a novel about her time working for the Swedish government. She says it's a political thriller that also "says something about the failure of the World Bank and the International Monetary Fund." I've heard her explain this on the phone.

"Even if it's no good, it'll get published," Mr. Peterson whispered to me once. "The owners of this apartment are dear friends of ours, Manny. And they both work in publishing. Lisa will be a proper author soon enough."

Mr. Peterson is the tallest person I've ever met. I'd guess he's six foot seven. I've never asked, nor have I commented on his height because my best friend in high school, Monique, was very tall, and I remember it irked her when other people drew attention to her height. Ever since, I've made it a point to never mention anyone's height, despite being tempted on several occasions. Mr. Peterson also has a direct communication style. Not mean, but serious and sometimes invasive, like the doctor who took out a piece of my father's intestine and told him to change his diet. "You keep your eyes in your books, Manny. You will break out of your circumstances," Mr. Peterson said. "This is what your country is known for."

I nodded along. What else is there to do in response to this type of misguided sermonizing? My mother, after all, runs a restaurant in Sunset Park; my father is the chess champion in our local park; my brother Javi went to Cornell and does cancer research at Mount

Sinai; Dahlia, my sister, is a physical therapist for professional tennis players; and Daisy, my baby sister, is at LaGuardia, hoping to go to Julliard. I'm the only disappointment in the family. I'm the one who took several years after high school to travel. I lived with my mom's cousin's son, Benito, in Sevilla, where I smoked a lot of hash and befriended loads of British exchange students who all thought I was Spanish or Roma. I intentionally avoided the American students because it seemed odd to travel so far and surround myself with more of the same. In the end, it proved to be much of the same: British and American cultures are both dominated by white people, mediocre pop music, and capitalism. As far as I could tell, accents and health care were the big differences, which worked in my favor because Benito's girlfriend lived in Manchester, and I joined my cousin on several of the trips to see her, and in the process had not one but three health-related emergencies: appendicitis, fractured wrist, and alcohol poisoning. It's true what everyone says about the British: they drink excessively. And when I was with them, I did too. Luckily, I had Benito to show me the way. Before landing on his doorstep, I'd only met him once, at our grandfather's funeral mass in San Salvador, but that didn't keep him from finding me work at the bar where he served oysters. My job was to shuck them and sometimes serve them directly to the customers who placed orders from the sidewalk. On my lunch breaks, I'd sweep the purple leaves of the jacarandá trees for several of the shops in the more touristy parts of the city. I'd also discard oranges that had rotted on the branches or had become jam beneath the hooves of the carriage-drawing horses.

This is all to say that I have ideas and layered perspectives, and my circumstances aren't dire. But neither am I interested in a life of subservience like the ones my parents and my aunts and uncles have led. I don't plan on staying with the Petersons or at BMCC. I'm just building some credits before I apply to bigger-name schools. Warm places, like California or New Orleans, now that I've had a taste for a more temperate climate.

My average shift with the Petersons is three hours long. There's nothing difficult or depleting about it. Halvar hangs out with Omar, Harald talks to his video games, and Hjalmar chills with me. The little one is cute as far as kids go—round and doughy—even if the eyebrows took some getting used to. Hjalmar can't hold a conversation in Spanish, but he repeats everything I say. *¿Tiénes hambre?* I ask. *¿Tennis umbree?* he replies. The little guy's accent is horrendous and probably irredeemable. Some people just don't have an ear for new languages—another thing I recall about the British. These three kids have taken Spanish classes for years, but you wouldn't know it from hearing Hjalmar. It's like marbles in his mouth. On the other hand, when he sings in Spanish, which he does, he's quite passable. With my help, he's memorized Selena's entire catalog. The first time I played the Tejana superstar for him, he giggled, but after a couple of weeks, he was hooked—not only the videos but also her dancing and gestures. In fact, I suspect Hjalmar will be a performer of some kind—or maybe he's gender nonconforming with flare. From the moment he walks through the door after school, he runs to his room and changes out of his jeans and T-shirt or sweater and into a satin blue dress that he wore for Halloween—Elsa from *Frozen*. Then he skips around the enormous three-bedroom apartment singing. Hjalmar has no compunction about regaling the entire building with his renditions of "Bidi Bidi Bom Bom" and "El Chico en el Apartamento 512," his two favorite Selena songs. He gets a special kick out of singing the latter whenever he walks past apartment 512, which is coincidentally across the hall. But there is no boy in 512. There is no one in 512.

The tenant, Artie, died recently. He was eighty-eight. Pneumonia was the official cause. But it was loneliness too. He'd been living there for more than thirty years, the last two of which were alone. Artie was a tenant in the building since before my uncle started working there. "Mr. Artie is a very nice man" was how my uncle described him. In fact, in the two years before his death, Artie invited my uncle and the other super up for drinks every Friday night—this began before I started working with the Petersons. My uncle never went, and I wondered whether he'd resisted the invitations because Artie was gay. My uncle is a gentle man—everyone says it—but I remember him and my father making homophobic jokes when I was a kid. The sorts of things everyone felt comfortable saying, but wouldn't have ever said knowingly in the company of gay people. But they were jokes, nonetheless. The way I see it, there are jokes that intend to harm and there are jokes that don't. I guess what I'm saying is that if everyone who made jokes in bad taste, as opposed to those who were fueled by hatred, simply apologized and never made those jokes again, I think it would be okay to move on from the past, as long as the apologies were sincere, well crafted, and accompanied by some sort of restitution, like a retroactive tip jar or a constitutional amendment. Jokes, after all, add up.

"Did you never go to Friday drinks because Artie was gay?"

"¿Qué? ¡No seas estúpido! Mr. Artie was very good. A good people." Then my uncle explained that my aunt didn't like him to come home drunk, and he knew that whenever he had one drink, he'd end up having five. "I don't have control with alcohol," he said. In retrospect, I knew that. My dad is the same way.

I didn't know Artie well. Occasionally, I helped him with his groceries, when we both happened to be coming into the building at the same time. It's one of those buildings where you must go through two sets of doors to get in, and the second set doesn't open until the first one closes. But if you don't open the second in time, you have to go back outside and start again. A few times, I helped Artie when he got trapped in the vestibule.

Artie was a nice and interesting person—he was always dropping the names of famous gay guys he'd known; a few times, he'd show me the obituaries and tell me about a straight guy he'd slept with decades earlier—but I was primarily relieved to see him because his presence was in stark contrast to the gray, sparsely decorated, and cold of the building. And of its residents, whose bodies were perpetually tightening up and gazes darting downward, as if they'd been threatened, a reaction that fell somewhere between ironic and annoying since their fears felt like an assault on me. But when I was with Artie, I felt protected.

"Beer or vodka rocks?" he'd say when I'd set the groceries on his kitchen counter.

"I can't. The kids are waiting."

"Come back when you're done with the Nordics."

But I never did. In part because I didn't want to be in that building longer than necessary. I also worried I would give Artie the wrong impression. After all, I didn't know him apart from the lobby and hallway chit chat. What if, by accepting his invitations, I'd unintentionally send him a message. I didn't care that he was gay, but I didn't want to lead him on.

As it turned out, Artie invited everyone over. The building didn't have that many tenants to begin with: ten floors, six units each, minus the combined ones—on the tenth floor, a retired hedge fund guy built one enormous penthouse. Artie knew everyone. He'd been there since the beginning. "No one wanted to live in Tribeca when we got here," he explained to me once. "Just artists and junkies." Artie and his lover—his word, not mine—had moved into the building at a time when it was starting to be fashionable to live in Tribeca, well before it had been overrun with children's clothing boutiques, yoga and Pilates studios, and unaffordable restaurants, like the rest of rich Manhattan.

"Are you sure you didn't see anything suspicious?" Lisa and Eric asked me after the robbery. "Nothing," I responded. "What a relief Artie wasn't alive. Can you imagine if he'd been in there?" Mrs. Peterson said to Mr. Peterson matter-of-factly.

The whole building was talking about it—the robbery. At first, Peter, the Polish super who lived in the building, didn't tell anyone, but word got out because the realtor who was handling the sale of Artie's apartment was describing the robbery to someone over the phone, and one of the tenants overheard her in the elevator. "It was an inside job," said the realtor. Apparently, whoever it was had a key, and they were very neat about the whole thing.

My uncle suspected one person. Artie had lots of friends. Eighty-eight years' worth of friends. But only one of them had a key: Antonio.

Antonio and Artie met at a summer Shakespeare festival just before 9/11. They played the men who kill Banquo. Artie once showed me a framed picture. He and Antonio were in tights, standing to the side of a large outdoor stage. I don't know many plays, but I happened to know that one quite well. While I was in Spain, my cousin Benito played Banquo in *La Tragedia de Macbeth*. I ran lines with him.

> *Es extraño, no obstante:*
> *a veces, para llevarnos seducidos a la perdición,*
> *los instrumentos de lo oscuro dicen la verdad,*
> *nos cautivan con juegos inocentes para traicionarnos de una*
>   *manera irreparable . . .*

Antonio and Artie didn't work together again after *Macbeth*, but they had lunch once a week for the next twenty years. "Mr. Artie liked his routines," my uncle explained. He also told me that Antonio started coming over more often when Artie's husband died—they got married a few years ago, just after New York legalized it, about six months before Artie's husband died. That's around the time Artie started inviting the supers up for drinks.

At the very end, when Artie developed vertigo and couldn't do much on his own, Antonio was there every day. Other people helped too; neighbors dropped off meals and plates of cookies, friends visited, even Eric and Lisa did their part by leaving Artie a copy of the *Times* on his doormat every morning, which was something that Artie had, for years, done for the neighbors on the fifth floor. But it was Antonio who did most of the caretaking.

Illness did nothing to dent Artie's pride. He wouldn't allow a health aide to stay with him, no matter how weak he was or how often it was suggested by others, including my uncle, who, at one point, proposed that my aunt Gloria come clean his apartment and prepare him a few meals. Artie didn't mistrust people, but he preferred to do everything for himself. In that way, he reminded me of my grandmother, who famously swept her own bedroom on the morning that she died of gall bladder cancer. This unwavering streak of independence obliged Antonio to come by more often and stay with Artie for longer. He accompanied him to doctor appointments—there were plenty of those—to the market, to the barber, to the liquor store, to the ATM. They were always walking arm in arm. Like a man and his grandfather. Best I could tell, Antonio was in his early forties. I pieced that together myself from what Antonio had told me: "Acting was Artie's first post-retirement hobby, but *Macbeth* was my first job out of college."

Antonio was another of my hallway and elevator acquaintances, and a few times, we rode the subway together back to Brooklyn. I didn't say much during our interactions because Antonio always seemed so serious, and I realized that he wasn't really talking with me, he was just getting things off his chest. In his eyes, I was either safe or inconsequential. During one of his soliloquies, I learned that Artie had been a high school social worker and helped to organize the school plays. "After we did *Macbeth*, I gave up and went to grad school, but Artie did some off-off-Broadway stuff."

I have to admit something: the first time I saw Antonio, not long after I started working for the Petersons, I thought he was making a delivery. Tall, broad shouldered, and with a mustache like a small comb, he reminded me of the UPS guy that delivers packages to the restaurant where my mom works. Up to that point, the only non-white people I'd seen in the building apart from myself were the nannies, the maintenance workers, and people making deliveries. It was wrong of me to assume that the unknown brown guy was bringing dinner, but in my defense, Antonio was wearing a backpack, a baseball cap, and he was carrying a plastic bag. How was I to know he was a professor or that his husband was a tech guy? That first time I saw him, all I had were my assumptions, which I kept to myself. I also had my curiosity, which I fed by watching him through the peephole of the Petersons' apartment: he didn't hand off anything to Artie. Instead, they hugged as good friends do (warmly and for longer than I'd expected), and Antonio followed Artie into his apartment. I don't know how long he was in there, but it was long enough for me to confirm that he wasn't a delivery person. At that point—again, I'm not proud of this—I started wondering whether he might be an escort. The age gap between them was close to fifty years. Even in New York, I wasn't used to seeing that mismatched combination of people—young brown skin alongside a nearly transparent white veined with blues and purples. And yet, it made sense. Artie was unique. A really nice guy who said genuine hellos and held the door open and always had a recommendation ready for where to eat or where to go see a good dance performance and who always knew the weather forecast and took pleasure in hating the Republican party. His small talk was always medium sized. Not the burdensome kind that you wanted to avoid or the filler you quickly forget. Artie was, I guess, cool.

"That's exactly how I would describe him—cool," Antonio said to me as I was leaving the Petersons. He'd come by to drop off a large plastic bag of Artie's belongings a few days after he'd died—all the things Artie had taken with him to the hospital: clothes, eyeglasses, book, wallet, shoes, belt, and phone charger. "I was his health proxy," Antonio offered, when he saw me eyeing the transparent sack. "That means I made his medical decisions," he said, in his condescending way. "Artie asked me to do it, after his husband died. I agreed, but, between you and me, I'd hoped when the time came, I'd be out of town or that I wouldn't have to make any decisions. I kept my fingers crossed for a heart attack."

It was pneumonia in the end. Artie was walking around with it for weeks, and nobody knew. "I took him to the cardiologist, neurologist, even a podiatrist because his primary care doctor thought he might be falling due to arthritis in his feet. No one thought it could be a shortness of breath that was causing the vertigo. In hindsight, it makes perfect sense."

More than sad, Antonio looked drained. His eyes were the red of insomnia or hangover. His skin had an almost grayish pallor. And for the first time, I saw a shadow across his cheeks and chin, which were typically clean shaven. "What's wrong with doctors? Why couldn't they have pieced this together?" he asked himself in such a way that made me feel as if I wasn't a part of this conversation.

Antonio had spent most of the previous two weeks on the phone, carrying around one of those old-school leather-bound address books with gilded trim. He'd called everyone in Artie's life to tell them that he'd been admitted to the hospital; then, that he'd died. "Funny thing is all these people thought my first call was the death call. Probably didn't help that I started all of the conversations with, *You don't know me, I'm Artie's friend Antonio.* I mean, Artie was eighty-eight. It was never going to be about surprise birthday party, right?" Antonio attempted a chuckle but didn't fully commit to it. "When I called the next time, they assumed it was to give them an update. Do you have any idea how many old people I've heard sobbing in the last three days? It's unlike anything else. You'd expect them to be used to death. But every one of them sounded like a wounded animal. I felt like the fucking grim reaper—Sorry!" Antonio looked around to make sure that no one had heard him curse. As if we were kids in a library.

The funeral was somewhere on the Upper East Side. The Petersons didn't go, but they stopped at the reception in Artie's place afterward. "It was crowded and cosmopolitan," Mrs. Peterson later explained. She'd never seen such a mix of people in the building. I think she meant it wasn't all white, but I'm not sure. "There was smoked salmon enough for a battalion," Mr. Peterson said. "Lots of desserts very good too," he added, sounding a bit like someone who'd learned English after first learning another language. The day after the funeral, I saw my uncle with a stack of collapsed Zabar's boxes under one arm and a plate of lox, capers, and sliced purple onions in hand. Antonio had told him and the maintenance staff to take the leftovers. "¿Tiénes hambre?" my uncle asked while I stood in the threshold of the Peterson's apartment. Hjalmar, who was out of sight, on the couch in the living room, shouted "¡Yo tengo hambre!" so perfectly that I was proud. My uncle shouted back, "¡Muy bien, muchacho!" But Hjalmar was too busy watching *She-Ra and the Princesses of Power* (dubbed in Spanish) to engage in a conversation.

"They're coming to empty his apartment next week—Mr. Artie," my uncle said, while balancing the boxes and the salmon plate, and jutting his chin toward 512. My uncle affixes *Mr.* and *Mrs.* before the first names of all the tenants in the building. My dad does that too with customers and strangers. It's like living in *Downton Abbey*. In the case of Artie, it's alright, but whenever they attach the honorific to someone younger, it rubs me wrong.

The business of selling Artie's place began quickly. His relatives reached out to the building's co-op board soon after the funeral about hiring a real estate agent. They were going to organize an estate sale too. Antonio was upset about all of it, my uncle told me. "Mr. Artie wanted to donate everything, but the family doesn't listen. Greedy peoples." My uncle held up his hand and rubbed the tips of his fingers—thumb, fore, and middle—together.

A few days ago, I picked up Hjalmar and Harald from their respective schools uptown. On the subway ride home, Harald asked me—in English—whether I'd ever realized that I was *Manny the Nanny*. I explained to him—in Spanish—that I was their tutor and not a childcare worker. In response, Harald pointed out, by way of a series of rapid-fire statements, that tutors don't cook, clean, take kids to doctor appointments—only once, I did that—or take them to or from school. As Harald stated his case, Hjalmar continually repeated, to no one in particular, *Manny* and *nanny*, as if he'd just realized the joys of rhyming. Afterward, while we were making our way from the subway to the apartment building, I saw Antonio standing on the corner. He was wearing a large blue canvas bag over one shoulder and holding up a folded-up shopping cart behind him, the kind my mother used to take to the supermarket when I was a kid, in the pre-Costco days. Antonio looked very New York, but not very Tribeca. I thought he'd seen us, so I waved. But he didn't reciprocate. Instead, he turned away quickly and began walking north along Hudson. Antonio wasn't exactly a friend, but we had, over the course of the previous ten months, gotten to know each other. I hadn't seen him much in the weeks since the funeral, and yet, it was odd that he didn't say hello. A couple hours later, when I was leaving the building, I saw him again. He was seated at one of the benches in the small park-let where my uncle and I used to meet for hot-dogs. Antonio got up quickly and made his way toward me—this time without a bag or a cart. "I'm sorry about running away before," he said. "I didn't want the children to see me."

"Why?"

He didn't come up with a good reason. Instead, he explained that he'd left a few things in Artie's apartment—a book, an umbrella, and a bag of apples he'd picked up at the farmers' market on Greenwich on the day of the funeral.

"Could you let me into the building?"

"Sure, but how are you going to get into the apartment?"

"I'll ask your uncle or the other super."

And that was it. When the Petersons filled me in about the robbery, I pieced together what had happened. Antonio hadn't needed to ask my uncle or the other super to let him in. Antonio had a spare copy of the apartment key. I knew that because I'd found him in the hallway a couple of months earlier, casually jiggling the doorknob, biting his lower lip, nostrils fully flared, his breathing profound. It wasn't the frustration of having committed an error. It was the type of tension I felt whenever I stepped onto the elevator with someone I didn't know. Or when I was coming into the building behind someone who didn't recognize me. Antonio, I realized then, was also an interloper in the building, and he was, in that moment, without his shield. "I just helped Artie to bed, but I left my phone in there," he explained. "I'll have to go home to get my spare key."

The brief scandal about the robbery died down quickly. The co-op board asked Artie's family not to make a fuss. They didn't want police or attention of any kind brought to the building. The real estate agent responsible for emptying and staging Artie's apartment mentioned to Ms. Peterson that the few items that were worth anything—a copy of *A Streetcar Named Desire* signed by Tennessee Williams, a Shigaraki vase, a Dali sketch, a set of Danish nested end tables, and a laptop—were left behind. What disappeared were hundreds of books, three closets worth of clothes, dish towels, tote bags, and some utensils.

"I bet it was his friend—the Latin guy," said Mr. Peterson, who then glanced at me with the guilt of a hundred men, while he assembled sardines and pickles on a wooden serving board.

"Dad!" Halvar shouted in response, "It's Latinx!"

Omar, who'd been resting his elbows on the kitchen island, waiting patiently for the snack board, flashed me a look that communicated, if not sympathy, something approaching sympathy braided with awkwardness.

"Antonio—that was Artie's friend—is wealthy. I mean, he owns his home and he's a college professor. He didn't need to steal anything," I said by way of a retort. The Petersons and Omar all looked up at me with an unabashed and synchronized furrowing of their brows. I began immediately to regret my oversharing. A strange, guilt-like sensation took hold. I had, in my rush to defend his honor, betrayed Antonio by divulging the details of his personal life. I'd also incriminated myself and taken a sledgehammer to the entire mosaic of working-class people of color. And I might have set a bad example for Omar. To complicate matters, I'd been putting on my shoes in preparation for my departure when all of this happened, which made my exit appear unnecessarily dramatic.

I didn't see Mr. Peterson much in the weeks after the *Latinx affair* because Sweden had been tasked with trying to broker a deal to avoid the expansion of NATO. Halvar explained to me that the UN representatives from Sweden and Chile had laid out a plan that would reduce the size of the archaic organization so that Russia wouldn't feel backed into a corner and consequently inclined to expand its sphere of influence. Halvar hadn't heard this from his father. According to him and Omar, all of the kids at the UN school gossip regularly about the happenings at the General Assembly and Security Council. "They're both bullies, but the US has more leverage. To avoid conflict, the US has to cede some ground," Omar explained.

"Feels like you're giving Russia an easy out, O," Halvar interjected before stuffing a handful of pretzels into his mouth.

"Russia is just flexing because the US has given it no choice," Omar responded. "What did they expect?"

Robbing Artie's place would have been easy for Antonio to do because he had the access and familiarity with the building. He would have known about the cameras being out of service. He would have also known about the back entrance—an alley where one could easily and inconspicuously pull up in a car or a van. But the definitive proof for me was what was left behind. A real thief would have taken the autographed play and the expensive vase. This wasn't about money. When Artie's husband died, Artie donated his things to Housing Works. "That was very important to him. But first, he had all of us—his friends—over and invited us each to take one thing that reminded us of Greg. He made us try on Greg's clothes, and whatever fit was ours to take. I left with five oversized sweaters. That's exactly what we should have done with Artie's things," Antonio said before settling into a quiet that I abetted by looking away and continuing silently along Hudson toward the 2 train. Until Antonio began shouting: "O, treachery! Fly, good Fleance, fly, fly, fly!"

"What? Are you okay?"

"Who did strike out the light?"

"Oh!"

"Wast not that—

"¿No era acaso lo más adecuado?"

"There's but one down; the son is fled."

"La mejor mitad de nuestro negocio se nos ha escapado."

"Well, let's away, and say how much is done."

The next time I saw him was a couple of weeks later, the awkward day on the street when he asked me to let him into the building.

. . .

I stopped working for the Petersons in the spring, a couple of months after Artie's apartment had been emptied by the real estate company. It would be a few more months yet before Artie's relatives had the legal right to sell it. In the meantime, I got into Cornell, CUNY, University of Georgia, and University of Florida. CUNY made the most sense, financially speaking, but I hadn't yet accepted an offer.

College wasn't for another five months, but I quit the Petersons because I wanted to travel over the summer. The Petersons weren't upset. Mr. Peterson offered to write me a letter of recommendation. For what, I wasn't sure. "You are the kind of guy with lots of potential," he said.

On my last day, as Hjalvar and I were returning from the park, I noticed that the door to 512 was slightly ajar. I put Hjalvar in front of the television and sneaked across the hall. I knocked once. No one responded. "Hello!" I called out when I was already inside, but nothing was returned. I looked around quickly. Everything was unfamiliar. It was staged with new furniture, large abstract paintings, and yellow flowers. Near the front door was a tall basket full of umbrellas; on the wall was a row of hooks covered in logoless sports caps and tote bags emblazoned with the names of nonprofit organizations and magazines. In a moment of weakness—or possibly strength—I grabbed the largest of the bags and filled it with five umbrellas, four hats, and a beige canvas bag with green straps. I justified the theft to myself: there wasn't a single unbroken umbrella at my parents' house; my mom was always encouraging my dad to wear hats to protect his face from the sun; and I was trying to promote reusable bags at home. But just before I stepped out into the hallway, I panicked—it crossed my mind that the real estate agent might have snapped pictures of the place. I rushed to put the hats, umbrellas, and tote bags back exactly as I recalled them. Then I put my ear to the door and listened for sounds. When I heard none, I stepped outside and softly pulled the door within an inch of its jamb, just as it had been before. Then I made my way across the hall, back to little Hjalvar whom I'd left singing along to Selena.

THE CARETAKERS

PEOPLE CONTINUE STREAMING ONTO THE platform, somehow finding the unfilled spaces. The subway station, like the neighborhood above, teems with South and Central Americans, Asians from Russia to Indonesia, a smattering of Eastern Europeans, a few mixed couples with their ambiguous progeny, and a half-dozen elderly Hibernians. It's 5:49 p.m. I've just left my aunt at a hospital in Queens, the sort of medical establishment that resembles a prison on the outside and a Star Trek vessel on the inside. The transportation app on my phone flashes a warning about the F train: it's been rerouted and delayed. In other words, one can be late for a place they never intended to visit. After a few minutes, a boxy, steel caterpillar with enormous glass eyes rolls into the station. It's the R train, the one train I can count on to arrive whenever I don't need it.

It, too, is Brooklyn bound, but slower. This one is also older, of the antiquated variety that keep their through-doors locked, preventing passengers from moving between cars. I get on anyway because it's here, it'll get me home eventually, and very few people seem to be interested in this train.

The doors close.

Despite the train's relative calm, I put on my headphones. I owe this intervention to Gerardo. We barely keep in touch since I got married and had kids. Except for birthday wishes. To be clear, for many of the last twenty years, I have texted him on his birthday. Gerardo usually responds something along the lines of *Mi'jo, I can't believe you remembered!* Then another year goes by, during which he never acknowledges my birthday, leaving me to think that what he really meant was *Mijo, why do you keep making this outdated, performative gesture?* I don't mention this now in order to recriminate; it's just an observation. Besides, it's not only Gerardo. I have this asymmetrical relationship with many people.

Anyway, the headphones. Gerardo visited New York a couple of years ago. We met in the East Village and drank martinis at a dive bar on 7th and 1st, before feasting on fried oysters, duck-fat drenched potatoes, and grilled pigeon at a restaurant near 1st and 1st. I chose that particular place, with its cramped tables and wobbly bentwood chairs, because Gerardo appreciates spectacular meals in understated dining rooms. He was also friendly with the lesbian pair who owned the place, and I knew we'd get undue attention. It was during this dinner that he said I should visit him in LA.

"It's *thee* place right now. It's laid back and vibrant. You can't find that here."

"I prefer my cities to pick a lane. Either you're laid back or you're vibrant."

"Our people are there!"

"Our people are here too."

"Yeah, on the outskirts and in the kitchens. There, we run shit, in addition to being on the outskirts and in the kitchens. It's nice to have a balance."

"Have you given up on New York?"

"This place has lost its way. The food is shit, the culture is shit, and the men are all shit."

Gerardo was bitter about the way things had ended for him here. He'd suffered a broken heart as a result of a broken rule—his cardinal rule: never date a white guy. Officially, he and Tim broke up because a pair of hedge fund guys offered Gerardo a buttload of money to open up a high-end vegan Mexican restaurant in LA, but things with Tim had soured much earlier, after Gerardo stumbled upon Tim's porn browsing history: *latino bottoms, latino twinks, latino big booty, latino threesome, latino 3some, latino fisting, latino felching, gay latino housekeeper, latino gangsters, latino gang banging.*

Latino housekeeper was the tipping point.

"Trust me, you'd love the West Coast. Everyone is fit and passive aggressive—Your favorite."

"I haven't been on a plane in over two years. And I have no desire to fly."

"Two years!" he half-yelled.

It was a good thing I'd just stuffed the last oyster into my mouth because I might have otherwise shushed Gerardo. I detest that sort of attention-drawing loudness. And he knows it. In fact, I'm convinced Gerardo does it intentionally—his way of loosening me up.

"That's insane," Gerardo said. "You can't not travel because you're afraid of flying."

I tried to explain my fear, but Gerardo wasn't particularly sympathetic. He just kept repeating that it was the safest way to travel, that it was more dangerous to drive, to walk, to go to a high school

in the United States, as if I didn't already kn[...]
ever, offer a solution: noise canceling headph[...]
deprivation is exactly what you need," he said. "I s[...]

That was two years ago, and now four since I've [...] a plane.

To complicate matters, the anxiety that was once [...]e dominion of air travel has now crept into the subway. The train doesn't even have to be excessively crowded. I am nonetheless consumed by a sensation best described as constriction—what I imagine death by large python to be. A few weeks ago, it got really bad. I became insatiably desperate for more space on the Q train, and the only available option seemed to be the floor. Knowing that I couldn't spread out on the floor of the subway during rush hour only made my mind latch onto the notion with more intensity, until I descended into a sort of contained lunacy. The other passengers were watching videos or playing games on their phones, a few read, a few others stared ahead or down at their feet. The contrast between my internal reality and the external one only made the situation worse. As I waited impatiently for my descension into hell to be complete, I tried everything: I tucked my head between my knees, pinched my inner thighs, held my breath, pulled out a nose hair, clenched my stomach, jaw, and ass, and counted all of Roger Federer's grand slam titles, in chronological order: Wimbledon 2003, Australian Open 2004, Wimbledon 2004, US Open 2004 . . . By the time I got to the French Open 2009, we'd reached my station.

Since that day, whenever I board a train, I feel as if I'm taking my life into my hands. The panic is undoubtedly precipitated by something other than the train itself, but because my brain has entangled the two, the severing will require some effort. I should return to therapy, but I won't. I am by no means opposed to this type of intervention; it's the search for a therapist that has proved insurmountable.

...................at the noise-canceling headphones help, and
pe............make me think of Gerardo, who, ironically enough,
I for............ge last week, on the occasion of his birthday.

"They think she'll die soon. Sepsis," my father said, yesterday
afternoon, over the phone. "Maybe a few days is all she has. I'm
going to see her tomorrow morning."

"Do you want me to go with you?"

"It's up to you," he said, his voice thin, sheepish. "I know you're
busy with your work."

We agreed to meet at ten so that my father could have enough
time with his sister before his shift at the restaurant, but we both
arrived nearer to eleven. There were families of three, four, and five
scattered about the lobby's benches and hovering around the reception desk. There were no fewer than seven ethnicities represented in
that waiting area. Most of the groups could be defined by their shared
skin color and height, but there were a few jumbled families that
made me wonder about the epigenetic effects of living in this country. Was it the US diet that caused children to be so much taller than
their parents? Was it the US economy that aged parents quickly?

It was in this human tapestry that I spotted my uncle. He was
tucked in a corner, backlit by a vending machine, standing near an
It's a Boy balloon—already a pressure and a reminder of gender's pre-
eminence. My uncle was unchanged since I'd seen him last, five or
six years earlier at his granddaughter's baptism. Physically, my uncle
is a stretched version of my father—taller, thinner, shaggier. Unlike
my father, he's a persnickety man, wary of germs and their primary
vector: humans. He spotted us immediately.

"¡Hola!"

"¡Hola!"

"¡Hola!"

We made our way toward the bank of elevators.

The ICU was clean, transparent, and made of glass—walls, partitions, windows. My aunt was alone, supine on her bed, and strikingly damaged, bloated and, in a way, stranded. As we approached, she squinted until her eyes vanished between lids and upper cheeks. My uncle stepped forward, bending to kiss his sister's forehead. My dad tried to lift her hand, but the act triggered a sustained, mumble-ridden agitation.

";Qué pasó?" he asked.

"¡Imbécil!" she managed to enunciate through her sedation and her swollen tongue.

My father hadn't spoken to her in five years. A misalignment that had become a cold war. Typical of my father's family. Siblings who don't talk to each other. Fathers who disown sons. Daughters who freeze out mothers. Then, without warning, a thaw.

I kissed my aunt quickly, venerably, like a pilgrim visiting a religious artifact. Her skin was warm; her hair, oily and wayward. Her wrists, ankles, and feet were ashen and cracked like the bark of a tree. If she had been in clear possession of her faculties, she would have been mortified at her slovenly appearance. Furious, too. My memories of her were of a bon vivant with fastidious tastes and a cigarette cemented between her fingertips. My aunt never forgave a strand of hair for slipping from its place—she seldom forgave anything. She'd been, all her life, held to a standard—a woman, an immigrant, a mother, a woman, a woman, a woman—and she'd turned that lens onto everyone else.

We sat awkwardly in the sun's direct and reflected brightness, alternating between peering at our phones and decoding my aunt's utterances. My father interlaced his fingers and slouched in his chair, like a troubled teenager playing aloof. My uncle fondled nervously the zipper of his thin jacket, rarely looking up at what remained of his sister. The discomfort of men and their feelings filled the room. I began to feel self-conscious about the urge to care for my aunt, to caress her hair, to pat her hands, to embrace her. I was officially the queer one in the room, an implication that my humanity was a performance, risible, expected, and somehow required. The weight of it kept me in my seat.

At one point, my aunt slipped into a pronounced fit of agitation. "She's dead!" she cried out.

Apropos of nothing, my aunt had convinced herself that her sister, another of my aunts, had died. Through tears and labored heaving, she was trying to convince us too.

My uncle looked at my father and me with peculiar eyes, full of gall and disbelief. "No," he shouted. "Nilda's fine! She's at work. She'll call during her lunch break. It was just a dream," he said, before patting her hand quickly, like a hummingbird who's been recorded and played back in slow motion, a gesture of penance for temporarily raising his voice.

My aunt insisted for a minute longer before shutting down abruptly, exhausted, her words mid-formation, like a robot who'd spent its battery. We all studied her torso waiting for it to move up and down. It did, and we exhaled.

At Queens Plaza, the doors open, riders board, and the doors close again, all of it efficiently, as if our mass transit system were well funded. I make an effort not to scan the car, but it's too late. A gray-haired couple with curved spines dodders a few feet away, and I feel an obligation to relinquish my seat. If I weren't in my current state, I would, but sitting here (folded at the knee and waist; the wall a supplementary backbone) comes with primordial comforts that I am unwilling to sacrifice. I peer up again. A young couple with bright eyes and enviable posture has offered the elderly pair their seats.

At 57th Street, a woman pushes a pram-like stroller onto the train, not without difficulty. Whatever guilt I feel isn't enough for our eyes to meet. She remains by the open doors, almost paranormally oblivious to the people who attempt to board behind her. She fumbles at locking the wheels of the stroller, repeatedly tapping at a red lever with her foot but missing. Three, four, five sluggish tries. Her condition becomes apparent. Drunk—No, high. The lack of cognizance in her eyes, her sallow skin, and her absent teeth tell me this is a lifetime of being high. The cradle of the stroller lies horizontal, cocooned by a blanket—a ragged thing dappled with a meager selection of farm animals: cow, chicken, pig, sheep, cow, chicken, pig, sheep. She finally locks the wheels. Through it all, her empty eyes remain low and hidden. Her lips are painted a shade of red I can't name, nearer to pink than purple. Is this fuchsia? The makeup-less splotches on her face reveal a cadaverous whiteness. She might be my age, but she might be twenty years more.

I pull one headphone from my ear. The combined din of scattered conversations and an old train lurching along outdated tracks doubles as white noise. The baby is silent. I sense something eerie afoot—a foreboding that has become typical of these trips, but is somehow different today. Also typical: believing that today is somehow different.

Hold my hand, I consider saying to the stranger beside me. I've just spent six hours in a hospital trying to provide comfort to someone with whom I couldn't recall ever having a proper conversation. Could you do the same for me?

I also consider shouting at full volume a litany of my fears. I'm afraid of losing my mind. I'm afraid of violence. I'm afraid of suffering. I'm afraid of my children being bullied. I'm afraid of illness. I'm afraid of dying. I'm afraid of dying before there is any meaningful reparation of the world.

Puddles and premature warmth made for an unpleasant spring day, the first one of the season easily mistakable for summer. The hospital, too, was balmy in the places lit by the sun.

In retrospect, my aunt had clearly been saying, "Agua. Por favor." But it took a few tries for us to understand.

The nurse, a trim Filipina with a pageboy cut and amber eyes, explained that my aunt couldn't have any liquids. She said it apologetically, albeit at a rapid pace, with a mild accent that left me wondering if, like many foreign-born clinicians in the United States, she had been trained in her country of origin. A colleague of mine studies this phenomenon: the siphoning of professionals from abroad. It's called *brain drain*, and it contributes to skilled labor shortages in poorer countries. The Philippines likely subsidized this nurse's schooling, and we poached her. To be fair, she might have wanted to be poached. But now the Philippines is short one nurse and probably thousands.

"Ice chips," she said, "I'll bring them to you shortly."

Another nurse eventually arrived carrying a plastic cup and a white spoon. She approached my aunt and caressed her face and arm with an unquestionable kindness that highlighted how ineffective the rest of us had been. After measuring her vitals and scanning the clipboard that hung from the railing of the bed, the nurse asked if she could have thirty minutes to bathe my aunt. My father, my uncle, and I walked to a nearby restaurant with lime-green tables. We knew the portions would be enormous, so we skipped appetizers— an example of a new, health-conscious decision-making—and instead shared one order of cow tongue in sofrito and one of tripe stew. The conversation centered primarily on my grandmother, who was still in Colombia, and by all accounts, in better health than most of us. I knew little about her, except that she'd married young, was quick to anger, and had an errant bullet permanently lodged in her chest—her kitchen window in Bogotá, where she often sat for lunch, looked out onto the military school's courtyard.

We ate quickly. When the bill came, each of us reached for his wallet, but I made the grander gesture.

"Qué buen hijo," said my uncle to my father. "Qué generoso."

This one act of kindness led to a hagiography that lasted the two blocks back to the hospital: the best grades; always had a book in his hand; a professor with job security. I was proof, in a way, that they had been right to come to this country. Right to have endured. They probably weren't right, but it's done now, and besides, the choices were few—then as now.

We approached my aunt's room. Her arm, trapped in a web of cables and tubes, hung lifeless a few inches from the reflective linoleum, giving the illusion of two people about to touch. "Shit," my father called out as he sped toward her. While he was disentangling her arm, she roused, and my father let out a high-pitched sigh, like a balloon that had been recently untied.

"¿Quién es?" My aunt's voice was silty, but the words now sluiced out clearly, no doubt because of the ice chips. She inquired again about the dead sister who had not died and, then, about a childhood pet that only my uncle recalled vaguely. After everything, she winced.

We sat for thirty minutes more before my father announced that he had to leave. He'd be late for his shift at the restaurant, a suburban Italian place where he'd worked since I left for college. He offered me a ride to the subway station only a few blocks away, but I told him I'd stay longer. He squeezed my shoulder and pulled the wallet from his pocket, for what reason, I was unsure.

"Please, Dad. I'm fine."

"Are you sure?"

"Yes."

Whether I was guided by love or guilt, I didn't know. Maybe it was responsibility. My father shouldn't be working at his age, and frankly, I had nothing pressing to do, least of all carrying trays of heavy plates and precarious cocktails. I remained for him. And for her. Death, after all, was in the room, and our presence was keeping it at bay. Leaving would have made me an accomplice.

At Union Square, a family of Nordic-looking people wearing small backpacks and carrying travel guides squeezes inside a now packed train. The children have blond eyebrows and exhibit the sort of inoffensive confidence one expects of democratic socialism, where people aren't afraid of one another. Neither child clings to their parents. Their delicate fingers clasp a metal pole as their eyes scan the advertisements above (immigration lawyer, dermatologist, moving company), the irreparably scratched windows, and the seat stained with dried blood that remains empty. This quartet of Danes, Swedes, or Norwegians came to marvel at the grandeur of New York, but the scenes of inequality and second-tier modernity have surely captured their attention. I'm embarrassed.

The lady with the stroller now sits across from me. Her neck is rounded and her head hangs low, like a cursed swan. Her lips droop, slightly agape. She's wedged a leg protectively between the stroller's axles and one slack hand inside the carriage. Again, I pull a headphone from my ear. No sounds of a baby, still. I expect the child to be awake, to be fussing. The loudness of the train is incontestable. Then again, the womb is chaotic—I've read—which is why newborns sleep well with white noise and in motion. Or maybe there isn't a small child in the stroller, but a dog instead. I've seen that before.

This train has made an inordinate number of stops, and I am reminded of why I avoid the R. But the time between stations is brief—a newfound reason to appreciate the R. It's all going well. Too well. What if we stall? One minute I can bear. Five is another story. Ten is a panic attack. *Leave now, before the doors close—No, stay! On Saturdays, every train will be as crowded as this one.*

The doors close.

I turn up the volume. I'm listening to *Get It Right* by Aretha Franklin, an underrated, percussion-heavy album produced by Luther Vandross. The 1980s was a prolific decade for Franklin—six albums, nine Top-40 hits—often overshadowed by her years at Atlantic Records.

My aunt dozed off, leaving a silence that my uncle and I were obliged to fill. We talked for a few minutes about my work, about my cousins, about my kids. I showed him pictures; he told me they were beautiful and that he could tell from their eyes that they were full of personality. Then, like many other people his age who I have met since having children, he warned me that it would all fly by quickly.

I couldn't recall another time in my life when my uncle and I had had a conversation that lasted longer than a few pleasantries or a few humorous observations. He's nice enough, but he's never been much of a talker. Once, when I was seven or eight, he called me a fag for walking around in my mother's heels, as I entertained a roomful of Uno-playing adults, like a USO performer. He meant it innocently enough, but the words stuck with me.

When it seemed we'd run out of things to share, he said, "It's a big room, no? Who could afford this sort of hospital stay without insurance?"

I responded with a few talking points about the inefficiencies of our health care system, but immediately I feared I had come across as pedantic or, worse, combative. I retreated: "Just make them all government employees and negotiate drug prices. Who cares about longer waits."

My uncle let out a brief laugh that seemed to erupt from his belly. "¿Eres Chavista?"

Chavista was his shorthand for leftist, socialist, communist, pro-Fidel, anti-imperialist, etc.

I played it safe: "No. Not really. I agree with the ideas, but the corruption is too much. On the other hand, who's to say how things would have turned out if the US minded its business." What I wanted to say was that the vilification of socialism in the Western world rests solely on a flag-waving fear of abrogated individual rights and liberties, but a bit of collectivism would do us all well.

My uncle nodded without revealing his opinion on the matter, which only forced me to say more: "If it were up to me, presidents wouldn't serve consecutive terms. And instead of four years, they'd serve six and disappear. Look at Chile. Or Uruguay. They have one-term limits."

"Peru too, but all its former presidents are under investigation," my uncle responded.

"Maybe they shouldn't allow reelection at all," I said. "Or private campaign financing."

My uncle reeled in an extended leg and shifted in his seat. It was the first political conversation I'd ever had with him, and I feared it would be the last.

"I mean, those are just my unformed thoughts," I added timidly. "What do I know?"

I looked over at my aunt and wondered why she'd picked that moment to sleep soundly.

"All of my politics are on the fingers of this hand." My uncle wiggled his digits, as if he were becoming acquainted with a new prosthetic limb. It was his left hand.

It was an odd way of putting it, but his declaration brought relief and camaraderie into the arena.

"If you ask me, a parliamentary system is the way to go," he continued. "But mi'jo, don't hold your breath. People like us are good at only two things: worrying and hablando mierda. Never action." Then he patted my knee and returned to his phone.

People like you and me . . . ?

I went to the bathroom. When I returned, my uncle was angled over his sister, saying goodbye. Whatever she was saying had turned his cheeks and eyes red. I took advantage of the moment to grab my things, but my uncle noticed. "Please," he whispered, "don't leave her alone."

On the bridge between Manhattan and Brooklyn, the train stalls for seconds; then, minutes. My intestines contract. I do my best to ignore the twenty-first-century reality of being trapped inside a twentieth-century contraption while suspended on nineteenth-century engineering. I attempt to funnel all of my scattered energies into my auditory nerves. I focus on George Michael—"A Different Corner," a song from that brief period when he sang alone but was still technically part of Wham! I try to assume its docile energy, sway my head, and in the process, redirect serotonin. It seems to work, but I don't know for how long. At least the car is no longer crowded. Two, four, seven, nine, thirteen, fourteen, sixteen people are left. Many of the orange and yellow seats were abandoned somewhere before Canal Street, when the conductor announced that the train would begin running express.

The baby stroller remains across from me, along with its slumped caretaker. I'm concerned that what little air circulates in this warm car is incapable of penetrating the fabric enveloping the pram. It has crossed my mind that the child is dead. If we are truly part of a multiverse, then there is another universe in which I approach this person to ask if she is okay. In this universe, however, I've fulfilled my caretaking duties for the day and don't meddle in the affairs of others.

Inhale for four: one, two, three, four. Hold for four: one, two, three, four. Exhale four: one, two, three, four. Hold for four: one, two, three, four.

I message my husband: "On bridge. Stuck. Almost home."

I message Gerardo: "A belated happy birthday to you, you silly old thing!"

I refresh a page of tennis scores, but it's the European clay court season and all the matches finished hours ago.

That takes all of forty-five seconds.

My husband responds: "Sorry, hon. Remember the breathing! Kids are in bath. See you soon."

It dawns on me that the person sitting across from me gets high to cope with her anxieties; I count breaths and listen to pop music. Currently, her treatment plan feels more effective.

I decide to walk to the other end of the car, hoping movement will quiet the trill of madness. I half rise before the train judders abruptly. I sit back down.

After each ice chip, I wiped away the excess water that dribbled down my aunt's chin and cheeks. I imagined her decades earlier, spooning food into my mouth and dabbing the corners of my lips. There were weekends when my parents worked late, and my aunt babysat. In her apartment, air freshener and cigarette smoke collided mid-air, creating an aroma distinct enough to qualify as an emotion decades later. I imagined, too, a time before I existed, when my aunt was young, still in Colombia. She'd been, briefly, an actress. Almost famous, my father told me once. She was also good with numbers. La calculadora, they used to call her.

She twitched violently in her sleep. When she woke, I offered music. She accepted but almost immediately shook her head like a willful child until I removed the enormous headset. She toggled in quick succession between fitful sleep and fussy consciousness. At one point, she began confessing and apologizing, most of which I didn't understand; some of which didn't require any deciphering.

"You were always a smart boy, but also the most annoying kid I've ever met," she said with a straight face.

"I don't think much has changed," I responded.

We both let out abbreviated laughs; hers morphed into a coughing fit. She asked about her husband, my uncle—a super at a nearby apartment building. I explained that he was working and would be arriving soon.

"¿Y mis hijas?"

They'd both been there in the morning before I arrived. They were also working, and I wasn't sure if they were coming back. "Más tarde," I said, conscious suddenly of how many people in my family work on the weekends.

I was thinking just this when my uncle walked in. "Hello, beautiful," he said and kissed the top of my aunt's head. He then pivoted toward me—"¿Qué hay, mi'jo?"—and extended a bandaged hand. He'd pinched it between a refrigerator and a wall, he explained. I sidestepped his masculinity and put my arms forcefully around him. The tonic of harsh soap and pungent aftershave was strangely comforting. His thin hair was freshly wet and combed, and he wore the same mustache he'd had when I was five, but now gray.

While my uncle and I exchanged hasty life updates, something inchoate began to unfurl inside of me, like tendrils of fear: one for her, one for them, and one for my trip home. My uncle spotted the uneasiness in my face and told me not to worry. "It's just the effects of yesterday's anesthesia," he said. "She's seen the worst of it. Come to the apartment when she's better. I'll make a pot of mondongo for you."

"Sí, pronto," I replied. But I knew this might be the last time I saw my aunt. While she slept, one of the nurses had explained to me that someone with my aunt's comorbidities—diabetes, hypertension, kidney failure—doesn't usually recover from sepsis. "Her entire system is fighting her," she said. "Prepare for the worst."

As the station's lights appear, a combination of accomplishment and relief fill me, like wine coating an empty stomach. The train slows, and I surf my way to the doors. I am in the first car, and we're moving fast relative to the platform. Too fast, if you ask me. It's 6:51 p.m. My children are usually in bed by seven, but awake for a short while longer. If I hurry, I can catch that brief, hallowed window of time where they're not yet asleep but not awake enough to be reenergized by my presence.

We come to a hard stop, but the doors don't open. The old train jerks violently and halts again before expelling a cold hiss. A muffled commotion commences. I turn to find the sleeping mother tipped over, sprawled across a few seats, her open mouth revealing a darkness, a mini-golf hole without adornments. Her arm is limp, her fingers curled, knuckles barely brushing the floor. The stroller remains upright, her feet tangled in its base. A few people approach her slowly, a trepidation born of urban living. Before they reach her, the doors on which I am leaning open behind me. I stumble and catch my heel in the space between the train and the platform. My headphones fly off just as my ass hits the platform.

"She's dead! Oh my god, she's dead!" I hear someone inside the train shout.

"The baby!" someone else yells.

The child's cries are alarming and distant, like those of an injured cat through an open window. I remain on the ground with an obstructed view, but I am able to see two women gently paw at the mother, while a third walks toward the stroller and reaches inside. She pulls out the child and now the farm animals are dangling from the stranger's arms.

An odd thought enters my mind, one that suggests that even an atheist can be Catholic: This woman died so that my aunt might live. Somewhere they have traded places.

The chaos around me does nothing to interrupt the train's business. The doors attempt to close despite half of me remaining inside. They press on my legs and I start pulling, softly at first because I know the train won't leave while my torso juts out onto the platform. But then I hear the conductor say, "Next stop, Atlantic Avenue." I begin to pull with more force, frantically. From nowhere, it seems, hands appear under my arms. They are attached to urgent, commanding voices: "Open the doors! He's trapped!" Two people are lifting me; several others are screaming and pounding the train car with their hands and fists.

The doors open long enough for all of me to escape. I see the dead woman. She's upright and disoriented, with heavy eyes. No longer dead. I don't see the baby, but I hear its cries.

"Are you okay?" ask the people who bring me to my feet. One of them bends down to pick up the headphones.

I feel tears in my eyes, my chest barely able to contain the heart beating violently inside of it. A small pain shooting up my spine from the place where my body hit the platform. "I'm fine," I say. "Thank you."

In an instant, the chaos recedes to a level indistinguishable from the norm. A controlled voice wrapped in static cuts through the noise. The conductor is calling for assistance. I hear the strident sounds of indignation and relief. The train remains in the station, but I don't look back anymore. I turn and walk up the stairs slowly at first. Then through the turnstile. Then up another set of stairs.

There's still sunlight but I cannot see the source because of the skyscrapers that keep sprouting like capitalist bamboo. Across the street, one third of the building's façade is occupied by a clock that reads 12:15—years of this. My phone says 6:55. It also says I have a new text message. From Gerardo: "Mi'jo! Grassy-ass! I was wondering what I'd done to not get birthday love:-) Talk soon. xo."

THE SIX TIMES OF ALAN

ALL OF THE OTHER CHILDREN were white.

I considered leaving, using the tantrum-proof promise of ice cream as an exit strategy. Instead, I held my breath for ten seconds, exhaled with intention—just as Alan always tells me to—and allowed Jules to wander off and play. In this regard, I'm unlike my husband, who thinks children should be left to interact with the world on their own terms and spends most of his playground-parenting lost in his phone, occasionally glancing at the exits. I'm too busy invoking ancestors and casting protective spells. But it's been a couple of years now of parenting, and very few people on the playground have proven to be anything worse than casually horrid or vaguely racist. Which is probably why I let my guard down.

This all took place three Fridays ago, at a small park in Manhattan—specifically, where Bank, Hudson, and Bleecker meet.

The pristine tangle of primary colors was encircled by a ring of car traffic, chic boutiques, and restaurants that opened only for dinner. The neighborhood had become more upscale and less appealing in the twenty years since I'd known it primarily as a nightime cruising ground: besotted kisses and furtive, moonlit hand jobs, most of which took place on the Bleecker side of the playground.

Last month, however, there was none of that. What I remember is Jules wheeling around a rusty toy stroller that had been discarded. I recall, too, another stroller-pushing child of similar size and shape, but blonde and white. I remember feeling that everything was going smoothly enough for me to get lost in my email.

I fear I'm being redundant, but this is as propitious a time as any to explain that my skin color, like that of Jules, sits on the spectrum of brown. I occupy a lighter nodule, a decidedly Central and South American mestizaje of the Indigenous-European variety. Jules, too, is a mix of identities, the most identifiable of which is Black—the ethno-racial-political category, not the absence of light. I bother to mention this at all because I've noticed on several occasions that this sort of phenotypic asymmetry within a family sows confusion, especially for the other guardians at the playground, who look around curiously, and sometimes with blatant alarm, whenever they don't see a corresponding Black adult for Jules. Not in an *Are you okay, honey?* fashion, but more of a *Who is guarding this unknown variable?* fluster. It doesn't matter if I'm interacting with my baby in an unambiguous parent–child fashion, the other guardians stare (me, Jules, my face, Jules's face, then mine again), searching for commonalities, desperate to understand or to prove. There's no two ways about it: racial discordance unsettles people. And it often casts me as an unwitting eavesdropper.

"This kid . . ." blared a man in a sweater vest and dirty blond eyebrows a few feet away, before he caught himself and began again, but now in a hopeless, stakes-raising whisper. "This *black* kid just tried to jump Taylor and steal her stroller, but she wadn't havin' dat. Nuh-uh," he said proudly and patois-y to his wife, a similarly handsome woman sitting beside him and breastfeeding their younger child beneath a white sheet decorated in cartoon rainbows. Then he dragged his hand through the air in a lazy, sass-less semicircle that ended with soft finger snaps. Whether the throwback pantomime was his misguided homage to Black women, gay men, or the resurgent era of drag queens is unknowable.

What was clear was the way little Taylor's father had manipulated the register of his voice to talk about Jules. It changed me. I detest physical violence—I caught a glimpse of a UFC match at the barber last week and I got woozy—but in that moment, I contemplated digging a grave in the sandpit for the whispering racist. In fact, it took every breathing and mindfulness exercise Alan had ever taught me to keep me on that park bench.

It bears repeating that my child is two years old. Two-year-olds cannot steal. It's not possible. They don't yet understand ownership or capitalism. This isn't to say that it's okay to take things, but I don't believe for a moment that the Klansman in Argyle would have mentioned it to his wife if my baby were not Black. There was racial pride in his insolent declaration; little Taylor hadn't only defended herself against the patriarchy, she'd vanquished the dark villain from a distant land—or public housing.

"Not everything is racism," says Alan. "I don't want to disregard how you're feeling, but on the face of it, he may not have meant any harm."

"But why characterize the actions of a toddler in terms of criminal behavior?"

"Granted, a poor choice of words, but probably empty words."

Frankly, I'm surprised Alan is staking this particular claim. It's not like him to—Actually, come to think of it, this is exactly like Alan. Whenever it suits his analysis, he speaks in a nested vernacular, where nothing is abstract or intangible—words within words, desires beneath desires, consequences of the consequences, like that—but when I want to peel back the layers of intent, he talks about "empty words." Now he's left me wondering if he, too, wears sweater vests.

"Why didn't you say anything to him?" Alan continues.

"To the guy at the playground?"

"Seems you missed an opportunity to engage and dispel your fears."

Engagement with the racist dad would have been impossible. After overhearing his *empty words*, I never again achieved the level of calm required for interaction with a perfect stranger. All the scenarios I concocted from that recently painted playground bench were loud and unevenly keeled encounters that ended with me in handcuffs. In some of the scenarios, I undoubtedly deserved to be arrested, but the stigma around being labeled racist is so libelous, even approaching little Taylor's dad with a diplomatic affect might have triggered a 911 call. No one, after all, admits they're racist. No one on a playground has ever said, *You're right, that came from a dank, unholy place deep within me that I need to exorcise.* And certainly never in a West Village playground. It's much easier to be racist, deny it, drive your accuser crazy, and accuse him of being crazy. And it was easier still to remind myself that I'd made a choice to be in that place.

That I was capable of leaving it whenever I wanted to.

That I had a savings account.

That I had an acupuncture appointment on Monday.

That I shouldn't get distracted by interpersonal encounters.

That this wasn't police brutality.

That reparations would one day close the wealth gaps that have sustained anti-Black racism for centuries.

I told myself all of these things. Then I whispered into Jules's ear, "Want Daddy to buy you some ice cream?"

Alan nods when I finish recounting the events of that fateful Friday. Then he scribbles something into his spiraled notepad.

I've returned to Alan (the fifth rapprochement in almost a decade) because I detest the inefficiencies of beginning a new relationship. Having to explain myself—Worse! Having to pay someone to listen to me explain myself: childhood, livelihood, fears, insecurities, coping mechanisms. It's enough to give up on therapy altogether. Alan is problematic, but he knows me, and that's invaluable.

"How did your parents meet?" he asks, apropos of nothing, midway through our second session of this, our most recent, reconciliation.

Alan is tall and lanky. His knees, one resting on the other, form a mountain of gently wrinkled khaki that peaks near his chest and gradually erodes as he sinks into the off-white cushions of a blond wicker chair.

Today, I was my usual early, in time to catch a glimpse of him playing solitaire on his phone. I make sure to arrive ahead of our scheduled time because Alan ends our sessions six minutes early. "Enough time for a trip to the bathroom and a call to my teenage daughter before my next client," he explained years ago, when I first started seeing him. "Quality not quantity," he said in response to my eyebrows. In the moment, the aphorism assuaged me; by the time his reasoning became fishy, I was already home. Addressing this minor injustice now would only confirm Alan's oft-repeated observation: I'm drawn to conflict but afraid of confrontation—he also thinks I'm petty. And digressive.

It was a timing issue, in a way, that led me to dissolve my relationship with Alan the first time. I used to arrive between 6:49 and 6:56 for our 7:00 p.m. appointments, but one time, I got there at 7:03, and instead of just sitting down and beginning the session, I made it a point to apologize profusely (a habit that feels at once involuntary and contrived) and, well, he took that as a sign of weakness and pounced. Not that he was consciously pouncing or exploiting weaknesses— and not that my uncharacteristic lateness on one day (ONE DAY!) should constitute a weakness—but humans do excel at capitalizing on each other's weaknesses, I've noticed. It's our way of taking or maintaining an upper hand, especially when Human A exhibits a character flaw that Human B (the one who pounces) also exhibits or suppresses in some manner, which I believe, in this case, Human B (Alan) has made a rather self-serving feather in his cap. How else can one explain his regularly ending our forty-five-minute session six minutes early but then having the audacity to comment on my one, solitary incident of lateness? Which is exactly what happened almost ten years ago.

"Have you ever heard of CPT?" he asked, after I'd finished apologizing for my tardiness.

"No. No, I haven't," I responded, dabbing at my brow and neck with a one-ply tissue I'd pulled from a ceramic box atop his djembe-drum coffee table. But I had (of course!) heard of CPT, only never in the context of a white doctor and a brown patient.

"You know, colored peoples' time," he said, very matter of fact, camouflaged in part by the enormous corn plant beside him. Whatever he uttered next didn't register because, by that point, I was too busy feeling microaggressed at a macrolevel.

I kept one more appointment with Alan after the CPT incident. I used the end-of-year holidays as cover for not returning: I had to leave town for Thanksgiving; in early December, it was my husband's holiday party; then, my holiday party; followed by Christmas. Alan called twice that January, but each time, I muted the ringing and stuffed the phone back into my pocket.

"How my parents met? Why?" I ask. It's been a few weeks since the playground incident. My legs, too, are crossed—a hillock of dark blue denim.

Alan lifts the mug of water from the drum's untreated rawhide. "It occurs to me that we've never explored the origins of your origins," he says and sips.

I won't tell him how my parents met. To begin with, it's none of his business. What's more, my mother would undoubtedly disapprove of my sharing her personal history with a stranger. But more to the point, I don't want him to know. Why does he want to know? It's a rather unremarkable story—they met at a house party in Queens. Even so, I know Alan will find some way to categorize it as a foundational moment. He'll remove his aviator eyeglasses and pinch the hypotenuse of his scalene nose, all the while practicing a measured bopping, as if he were speeding along a dusty highway, listening to the one decent Buffalo Springfield song. *That's useful insight. That explains plenty.* Then he'll attempt to decipher something that isn't coded.

"The story of my parents is somewhat complicated," I say without a plan.

"Complications are mountains we must climb to reach the rivers of truth."

Something about the lack of creativity in his metaphor angers me. It makes me want to give him the complications he so desperately seeks. I remain quiet as I scan the room. There are no fewer than six copies of the *New Yorker* on the short table beside me. Nothing comes to mind.

"They met at a house party in Queens."

Alan pulls off his glasses—"Uh-huh"—but doesn't pinch the bridge of his nose. Instead, he scribbles something into his notepad. I don't believe he's written anything at all. This is merely his way of completing a tiny circuit that took him nowhere. Doesn't matter. I'm not here for analysis. I want peace and, maybe, transcendence. Guidance, too. I want to better understand the origins of my weeks-long shitty mood. And I want a plan of action.

· · ·

Not even a year after I'd stopped seeing Alan for the first time—after the CPT encounter—I called and left him a voicemail. A week later, he left me a voicemail. The following Tuesday, I was in his waiting room by six-thirty for our seven-p.m. appointment.

My husband and I were going through a spell of asynchrony. Passive disagreements, differing priorities, long silences. It was as if Gus and I were on the same stage but somehow performing from different scripts—repertory theater gone awry.

"If you want, we could try couples counseling," Gus suggested, one Saturday afternoon, while repotting a basil plant that had flourished beyond our wildest expectations, but I knew that going to therapy together wouldn't work because my husband isn't much of a talker, and I don't do well with audiences.

To secure a new therapist, my insurance plan first required three preliminary sessions with an intermediary counselor who would, in turn, refer me to someone permanent. I argued that four or five sessions might be enough to solve the problem altogether, but the insurance company wouldn't budge, so I skipped the intake process and gave Alan a second chance. To his credit, he never questioned my ten-month hiatus.

"How is the sex?" he asked, during our second or third session of that first reconciliation.

"I mean, we both finish, so it's ultimately fulfilling, but I wouldn't say it's as thrilling as it used to be."

"Hmmm. I see."

"What does that mean?" I asked.

"What does what mean?" he responded.

"Well, what did you mean by 'Hmmm'?"

"Do you always believe that there are hidden meanings to everything?"

"No—Sorry, I just thought you were going to say something more."

"Have you tried fighting with your lover?"

Alan, whose brother was gay and had died of complications from AIDS during an early wave of the epidemic—something he mentioned casually during our very first session—has always referred to Gus as my lover, as if he were in the know, as if we were still in the mid-80s, or maybe as a tribute to his brother.

"Like a physical fight?" I asked.

"Sometimes, even in hardy relationships, time can mask small resentments. It's possible that you two have been too nice to each other."

"Too nice?"

"Partnerships ebb and flow. They're exciting, then naturally less exciting, then they're peppered with moments of excitement, but you'll never again have the exhilaration you had at the beginning. Take it from me, I've been thrice married." Alan chortled with the artfulness of a mall Santa.

After that session, I went home and picked a fight with Gus over his loud typing—his typing is indeed frantic, but it was just annoying and not something to fight about. The following day, I chastised him for leaving his rain boots in the entryway. "I keep tripping over them. Why don't you just put them in the closet with my shoes? Do you expect me to do it? Do you think you're better than me? Is this your way of saying that you don't want to be with me?"

Gus's emerald eyes went wide before settling into a squint, as if he were examining an exotic but harmless insect. "Are you feeling okay?" he asked.

In the days that followed, Gus took in stride my complaints about his runny eggs, cold feet, and his penchant for overplanning. But then, in the process of trying to fabricate a polemic, something authentic surfaced: I wasn't happy. It wasn't him per se; my beef was with the world, but Gus, in a way, represented that world. Apart from being a good listener, a good lover, and a good friend, he was also pedigreed and apolitical and a smidge pedestrian. I wanted someone who would inspire me to be a better human, someone who questioned power structures, someone to shake me out of my complacency.

I wasn't, in those days, able to articulate my needs, but the doubts had formed something wedge-like that was expanding. I attributed it solely to race. "Being in a mixed-race couple is tough. The world pits us against each other, and I feel it. It's too much for two people to bear."

"But have I done something wrong?"

"Well, now that you mention it . . . The other day, you didn't say anything when the server brought you the bill and handed you back the card, even though it was my American Express."

"I'm sorry, hon. I didn't notice."

"See! That's exactly what I mean. You're white. You don't have to notice."

Seems like a perfectly harmless and legitimate observation to make in the post-Obama years; back then, however, it hit Gus hard. His lips came together neatly; the rest of him looked wounded and droopy. We remained at opposite ends of the apartment until the sun set. That's when Gus emerged in a pair of white briefs—he knows what his soccer-player thighs do to me. Right there, on our wobbly gray ottoman, we had sex that was equally pliant, cathartic, and, yes, thrilling. Afterward, I apologized for being mean, and he apologized for unwittingly enabling racism. Never again did he allow restaurant servers to hand him the check. And I stopped seeing Alan. That was eight years ago.

"Have you been back to the playground?" Alan asks, his index finger pressing the tip of his nose up and down and then up again, as if he were alone.

"No. I don't want to interact with any of them anymore."

Between Alan and me, on the djembe, rests a bowl of candy corn left over from Halloween. The tricolor confections are appealing, and I'm feeling peckish, but I won't allow my hand into that nest of invisible bacteria and viruses.

"Them?" he says with a lilt and begins to stab at his notepad without looking down, as if he were casually creating a work of pointillism. "Painting with a broad brush makes you just as bad as the image you've concocted of the other father on the playground. Actually, worse, because your actions are premeditated."

Truth is, I haven't taken Jules to a playground since it happened—six weeks now. Instead, I emptied our hallway closet—old papers, buttonless coats, broken tennis rackets, stripped leather shoes, incomplete board games, obsolete CDs and DVDs—and turned it into a play space. I pasted glow-in-the-dark stars on the walls and lined the floor with cork panels. I also put two small chairs and a plastic kitchen-set in there. Gus was happy about the purge, but he was concerned about my propensity for avoidance.

"Your lover is right. And we should explore some strategies," Alan says, before flipping his pad closed and uncrossing his legs. "Same time next week?"

"You want the number for my therapist?" asks George. My ears and fingertips are cold. We're standing on the corner of 1st Avenue and Houston, not plastered, but technically drunk, and trying to hail a cab back to Brooklyn. "She's amazing, Filipina—a lesbian too."

I've known George for more than fifteen years—I went to graduate school with his wife—but only in the last couple of years have we found ourselves standing next to one another at social events. For a few months now, we've been meeting for happy hours. At first, our conversations seemed to be exclusively about everyday racism, but eventually we got to talking about books and movies and politics, all of which lent themselves to more productive conversations about institutional and structural racism. "Husbands of Color Convening," reads the subject line of all of his emails to me—his wife, like my husband, is white.

George is older, but I don't know by how much. His pop culture references (he saw the original *Dreamgirls* on Broadway with his mom) and the age of his daughters (both, teenagers) suggest ten years, as does his reticence toward car-hailing apps—"I'm not afraid of these cabbies," he's said on more than one occasion. George is half-a-foot shorter than me and weighs more too. He edits television programs, mostly sporting events, and he's won at least a half-dozen Emmy Awards, all but one of which he keeps under his bed, for fear of showboating. He's a lifelong New Yorker, in equal proportions direct and fragile.

"I had a white therapist once, and he told me I needed to 'trust people more.'" George is partial to air quotes. "'If you could just open up and let people in.' Can you believe that nonsense?" George asks, fingers curled.

"The nerve," I say.

"Get this: the therapist sends me to 'race-related' anger management classes. They're led by a super young conflict mediation and meditation 'expert.' A white woman who makes us do trust exercises. Entire class is Black men, and on the first day, we have to take off our shirts and give each other back rubs. Back rubs! Can you believe that? The second class, she wheels in white mannequins—honest-to-God mannequins from, like, a department store, all of them wearing striped polo shirts—and we're supposed to pretend they're real and engage them in conversations from scripts she'd written. When I get there the third week, there are small cages, the size of shoeboxes, in the middle of the room. Inside . . . hamsters. Fucking hamsters, man!" George, still one arm aloft, turns to face the street. Two empty cabs drive past. He accepts their insolence and faces me again. "Each of us gets one hamster. Mine is reddish, like old brick, with white streaks. Cute little guy. After petting them for like a minute, she plays something over the speaker system. A deep voice saying racist shit. I mean, really really racist shit that I can't even repeat, like a Tarantino movie. The instructor says that if the recording makes us 'feel anger,' we should take deep breaths and hold them for ten seconds, all the while hugging our hamsters. Then she tells us to stand on one leg, with one arm extended and the other still holding the little critters, 'like footballs against your chests,' she says. I looked like a fool. A damn fool. All of us did. That was it—the last class for me. Now, whenever I cross paths with a racist motherfucker, I tell him he's a racist motherfucker, and I get the hell out of Dodge. Then I go to the nearest bar and order the most expensive whisky they have. Used to be three whiskies, but Irene—that's my therapist—she helped me get down to one."

The entire time that George is recounting this, his arm has remained in the air. His eyes are as wide as the avenue before us. This stretch of pavement is at once alive, familiar, and threatening. I don't know if it's the alcohol, the night, or his vulnerability, but George looks older than I'd imagined all these years.

"Life's too short to keep giving these people the benefit of the doubt," he says convincingly, and points to a mustard-colored hulk with headlights, just below Houston. "This cab, right here." George gestures with his chin toward the other side of the street. "It's going to take a left. Get out there and grab it!" he insists, with an unfiltered urgency. "You're the 'safe' one in this scenario, mi hermano." George's exaggerated Pacino-as-Latino accent dissolves into a whistling laughter, a tea kettle boiling. He slides past me, into the narrow space between two parked cars, before nudging me onto the margins of the road. I throw one arm up and begin waving.

· · ·

According to some (but maybe all) neuropsychologists, fears are merely unprocessed traumas, often forgotten. To overcome the former, one has to invoke the part of the brain that stores the latter. This is done through a combination of bilateral stimulation and conversation, which allows for the unpacking, processing, and healthy repackaging of the memory.

The third time I started seeing Alan was because of my aerophobia. The fears of being trapped and of crashing had coalesced into mid-flight panic attacks and had all but decimated our vacation plans. I searched my health insurance website for therapists trained in this type of hypnosis, and there was Alan.

"We'll do some subtle exercises," he explained, "engage both halves of the brain. The source of your fear might be completely unrecognizable to you, something possibly sowed in your youth. Even while in your mother's womb."

Alan's solution was to swing a pocket watch in front of me, as I recounted every painful memory I could dredge up. During the third session, I unlocked an episode of high school bullying. During the fifth, I recalled a patch of turbulence on a flight when I was ten years old. During the eighth session, I was four and a neighbor's dog jumped onto my chest. During the ninth, as Alan was attempting to coax me back into my mother's uterus, I began to hear a soft, steady murmuring. At first, I imagined it was the sound of amniotic fluid encircling me, but then I realized it was Alan. He was snoring. He'd fallen asleep with his arm extended and raised, the pocket watch dangling, no longer in pendular flight. I stared as his torso grew and shrank subtly, as his lips pulled apart slowly, and as drool pooled in one corner of his mouth. His already long face looked longer, his shaggy gray hair, shaggier. For almost thirteen minutes, I waited quietly, occasionally checking my email, thinking that this was the first time

I'd ever gotten my money's worth. Then it crossed my mind that Alan might have had a stroke, so I hit the drum with force. He sat up straight away but didn't acknowledge what had happened. He simply cleared his throat and raised his wrist to his bleary eyes. "Alright, same time next week?"

I wasn't angry—the gold-plated to and fro was, admittedly, sleep inducing; plus the radiators had kicked in, producing a soporific warmth—but I didn't return after that. I asked my primary care doctor for a Xanax prescription instead. That was nearly seven years ago.

I don't teach on Fridays—just a morning faculty meeting and some paper grading. My plan was to take Jules to the park this afternoon. Until I read the morning paper. On the front page of the education section was an article (that should have been in the health section) about the overlapping research studies at twenty-five universities— the Ivy League, the junior Ivies, and some larger state schools—each of which arrived at the same conclusion: white people overestimate the age of Black children. The smallest misperception was four years; the largest was twenty. In other words, depending on the white person, a ten-year-old Black child is either fourteen or thirty.

(Thirty?) (Thirty.) (THIRTY!)

I was so overwhelmed by the findings that I missed my stop and had to walk an extra twenty minutes to work, all of which I spent thinking about the playground on Bank Street. Was it possible that little Taylor's father had thought my baby was six? Twelve? Twenty-two years old? No. It couldn't be. No way. Or maybe . . . That would certainly explain why little Taylor's father was so impressed at his daughter's ability to protect her toy stroller. A two-year-old defending herself against a twenty-two-year-old in diapers is, without question, an incontrovertible feat.

(What if all the other guardians believed my toddler was twenty-two?)

After ten blocks, the acrid thoughts coalesced into something knotted and searing. My throat felt like one of those neon puddles that streams away from a construction site. The brisk wind had been, only moments earlier, nipping at my nose and ears; now, there was a balmy lather between my clothes and my skin. Already, I was rehearsing the things I would say. Already, I was contemplating the handcuff scenarios. I called in sick to work, stopped by the market for some ice cream, and doubled-back to pick up Jules from daycare—a rookie move: the ice cream was soup by the time we got home.

"Your kid hasn't gone out in eight weeks?"

Alan blows his nose, which is reindeer red and dripping, like a cold or an addiction.

"Of course Jules has gone out. Just not with me. My husband has playground duty."

"How long do you think you can sustain this?"

I don't respond because I know Alan won't want to hear my answer: I am able to hold out for a long time. I've been, for most of my adulthood, inching towards this very isolation: seeking out carefully curated spaces where I might retain agency over my life; avoiding the arenas of over-encroaching whiteness to which I'd previously aspired; realizing, better late than never, that being outnumbered is a terrible way to live.

"Do you want your kid to have paranoiac tendencies? This is what will happen if you continue down this path. The world isn't against you." Alan is bellowing, but I'm not sure if he's chastising me or overcompensating for his congestion. He reaches for the tissues. "No one enjoys playgrounds. But this is what we have. Adapt, or die out," he says less aggressively. "Same time next week?"

I collect my things and say nothing.

"And remember the breathing exercises!" Alan calls out while fluffing the cushion of his wicker chair.

. . .

"I'm sorry, but that man sounds like a fool. Why do you keep going back to him?" George asks. "Is this Stockholm syndrome?"

We're waiting for our pastrami sandwiches in the basement food court of a new shopping mall in downtown Brooklyn. Despite the exorbitant prices, the place looks as if it were constructed in a high school shop class, everything wooden, rustic, uneven. George, too, is dressed down. Sweatshirt and sweatpants. I could never. Whatever comfort I might derive from soft loose-fitting cotton, would be no match for the flock of pointy-arrowed assumptions piercing me all over. Not George. He wears his lack of concern with a Boy Scout's pride and a peacock's pageantry. Sometimes he goes out of his way to look archetypically homeless. Tattered clothes, double coats, fingerless gloves. "I like to fuck with people," he said to me once. I look forward to this, to growing older and caring less, even if it means wishing away my youth. I look forward to wearing anything but dark jeans up to my waist and a button-down shirt beneath a V-neck sweater.

"You know what it's like to start therapy from scratch," I say. "Besides, this guy isn't all bad. He doesn't push pills."

"Why did you start going to him?"

"I told you, because of the playground."

"No. The first time."

"Oh. Lots of reasons."

"There's always one thing. A deciding factor or a—"

"My boss. Remember when I was working uptown?"

"Was that the cancer research?"

"Yeah. Well, one time, we were in the middle of a meeting, a dozen people around a table, looking over the results of the previous week's data collection. And he made a mistake, my boss. Something simple. And I corrected him. It was harmless. Not only harmless, it was expected. We're scientists; it's part of the culture to be accurate, to catch errors. He didn't take it well. His face tightened up, his eyes got small. I knew right away that I'd stepped out of line, in his eyes. And before I could autocorrect, he blurted out, 'You're not from here, are you?' I wasn't sure if he meant the city or the country."

"Fuck outta here!"

"Everyone else stayed silent. It was awkward as hell. I think I was in shock. But he kept going: 'You're an example of why immigration is good.' Then he moved on to the next page of the report. As if nothing had happened."

"People are nuts." George rests his elbows on the table and clasps his hands together. "You know what your problem is?" he asks. "Middle-class life. You're so focused on succeeding you didn't realize the room changed around you. My advice: quit trying to find that space between ignorant and hateful. The world is most certainly against you. You have to decide how you want to face it. Figure your shit out. And do it quick because what happened to Jules on that playground is just the tip of one iceberg. The sea is full of them."

"Number thirty-seven," calls out a voice from the gaggle of gangly employees crowned in green visors standing a few feet away. George bounds over to the counter, says something that makes the young workers laugh, and picks up both of our orders on an orange tray.

"Stupid. That's what it boils down to. People are stupid," he continues, as he plops down onto his sawhorse bench. "Remember I told you about that short doc I'm working on for PBS? It's about scurvy. Turns out, when England was 'a thriving empire,' more sailors died from scurvy than in battle or lost at sea. Millions of people. Millions! But then a ship captain realized that if he gave his crew lemon juice, they didn't get scurvy. Case closed, right? Nope. People continued dying from this completely preventable disease for like two hundred years. *Two hundred* years! Even after it was official policy, people resisted the lemons. How can you explain that?"

"Probably a number of—"

"I bet they were embarrassed their cure had been hiding in plain sight. Never forget, people are stubborn in addition to stupid."

"Is the moral of this tale that it's going to take two hundred years for everyone to catch up?"

"I don't know. I'm not an oracle. I'm just old. And my old ass can confirm for you exactly one thing: being allowed into a party is no fun if nobody wants you there." George cocks up one side of his face and sways his head from side to side.

I realize that despite George's leisurewear there really is no relaxing.

"Could be worse," he says in an almost whisper. "We could be broke."

I rekindled things with Alan for the fourth time about four years ago. My husband and I had gone to an adoption orientation meeting, at an agency that matched "Latino birth families" with "Latino adoptive families." Half of the crowded room was comprised of gay couples. The other half were straight couples and single women, most of whom had exhausted their procreation options before arriving there looking rather exhausted. In the weeks that followed, I wondered if it was too soon to be a parent. Had we truly come to the end of our lives as childless people? Would we regret this and, by extension, resent the child? And what of all the challenges—the racism, the homophobia, the misogyny? Was I equipped to steward a young life through a minefield that had left me limping through this world? Almost immediately, my eczema flared up, and I began sleeping fitfully. One time, I dozed off at my desk and drooled onto one of my student's papers.

I needed to talk.

Apart from one tasteless joke ("Who's going to breastfeed?"), the sessions with Alan were effective and uneventful. After a few months, I wasn't anxious anymore. In fact, the hassle of getting to therapy eventually outgrew the need for it. To escape, I told Alan our adoption classes were only available in the evenings during our scheduled session time. I said I'd be in touch when the adoption classes were over. "Whatever works for you," he responded. "I'll be here."

A week or so later, he left a voicemail. "Alan here," he began. "Remember, many less thoughtful people have been great parents. Don't overthink it. You'll do fine."

I was not expecting that kindness from Alan, even if it did in a way make sense. In his mind, I was the only thing getting in the way of myself.

Just over two years ago, I stopped seeing Alan again. Kind of.

It was early spring, and I was walking beneath scaffolding, thinking about how, seasonal allergies notwithstanding, I had a pretty good life. I'd just begun the tenure process at work, Gus was attending a group for anti-racist whitinos on Tuesdays, and we were next on the waiting list for a baby. I could have been in many worse places: the crosshairs of a drone in Yemen; a cell in Guantanamo; or the Middle Ages. I was thinking almost exactly this when, out of nowhere, a penetrating boom disrupted the expected cacophony of downtown Brooklyn.

Across the street, the two-story scaffolding affixed to a mid-construction high-rise apartment building had collapsed. No one, it seemed, had been walking beneath when it happened. Several people took out their phones and began snapping pictures, but most resumed their cadences immediately, as if all of it were acceptable, safe, and normal. They stepped around and over the rubble and through the dust plume, undeterred, eager to continue their commutes home. Even the small, round-faced man in a yellow hardhat, who clung from the remaining beam one story above, looked unfazed, simply mouthing softly, almost apologetically, his cries for help, as his coworkers rushed to prop up a ladder.

I tried to go about my business, but the heat traveling up my chest and toward my neck was paralyzing. Right there on the street, I removed my scarf and coat and rested my hands on my knees. It wasn't only the noise that unsettled me. The entire scene served as a reminder that the city was, at all times, on the verge of implosion. That we build endlessly without much foresight. That New York was bursting at the seams with money, but everything was done on the cheap. That it was the worst and best place to raise children. That the dangling construction worker who bore an uncanny resemblance to my father probably wasn't part of a union and probably wasn't from this country and probably had a child who would one day grow up to be middle class and queer and wary of doctors and playgrounds and any place where intentions might be suspect and that, despite his disposable income, he'd never truly enjoy his luxuries because even on planes he'd fear being trapped and he'd also fear the antiterrorism vigilantes that his distress and skin color might inspirit, and that no matter how much the experiences of father and son diverged, they would always be united by their outsider status.

After the construction dust settled, I took out my phone.

"How long has it been?" Alan asked.

"I don't know, more than a year?"

"What?"

"About eighteen months, I think."

"What?"

"Almost two years."

"I can't hear you well," he said. "Are you on the street?"

After some repetition, I deduced that he wasn't available on Tuesdays at seven.

"I could do Wednesdays, 7:15 to 7:45," he said, quick and crackly, like a drive-thru voice.

Of the thirty minutes he was proposing, I feared we'd only be together for twenty-four, and there'd still be a forty dollar co-pay.

"I'm away from my calendar right now. I'll recheck my availability and call you back later."

But I didn't call him back. Until seven weeks ago. After the playground.

It's Monday, and I've just left the Kinko's downtown, where I printed five hundred copies of the first page of the article about the research on white people's misperceptions of Black children's ages. With a neon green highlighter, I marked the section detailing how people interpret age-appropriate behaviors, like tantrums, as violent in the case of Black children. Five hundred times, I did this. Then I paid a small fortune to have each of those pages laminated.

In the days leading up to Kinko's, the article had circulated the faculty email list—in our department, any social science research that receives mainstream press becomes a conversation. The head of our one-person biostatistics department cautioned us about the study's results because of the potential for self-report bias—the tendency for humans to say what's expected or correct irrespective of the truth. The epidemiologist on staff responded that if in fact the study's participants had lied in order to make themselves look better, the discrepancy between the real and perceived age of Black children would be even greater. "At least the research is out there," she concluded. "Nothing to be done but wait for the information to diffuse."

(It took the British Navy nearly two hundred years to adopt citrus as an official treatment for scurvy. And longer than that for everyone to adhere to the policy.)

The faculty email thread got me thinking. If Taylor's dad mistook Jules for an adolescent or a twenty-two-year-old, he must have also thought my child had developmental issues. Jules is, after all, only two, an age characterized by stumbling, incomplete and often unintelligible sentences, spontaneous sobbing, and tyrannical arm-flailing. At times, I find Jules's behavior frustrating, and it triggers in me some sort of innate anger, until I remind myself that this is to be expected of a toddler. But now I wonder if the other guardians have spent the last couple of years assuming that I was being attacked by a young adult with a limited vocabulary and a choppy gait.

I've wanted to go back to the playground many times. In my mind, I have. Sometimes Sweater-vest Dad wears a peach-colored polo and boat shoes with no socks; sometimes a light-blue dress shirt, dark slacks, and brown leather slip-ons that match his belt's color and luster. Sometimes I hang back and study him, his square head, his parted hair. He's always immersed in his phone; periodically, he waves at little Taylor. Sometimes I approach angrily and challenge him to a duel—swords, those beekeeper masks, white jumpsuits— but I never get far because I don't have the requisite hand-to-eye coordination. One time, I blind-sided him with a sucker punch (jab? uppercut? I don't know), but the imagined sensation of my flesh and bone crashing against his flesh and bone left me queasy and with a crisis of conscience.

Sometimes we talk. It begins well enough: "Excuse me." But whenever I get to the meat of it—"The way you talked about my child belies a deeper pathology that you need to exhume before it ends up harming someone"—the exchange heats up.

Sometimes I bring Jules, who ends up playing nicely with Taylor, leading us to befriend Taylor's parents. Before we know it, Colin and Scarlett have invited us to their West Village duplex, and I'm thrust into a world of sweater vests and New England summers full of heirloom beach houses and tomatoes, which culminates, many years later, in a rehearsal dinner for Jules's and Taylor's wedding. And it's during the toast that I usually broach the topic, in a jocular-kinda way: "Imagine, Colin, if I'd let your ignorance stand in the way of our relationship? Huh, Colin? Imagine?" But Colin denies it, and the candlelit wine cave begins to laugh nervously. Then, he tells me I'm crazy, but his voice is in no way jocular-like. We're back to square one, minus the fencing accoutrement, and now, I have to look into Jules's eyes and say, "Honey, I'm not paying one damn cent for this ridiculous, overpriced, ill-fated affair. We're leaving this instant. These people are not welcome into our family."

"Alan?"

"Hiya! We still on for tomorrow?"

"Actually, I—uh—I won't be there."

"No problem. Would you like to reschedule, or should we just wait for next week?"

"Alan, I don't think I'll be coming back to therapy."

"Oh."

"I'm okay for now."

"We're all okay from time to time, but therapy is most effective if you stick to it. You're a prime example of that."

I remain silent, pacing my living room, wondering if he's lobbed an insult or paid a compliment.

"So, uh, same time next week?" he says and laughs. "I'm kidding."

"Okay. Thanks, Alan."

"Are you certain?"

"Goodbye," I say.

I call George and tell him about quitting Alan, about the laminated fliers, and about my plan to post them in playgrounds. He laughs, but then offers to help.

"Let's start next Wednesday after work," I suggest. "Instead of happy hour."

For a while, we discuss logistics. He offers to bring a holepunch; I volunteer zip ties. We agree to check in with each other in a few days.

Before we end the call, he gets quiet in a way that I don't expect from him. I assume he's having second thoughts.

"Something wrong?"

"No. All good," he says.

"Okay—"

"But if you want, I could pass along my therapist's contact info."

I'm touched by George's concern, but I dread the thought of starting again.

"Sure," I say.

WAITING

TYPICALLY, GUS WAKES BEFORE THE others and sits in the kitchen. Waiting for the water to boil, the sun to rise, and the others to wake. He used to pour the cereal or prepare the oatmeal, but the kids are old enough now to make their own breakfasts. And anyway, they want toast. Toast with jam, toast with peanut butter, and sometimes, toast with avocado and hummus. To budget time, he slices the sourdough and waits. His morning parenting consists primarily of reminders—to eat, to brush teeth, to pack. He diverts disagreements when they arise, or divvies up the final slice of toast, should they both want it. The children are well-tempered, and still, he has become adept at redirecting their energies.

For more than twenty years, he has been sitting in this kitchen. Once yellow with wooden cabinets, an old microwave, and a blighted refrigerator, it's now a bright, minimalist, magazine spread of a kitchen. In their eighth year of living there, the landlord, in a bygone overture, offered them the apartment under a rent-to-buy agreement.

"Doesn't seem right you should pay twice. I'll discount a portion of what you've been paying all these years from the total price," said Mr. Lester, a septuagenarian and, at the time, one of two remaining Black homeowners on the block. He'd bought the place during the era when no one wanted to live in the neighborhood, after the government had loaned all the white people enough to buy their homes in the suburbs. Mr. Lester had owned a vacuum repair business then. He had four children. A dozen grandchildren. A bundle of great grandchildren. He would have liked to rent his apartments out to *good* Black people, but they'd all left—some even by choice. Renting to a young gay couple—a white boy and a Latino, in this case—was the norm on that street. Every building had at least one gay renter, some of them not young at all. They were everywhere. He didn't like it, but he'd gotten used to it. At least this couple didn't cause trouble. No parties. They paid the rent on time. They helped with the garbage and recycling. Although he'd never say it aloud, Mr. Lester was relieved they weren't Black. That would have been too close to home. This is what other people did.

"This is very generous, Mr. Lester. You know the market rates—"

"I could kill an old lady in broad daylight, blame it on the market, and get away with it," he said with the voice of someone who'd smoked since he was young, and often.

The couple accepted the offer, bought the apartment, and renovated—added a bathroom, tore down the wall between the living room and the kitchen, got rid of a closet to make a small, third bedroom. "Maybe for a nursery," they said.

Gus sits alone by the window for up to an hour, depending on the season—in the winter, only thirty minutes. He sips his tea—English

Breakfast on Mondays, Wednesdays, and Fridays; Earl Grey, the other days—and sometimes reads the books everyone praises, but usually it's science fiction, which he alternates with glances out at the neighborhood. Always the group of elders moving briskly through the park, out of sync, but with shared purpose—some months in thin pants and visors; some months in puffy coats. By seven, the dogs have conquered the panorama. When they first moved to the neighborhood, it was dozens. Now, hundreds. He scans the fields, searching for those who don't clean up after their dogs. Every morning, a few. He shakes his head and continues reading, sipping.

"Papá, is that your favorite place?" his children would ask when they were younger. "Do you sleep there?" they joke now that their humor has grown sarcastic. He laughs along, marveling at their development, even when it bristles.

Gus doesn't have a favorite place, or a favorite anything really, but his routine is sacred. The skeleton on which the day fleshes out. A creature comfort he doesn't take for granted because he still recalls the brief period when he lived without it.

Years earlier—before the children fought over the last slice of toast; in fact, before there were children—he and Eduardo separated.

"You can have the apartment. But give me time to find a place," Eduardo said.

Gus's temporary sublet in Chelsea was small, smelled of cigarettes, and had a view of the neighboring building's fire escape. He feared he'd grow used to the convenient commute to work and the new environment, but he never did acclimate. Three months later, he returned to his chair by the window facing the park. Mr. Lester, who rarely commented on anything apart from the weather or the rats on the sidewalk, approached Gus one evening, not long after he'd returned. "Difficult to get used to being alone, but it happens" was the only thing he ever said about the matter. Mr. Lester's advice was rather magnanimous considering his wife of nearly fifty years had just recently died—colon cancer.

It wasn't particularly difficult to be alone, but neither was it pleasant. Or familiar.

Gus moved to New York when he was nineteen. And only a few weeks into his first semester of college, he met a boy—quiet, face full of freckles. They were lab partners. Together, they dissected a small shark. Together, they were struck by how large and oily the liver was. For buoyancy, they learned. Oil, after all, is lighter than water. One mid-semester night while studying, the biology turned to, well, chemistry. They were together for nearly three years, until Gus came home early to find the quiet boy with freckles under another boy—no freckles. He was neither jealous nor heartbroken. "I'm disappointed, that's all. But if you want to try and make this work, I will." The boy, however, was ready to move on. Gus ran into Eduardo a few months later, at party in the days before graduation. They'd seen each other on campus before, but that was their first conversation. "Have you always been this good-looking?" Eduardo asked him during a lull.

From the beginning, Gus was disarmed by Eduardo's honesty and curiosity. Never satisfied by the surface of things, Eduardo investigated everything, including the quotidian. "Do you really want to do this, or are you trying to please me?" he might ask of his choice of restaurant, movie, or vacation destination. Couldn't both things be true? Gus wondered over the next decade, more amused than concerned.

They lived contently, on occasion veering toward complacent—Eduardo liked to joke that their routines had routines. But their love was pleasant, well-kept, and unobtrusive, easily taken for granted.

The changes were gradual but they appeared to Gus as sudden. Eduardo was different, he thought. He seems unhappy. Never quite present. Scowling at everything: what they ate for dinner, what they watched on TV, what they did on the weekends. He was also suspicious. First, of the world; later, of him. What had once been refreshing transformed into something else.

"Did you see that the sales clerk followed me around the store?"

"The lawyer didn't look in my direction once during that entire meeting."

"Have you noticed that customer service folks call me 'man' and 'bro'? They call you 'sir.'"

"Don't tell me that taxi didn't see me?"

Gus made an effort to be aware. *Be proactive*, he read online and in books about how to be an ally. He was authentically angry about the injustices of the world. He found himself growing preemptively upset at his fellow white people. Because the social ills felt intractable, he focused on saving Eduardo. He took to hailing their cabs in the cold and rainy months. He made an effort to notice when others ignored Eduardo or made assumptions about him. When it came to official business—loan officer, doctor, general contractor—he allowed Eduardo to do most of the talking. Or he'd overemphasize that Eduardo was his *partner*—later, *husband*. But this, too, discomfited Eduardo: "It's awkward," he said. "It's exhausting too. Plus, it feels classist."

Gus's teas lived always on the second shelf of the middle cupboard because Eduardo believed spices, cooking oils, and glass containers should occupy the low shelf. After Eduardo left, he relocated his teas to the counter, in plain sight. He also brought his sweaters, hiking boots, and the rest of his science fiction books up from the basement and filled the newly empty spaces. The future nursery remained an office.

The morning routine also stayed as it had always been. The water boiled, he submerged the leaves, set the timer, warmed his milk in a small saucepan, and assumed his position by the window. The early hours in the park were leash-less ones punctuated by stern shouts of names that were at once modish and anachronistic—Buster, Otto, Sylvester. Countless dogs racing past, through, and onto each other. Humans begging and cheering and bellowing at their four-legged mates, doing their best to rise above the interspecies indignities.

"I'd find it difficult to get up this early for a dog," Eduardo used to say. "I bet you there are many affairs happening in that park. Maybe we should get a dog. Just to spice things up." He must have been joking, Gus thought, because Eduardo was allergic to dogs.

From his place by the window, Gus never spotted anything that amounted to amorous. Licentious, yes. He fixated on the handful of people who didn't clean up after their dogs. The transgressors, he noticed, were types. The imperious ones who walked away from their messes, as if they were doing the grass a favor. The artful ones who went through the motions of searching their pockets for plastic bags, before walking away sheepishly. The cowards who scanned their perimeters quickly before speeding off, heads bowed. Some offended repeatedly. Most didn't. In a city of nearly nine million people, if each dog owner had one infraction, Gus calculated, the result was a lifetime's worth of shit. Eduardo had always been less forgiving: "Covert, lazy racism. They do it because no one expects it of them. They know what the assumptions will be." In the year before they broke up, Eduardo took to shouting, "Clean up your mess!" from the kitchen window before ducking away.

Gus didn't tell anyone but his parents and a few telemarketers about the separation. It was Eduardo who emailed their mutual friends, most of whom responded with the same sentiment: *I'm here for you both.* But it was Eduardo who kept the friends, which was fine because Gus had never been good about initiating any sort of socializing.

In the weeks after the break-up, his parents offered to visit. He demurred. Although they'd grown used to his relationship with Eduardo, they'd opposed it at the outset. "He doesn't complement you," his mother said to him after their first visit years earlier. "Are you sure he makes you happy?"

Happy? Sure. But Gus questioned the importance of happy. He was content. And maybe more important, comfortable. He enjoyed Eduardo's company. He liked sharing a home, a couch, and a bed with him. The sex was superb, even if at times wilder than he would have liked. He looked forward to their summer trips in July—France, El Salvador, Japan. He'd adjusted to Eduardo's dedication to cilantro and to his overconsideration of perfect strangers. He appreciated how Eduardo could turn the most ordinary situations into a primer on racism and class warfare. Gus depended on his reminders—to put on sunscreen, to exercise, to floss.

What did happy have to do with anything?

"You don't seem yourself," said Ellen, without making eye contact— an accepted trait in a room full of coders. Ellen was a recent transplant from Salt Lake City, and one of only three women in Gus's department.

"This may be super inappropriate, but I heard you broke up with your boyfriend—"

"Husband."

"Husband, sorry. I'm sorry. I wasn't—Anyway, I—If you're ready—When you're ready. My best friend from college just moved here—He's single. A doctor. He's really nice and cute. Doesn't have to be a date. He's also looking to make friends."

Louis was indeed friendly, handsome too, in an outdated fashion characterized by neatly parted, gelled hair. He talked endlessly during the sushi dinner, periodically interrupting himself to say,

"Now, tell me about you," before finding a way to steer the conversation back to himself. He was a dermatologist, he wasn't allergic to gluten but did his best to avoid it anyway, he was taking a capoeira class, he liked to go kayaking in the Hudson River, he lived in Harlem ("but in the nice part"). A few times, he proclaimed his love of Asian food, as if the entire continent were a stuffed animal. Eduardo, Gus thought, would have left after the Harlem comment. He wasn't particularly attracted to Louis, but they'd drank two large bottles of sake, and since he hadn't had sex in over a month, not since Eduardo had come by unannounced one Sunday to pick up his mail, he said yes when Louis invited him back to his place.

The roleplaying had made him cum sooner than he would have liked. Louis wanted his face and ass slapped and his hair pulled. "Harder," he said throughout. Gus obliged the dermatologist from Utah, marking his colorless skin red and taking fistfuls of stiff dark blond with confidence—ease, too. Eduardo would have been pleased, he thought. He'd always encouraged this sort of abandon during sex.

Afterward, on the walk to the 2 train, he was struck with an unfamiliar feeling. Not fully guilt or shame, but hints of both. Primarily, it was sadness. A hazy sort of sorrow that began in his intestines. It was neither grave nor heavy. Vague in all its dimensions. Gus closed his eyes and felt the sensation spread across his chest and his face. It throbbed lightly, a mild storm. It reminded him of the death of Washington, the border collie he'd found on the beach as a kid. He was with them for three years, until he escaped from their yard and tried to run across the road that separated him from the beach. Washington had only lived with them during the summers—in fact, with the staff of the summer house—but Gus had grown accustomed to him nonetheless. When his parents told him, he didn't react much, but he recalled the small weights on his chest. It was something like this that he felt now on the train.

Louis texted a few days later. He had an extra ticket to *Hairspray*.

"I had a good time the other night, but I'm not ready to date just yet."

"No biggie. But if you just want to fuck some time, I'm cool with that too."

There was a time when Eduardo had wanted to go to the theater often—*Spring Awakening, Spamalot, The Producers*—but at some point, he read the first chapter of a Frantz Fanon book and forbade himself art made by colonizers. Then he only ever wanted to talk about collective liberation. "Everything is made through a white supremacist lens. We can't free ourselves if we don't seek out other perspectives. We have to saturate ourselves with experiences that we've been denied all along in order to make a dent." Eduardo's logic was sound enough at first even if annoying. "What about *In the Heights* or *Passing Strange*?" Gus offered. "That's a start," Eduardo replied. But he eventually found reason to hate Midtown. Then, he could barely tolerate Manhattan. "The whole city's a caste system, but at least there's a whiff of egalitarianism in the outer boroughs."

In the last year of their relationship, it became unusual for them to leave home. It had become impossible to disregard the changes. The only place in their lives where Eduardo had become more adventurous was in bed. A little louder, a little rougher, a few toys, a threesome, a warehouse party in Bushwick.

The explorations couldn't mask Eduardo's growing discontent, but neither was he making an effort to conceal anything. By the end, he took to punctuating even minor disagreements with "This isn't working," before walking into another room, leaving Gus to wonder if this was it. He found himself repeating the same questions: *What exactly isn't working?* and *What do you want to do?* Usually, Eduardo had already left the room, but one time he responded. "Maybe some people just don't fit together." That, too, made sense.

On the 187th day of living alone, Gus didn't drink his standard tea. He squeezed, instead, a bit of lemon into a cup of chamomile because of an ambiguous pain in his gut. He hated chamomile. It tasted like water wrung from old grass, he thought, as he stared out at the dogs and their humans.

There walked the elders with their swinging arms, like robots with flair, as he waited for the toaster oven to ding, so that he could begin to spread the butter.

Before leaving for work that day, he watered the herbs, including the basil Eduardo had bought at the farmers' market last year, despite Gus's protestations: "They keep dying." He ran the dishwasher with a week's load, gave the area beneath the kitchen table a half-hearted sweep, and tucked four scattered shoes into the hallway closet. He folded clothes, made his bed, and gave the toilet a cursory scrub before remembering that the cleaning person was coming that day. He searched his dresser for a few condoms, checked their expiration dates, and placed them into his bedside table. He showered, did twelve push-ups, got dressed, and left for work.

That afternoon, he sent Charles a message, "Confirming tonight."

"We're on. Looking forward to it."

He'd been chatting with Charles sporadically for a couple of weeks, trying to find one night where both of them were free. Charles was a biostatistician, he was vegan until dinner, and his profile listed Gloria Trevi and Toni Morrison as *favs*. He was versatile, but was going through a "bottoming spell." He had large dark eyes, a wide nose, and a hue of brown skin similar to Eduardo's. "See! It's a fetish!" Eduardo had said to him the previous summer while they lay out on the beach remarking on the men who walked past. What would Eduardo have to say about Charles, never mind that they both worked in public health? But Gus disputed the idea that he was fetishizing anyone. What he had was a clear preference for men who reminded him of Eduardo. In his eyes this attraction was a compliment, but he knew Eduardo wouldn't have agreed. And frankly, it might all be a fetish, attraction and superiority braided so tight they'd become indistinguishable from one another. No, he thought. Something doesn't have to be true just because it could be.

He left work early, went for a haircut, and splurged on a beard trim. Afterward, he went to the gym, showered vigorously, making sure to shake and scrub the loose hairs from his scalp and face, swam for exactly twenty minutes, and showered again. He arrived at the bar in the East Village fifteen minutes ahead of schedule.

"What do you recommend for an upset stomach?" he asked the bartender, a hefty man wearing a plaid flannel and brandishing a tuft of chest hair.

"A nap."

"I'll have a tonic water, please."

The bar was empty but for a cluster of men perched on stools, and one outlier who hovered alone near the billiards table. The smell of ammonia hung cloud-like. Gus asked the bartender for change and walked over to the jukebox, where he became inexplicably giddy. It wasn't the impending meeting with Charles; it was the power he felt at being able to determine what everyone else would be listening to for the next fifteen minutes. He chose Pet Shop Boys, Depeche Mode, and the Smiths.

Charles walked through the door five minutes late. He wore a long, beige coat and a mustache that he didn't have in any of the pictures. It was an unobtrusive strip, without any of the performative specter of the other ones in the bar, in the city, or online.

"I don't always know when it's going to happen," explained Charles, while pointing to his own face. "Sometimes, it's just because I'm lazy about shaving. Sometimes, it's because I get into old porn. Sometimes, I just want to see someone different in the mirror—Too much?" he asked, pointing at himself.

"No."

"Good."

Charles raised his eyebrows briefly and stared at Gus until he looked away.

"You're cute."

"Thanks," Gus replied.

"What are we drinking?" asked the bartender.

"Rye Manhattan. Straight up, with a twist," said Charles.

"Bourbon preference?"

"Surprise me."

"And you? More tonic?"

"With gin."

The bartender set one cocktail napkin before each of them and walked to the other end of the bar to ask the men huddled at the other end if they wanted more of the same.

"A rye Manhattan usually takes a cherry, not a twist."

"I don't like cherries," Charles responded. Then he removed his overcoat and folded it onto his lap. He reached into his pocket and set a twenty onto the bar. "Be honest," Charles continued, "do you really like this place, or did you just agree to come here because I suggested it?"

There was a familiarity in Charles' directness. Gus searched his face for something else that he might recognize, but there was nothing. "I like that it has a jukebox. But I probably wouldn't have suggested it."

Charles pointed vaguely into the air. "So you're the Morrissey fan?"

"Smiths."

"Huh. Well, I've never been able to tell the difference," Charles said playfully.

Eduardo hated it when Gus corrected him, especially in front of others. "The whole world is against me. I don't need you criticizing me too," Eduardo had said to him once on the subway, on the way home from a friend's wedding or the opening of a friend's restaurant. But correcting the record was involuntary. Whether it was a software bug or a human, it didn't make a difference to him. It would never occur to him to be offended for being proven wrong.

They took a cab back to Gus's apartment because it was closer to the bar.

"Would you like something to drink?"

"More bourbon, if you have it." Charles leaned against the kitchen counter, his button-down shirt taut across his chest; long elegant fingers extending from soft hands; dark eyes a bit bleary. "It's a beautiful apartment," he said.

"I wish I could take credit, but my ex was responsible for most of it."

"He's an architect?"

"No, I just mean, a lot of it was his idea."

"How long has it been?"

"Since we've—I've—been here, or since the break-up?"

"The break-up."

"Almost six months."

"Were you together a long time?"

"Several years."

"Oh, wow."

"How about you?"

"Nope. Nothing."

"Is that him?" Charles pointed toward the stainless-steel fridge, its façade under an array of magnets, receipts, a calendar, a notepad, and a small picture of him and Eduardo in shorts and wearing backpacks while standing on the Equator—the previous summer's trip. "He's cute. I see you have a type."

"Not really," Gus responded calmly, but the rosiness that had already been there after the third gin and tonic had now intensified in his cheeks. "Listen, I'd rather not talk about my ex."

"That's fine by me." Charles didn't appear to be offended.

"It's just that—"

"No need to explain. I get it. I'm nosy." Charles raised his glass, emptied it, and set it back onto the table. "You know what I'd really like? I'd like to get naked and fuck."

Charles disappeared into the hallway before Gus could point him in the right direction. He began to follow but doubled back and grabbed both glasses, put them in the sink, and ran a bit of water in each.

Charles was already naked and on the bed, facing away from the door, kneeling, resting gently on his heels. Gus unbuttoned his shirt quickly and unclasped his belt. He placed his hand with force between Charles's shoulders, who landed face down and let out a sultry moan.

"Too rough?"

"Not at all."

Gus reached for the drawer of the bedside table and pulled out a bottle of lube and an array of condoms. They were the ones that Eduardo had collected over the years—Pride parades and health clinics. The lube, too, had been Eduardo's choice—extensive research about differences in health effects between water and silicone. Even the bedside table was Eduardo's doing—his weekend surveys of the neighborhood's stoops to salvage gently worn furniture, immaculate soup bowls, and once-read books. The bed was Gus's only contribution—something firm yet forgiving for his stiff back.

"We don't need those. I'm on PrEP," said Charles, when he saw the condoms.

Gus, too, disliked condoms, but in this instance, he couldn't rid himself of Eduardo's voice and his decade-long stream of PSAs. "I'd rather we did," he said.

"Suit yourself."

Gus positioned Charles at the edge of the bed, his back arched in a way that elevated his ass and spread it just enough to offer up a flash of a raw, pinkish flesh. He lowered himself onto the floor and buried his tongue inside of Charles, who was now grunting wildly, despite having wedged a section of the comforter between his teeth.

"Don't stop, that feels great," Charles said.

But Gus couldn't help it. A cramp or spasm had shot through his abdomen. Charles turned onto his back and sat up to find Gus squatting on the floor, still in his underwear, his gladiator thighs and calves pressed against one another. "You taking a break already?"

"I'm sorry. My stomach."

"No rush. If you need to go to the bathroom. I'm okay to wait."

"It's not that kind of pain. Listen, I hate to do this, but can I have a rain check?"

"Serious—"

"Ahhh!" Gus wailed and spread himself onto the floor. He kept one hand on his stomach; the other masked his face.

"Where does it hurt?"

He pointed to the subtle dip above his pelvis.

"Huh. Have you had your appendix out?"

Gus shook his head.

"Could be. My roommate a few years ago had a similar thing happen. His appendix burst. He could barely walk. I had to carry him down the stairs. On a scale of 1 to 10, where's the pain?"

"Seven. Ahhh, ahhh"—he winced and arched his back, as if the floor had suddenly become unbearably hot or cold—"eight and a half."

"I think you need to get to a hospital." Charles pulled up his underwear and pants, and retrieved a phone from his pocket. "I can call you a car."

"It's okay. I can do it." But when he tried to roll over, the agony forced Gus onto his back again.

The hospital a few blocks away had a bad reputation, even after a dizzying decade of gentrification. Every year, there was a story about someone refusing care and instead dying en route to Manhattan. Gus had been to this hospital a few times. Once, a case of food poisoning. Another time, when Eduardo sliced his finger while cutting potatoes drunk. And most recently, for post-exposure prophylaxis, after the condom burst during a threesome with an art critic they'd met in Williamsburg. The hospital's fluorescent lighting, faded pastel walls, and the lingering scent of restrooms overused by local vagrants made for a lugubrious setting, but the clinicians had been amiable and competent during his previous visits.

"Do you want to go in with your partner?" the nurse asked Charles.

"Oh, he's not my partner. He's a, uh—"

"No need to explain," said the young square-headed nurse, whose badge read, *David*.

Charles wasn't going to explain. Gus had absolved him of any guilt on the cab ride over. There was no expectation that he should wait, and he had no intention of staying.

Around three in the morning, the nightshift nurse with curly gray hair and a prominent mole on her chin, came out to the waiting room where only three people waited. Her badge read, *Gladys*. "Eduardo!"

"Yes. Here."

"Are you family?"

"He's my husband."

Gladys dipped a hand into the front pouch of her white smock. "The surgery went well. He won't be feeling much of anything for a few hours. Expect soreness."

"Can I see him?"

"Of course, but he'll be drowsy. May not recognize you right away."

Eduardo knocked lightly on the door before tiptoeing into the room. There he was beneath a worn baby-blue blanket that rose and fell subtly with his chest. Gus looked yellow beneath the harsh glow in an otherwise dark room. Eduardo lifted an unwieldy chair over from the corner of the room and angled it beside the bed. He caressed Gus's hand, careful not to touch any of the various tubes or cables. He studied his face. His thick, salt-and-pepper hair was in disarray, his lips were crusted with saliva, and his beard was thinner than he'd seen it in years.

"Hon?" Gus whispered a few times, before finally reaching through the slats on the bed's rail and touching Eduardo, who had fallen asleep with his feet tucked beneath the stiff mattress, a coat draped over his legs.

Eduardo opened his eyes and sat up. "How do you feel?"

Gus tilted his head to one side and back to center. His eyes only half open.

"The nurse said everything went well. I like her. Gladys. She's like a sitcom but serious."

"How did you—"

"The health proxy card in your wallet. And you told the anesthesiologist to call me."

"Really?"

"You managed to give her my email and repeat my number several times before you went under. They were impressed."

"I don't remember."

"You hungry?"

"Yes."

"It's almost seven. Cafeteria should be open."

"I don't know what I'm allowed to eat."

"I'll check in with my new best friend: Gladys."

Eduardo adjusted the wool cap over his shock of dark hair and pushed his glasses up the bridge of his nose. He rose and squeezed Gus's foot through the bed covers.

"Tea, please."

"English Breakfast or Earl Grey?"

"Whatever they have."

"If they have both?"

"Surprise me."

Eduardo put on his shoes, checked his pockets, and walked to the door before turning back. He remained there in the frame, one foot in the hospital's brightly lit hall, the other inside the dim room, staring back at Gus, who could barely keep his eyes open. They were looking at one another, Gus assumed.

"Wait here," Eduardo called out before walking away.

Gus did his best to laugh, mustering only a smile before drifting.

COMRADES

TO THE POINTDEXTER

41 y/o, 5'9", 150lbs, single

Health researcher

FUN FACT: Stress of inequality is leading risk factor for top
10 causes of death

PAST: Imperialism, settler colonialism, genocide

FUTURE: Truth, reconciliation, reparation, repatriation

HOBBIES: Reading, running, friends, civic engagement,
protest, op-ed writing

IN BED: Anything goes, except tickling or water sports,
vers top

SAFETY: . . . is an illusion in an uneven society. #FTP. But
yes to condoms.

PREFERENCES: People who think about upstream causes & solutions; solidarity; +/− 5years; no pets; no racists; in-person meetings over online chatting.

POLITICS: Far left of center

CLAIM TO FAME: I once gave Angela Davis a tour of Liberty Plaza—but I don't do cult of personality.

ABOUT ME: Recently ended a long-term relationship. We weren't politically aligned. I'm middle-aged. I hate people, but I'm ready to fight for our liberation. No white men, pls. No couples. No shade.

#SeriousRepliesOnly #BrutalHonesty

COLLECTIVE[G]LIB

40 y/o, 5'10", 150lbs, single

RN

FUN FACT: n/a

PAST: Still recovering from my suburban adolescence

FUTURE: Looking for Mr./Mx. Right Now-ish, but open to Mr./Mx. Down-the-Road

FREE TIME: n/a

IN BED: Flex, open-minded, sometimes rough

SAFETY: PrEP, condoms

PREFERENCES: Not interested in "preferences"

POLITICS: Well left of center

CLAIM TO FAME: I went to school with Jared Kushner and hated him then too.

Tonight's been great. I don't know if it's the gin talking, but I feel a connection.

I'm glad it's mutual. Relieved, actually.

I know it might be a bit forward, but do you want to come back to my place?

Interesting that you've been interrogating me online for a week and now in person for two hours, but you consider this part forward? Frankly, if you didn't invite me over, I'd be disappointed.

Oh, you would, huh?

Should we jump on the G or catch a cab?

Cab would be nice. I think the G is running in two sections and with delays.

Perfect. Shall we?

Okay, but before we go, I'm curious about something.

More questions? I thought I'd answered all of them already.

Nearly there.

I'm kidding. I don't mind at all. I think it's adorable. And I don't mean that in a condescending way. I honestly appreciate a grown-up conversation. The last guy only wanted to talk about the *Golden Girls* and real estate. I want more substance.

I couldn't agree more.

So what's your question? Shoot.

Well, it's about Palestine and Israel.

Oh.

I know, sorta heavy. But just curious about your position.

Vers bottom.

What?

I'm kidding! I don't know. I don't really think much about Israel.

What about Palestine?

That's what I meant.

But you must have some opinions on the matter.

Not really. Honestly, I think their conflict takes up too much space in the political discourse.

I see. But our billions in military aid to Israel every year . . .

Well, that's bullshit. We shouldn't do that either.

Cool.

On the other hand, I can understand why Israelis would want to defend themselves. I mean, rockets landing in their backyards. Suicide bombers on the commute home—

Israel has nuclear weapons. You know that, right? A massive army too. And US support. Not to mention the support of several other countries in the region. Palestinians are subhumans in the eyes of Israel. It's impossible for them to return to their homes; meanwhile, any teenager in Schenectady can claim that their great grandmother's third cousin was Jewish, and they get a free trip to the motherland. Is Israel the dom or the sub? It can't be both at once.

You don't fuck around, huh?

My ex's family was Zionist, and for nearly fifteen years I held my tongue. I'm not doing that anymore.

Oh.

What?

This is a rebound thing?

No. Not at all. I don't think so.

Geez. Listen, like I said, I usually don't give this much thought. Also, I have a lot of Jewish friends, so—

I've probably had sex with five times as many Jewish men as Muslims, only two of whom were Palestinian. It's New York.

I'm not giving oppression a free pass, but the way I see it, the Jews in Israel aren't going anywhere. And I know everyone says this, but the Holocaust was a game changer. The same rules don't apply.

Just fuck all the Palestinian homes and lands then?

No, but why get caught up in what's happening thousands of miles away? And why pick on Israel of all places?

How much time you got? *A*, we're not an isolationist country; we mind everyone's business. *B*, haven't you noticed that it's, like, a precondition for our elected officials to declare their abiding love for Israel? We couldn't ignore Israel if we tried. *C*, you're *supposed* to let your friends know when they're messing up. They're the ones you can influence most. If your neighbor isn't sealing up their trash bins properly and rats are chilling on your stoop as a result, are you going to pick a fight with the guy ten blocks away whom you've never met because they're playing their music too loud?

What? Is Israel the neighbor or the guy ten blocks away?

The neighbor.

I don't understand. Honestly—and don't hate me for this—I guess I just don't care enough—

Wha—

Which doesn't mean I can't *learn* to care about it.

Or maybe your position on this issue is indicative of others that will come to light over time?

Did you just ruin a decent date over Israel?

Is it ruined?

I might let you fuck me if you stop talking.

I'll do my best.

PRINCIPAL SKINNER

36 y/o, 5'11", 160lbs, single

Elementary school educator

FUN FACT: I can play most of *The Miseducation of Lauryn Hill* on the harmonica.

PAST: n/a

FUTURE: I'd like to be married, have kids, and own a home before 40.

FREE TIME: Soccer, mystery novels, karaoke, DSA

IN BED: vers; leather; spitting

SAFETY: PrEP

PREFERENCES: ;-)

POLITICS: Bernie's politics; Elizabeth's practicality

CLAIM TO FAME: n/a

What are you drinking?

A martini: gin, straight up, three olives, stained.

Stained?

Just a splash of olive juice, not all-the-way dirty.

So you like it a little dirty, huh?

My drinks, yes. What did you get?

An old fashioned.

I guess if I'm my drink, then you must be yours.

In some ways, yes, I am traditional.

How so, apart from your suit and tie and the perfect side part in your hair?

Very funny.

I'm not making fun.

I have to be this buttoned up for work.

So what do you mean by traditional?

Well, like my profile says, I'd like to get married.

I guess us gays getting married has become mainstream. The era of queer communes and cooperative child-rearing never really materialized, did it?

Communes? That appeals to you? I mean, not for nothing, but clean shaven, salt-and-pepper daddy hair: you're not exactly a radical fairy.

You're right. In theory, the idea appeals to me, but not actually. It's just one more post-revolutionary construct that's wonderful in a vacuum, but doesn't work well in practice. Not in a pre-revolution context.

Post-revolutionary constructs in a pre-revolution context . . . ? Now you've piqued my curiosity. Give me an example of these constructs.

I'll give you two: polyamory and Madonna.

Madonna, I understand, I think. But polyamory?

It doesn't work.

C'mon—

Maybe in Canada or Uruguay polyamory is common and success-ful, but not in this imbalanced hierarchy.

It doesn't have to work for an entire people. It only has to work for the people involved.

It doesn't always work for the *people involved*, trust me.

Care to elaborate?

Well, no—Hear me out: Imagine our date tonight leads to a sec-ond date, then a third, then we fall in love, then we move in together.

Sounds nice.

Right? Well, let's say it's Tuesday night and I want to watch the new episode of *Pose*, but you're nowhere to be found because you're on a date with Richard, who you see on Tuesdays.

Well, *Pose* is no longer. We can stream it whenever. Doesn't have to be Tuesdays.

But Tuesdays are my rough day at work. Every week, I make a two-hour presentation to my team, after which I facilitate a discussion on the findings of the previous week's data collection. Maybe for another person this isn't a big deal, but public speaking isn't my forte. I invest a lot of energy preparing for Tuesdays. And at the end of those days, I'll want to come home to you and the nice dinner that you've made—obviously, dinner making is a shared responsibility, but you would make it on Tuesdays, or at the very least, oversee Tuesday dinners, which can be ordered. For the rec-ord, I have no problem ordering out occasionally, but I prefer to cook at home because I like to know the provenance of my food; I like to select my own ingredients; and I like to control how much salt and fat end up on my plate and, more importantly, in my intestines. That, by the way, is another phenomenon better left for the post-revolutionary era, this foodie culture, with its fats and salt. That sort of gastronomical indulgence can't work in a society where chronic cortisol is already the equivalent of at least one high-fat, high-salt meal per day. Sometimes, we just have to accept our context and steam broccoli and sprinkle some vinegar on it. In any case, I'll eat whatever nourishment you end up procuring for us on Tuesday nights.

Wow. I'm, uh—Listen, I'm health conscious too, and all your other concerns have simple solutions: I have my dalliances with Richard, or whoever, on Wednesdays, and on Tuesdays, I make you my famous vegan tacos.

You're missing my point.

What is your point?

There'll be conflicts. And those conflicts will lead to insecurities and resentments, even if you begin with two secure, non-jealous people.

There's conflict in monogamous relationships, too.

Yes, and isn't that enough?

Enough to adhere to outdated, inflexible standards for what constitutes respect and commitment?

Don't get me wrong, I'm open to being partially open. Threesomes, foursomes, orgies, sex clubs. All that sounds great from time to time. And if we occasionally have work trips and mess around with other people, I'm okay with that too, so long as we're careful. Safe, you know. But what I don't want is for my partner to have a double life.

Double life? Aren't you—

At some point, Richard is going to say, I need more from you. Trust me, he will. And you're going to want to give him more, but our time together is already so limited because of work and other commitments. And you're going to start meeting him at other times. And then he's going to want more. And he deserves more. Richard is great. Lovable, quick witted, sexy: the whole package. But I'm not interested in sharing you that way. I don't want you to be constantly staring at your phone, waiting for the next message. I don't want to share custody of you with another person. And look at you:

beautiful brown eyes, pouty lips, large hands, and your shoulders are practically busting out of your shirt. How many times do you go to the gym per week? Three, four days?

I lift at home, six days a week.

It shows. And I'm sure you have a coterie of men following you around.

Let me guess, your ex had a Richard.

A Jeff.

I see.

Before you say it, this is *not* a rebound thing. We ended things almost a year ago. I'm just making sure not to make the same mistakes as before.

Listen, I think you got this all wrong. I'm an assistant principal at an elementary school. I get up every morning at 5:45 a.m. I'm certainly not suggesting a clandestine life that runs into the wee hours. But I also can't commit to a lifetime with just one person. You'd be my primary partner, but I can't be monogamous. There are too many experiences to be had and connections to be made.

Okay.

This isn't going anywhere, is it?

Probably not.

I think you're making a mistake. Not about me, per se, but about closing yourself off to connections. What if it's you who meets a Jeff? What if he helps you discover something about yourself?

What if we don't live this life trying to maximize every single possibility? What if we cherish and nurture the good things we already have?

Agree to disagree?

I guess.

You want another martini?

Not really.

Good night, then?

Yeah, I—

Actually, what did you mean by post-revolution?

I imagine there will come a time when everything is even. When there's been atoning for past sins and income gaps have shrunk to an insignificant degree and everyone is on even ground. In that world, we can reorganize and reconfigure many of our institutions, including romantic relationships—maybe we have a throuple with Richard and he co-parents our children—but as long as our society doesn't support this degree of queering, it won't work on a mass scale.

I say again, there's nothing mass about it. We're talking about two people, just us.

We're literally talking about no fewer than three people.

Okay, you've made your point. But tell me, how does Madonna figure into all this?

In the post-revolutionary world, you can try on other peoples' cultures for effect because each culture has already been given its due, in a way, and it won't feel like theft whenever she puts on a kimono or slaps on a bindi.

So you didn't like *Ray of Light*?

MR. BUILD-IT WANTS 2B DEMOLISHED
29 y/o, 6'2", 175lbs, single
Architect
FUN FACT: I repeated 2nd grade and skipped 6th grade.
   All good.
PAST: n/a
FUTURE: n/a
FREE TIME: Crossfit, travel, going out with friends
IN BED: Bottom who can tolerate pain
SAFETY: PrEP
PREFERENCES: hung tops, spit over lube

CLAIM TO FAME: I helped design Meryl Streep's daughter's apartment in DUMBO.

Isn't it warm in here?

Sorta. Why? Are you uncomfortable?

No. It's just that you haven't taken off your coat since you arrived?

Oh, well, I never get to wear this.

It's a nice coat. Full length?

Yeah. Pure wool.

Is that houndstooth?

Yes.

Nice.

Thanks. So research, huh?

What?

Your profile. It said something about research.

Oh. Yes. Stress.

It's hard work?

Sort of, but I meant it's research *on* stress. That's what I do for a living.

Like how it works? Or . . .

We look at the effects of stress on health.

I assume it's no good.

Chronic stress is bad for the body, for sure. I study how hierarchies contribute to stress.

Sounds interesting. And probably depressing. I can't imagine there's a cure for hierarchy.

I remain optimistic. Many other countries have done it.

Interesting. Do you travel a lot?

Mostly conferences. I used to take long vacations in the summer. My ex and I, that is.

Oh. Well, I love to travel.

Cool. If you could go anywhere . . . ?

Anywhere in the world?

Anywhere.

I have a list actually.

Shoot.

Iceland, Australia, Thailand, Machu Picchu, and Africa.

Machu Picchu is in Peru.

Right. That's what I meant.

And Africa is an entire continent with more than fifty countries. You have anywhere in particular you want to go?

I don't know. For sure somewhere with beaches. And preferably not war-torn.

Fuck's sake.

What?

You sound like a third grader.

Because I don't know all the African countries?

And "war-torn"? You said that.

I'm sorry, what? Who the fuck—You had a boyfriend once?

Yes.

How long were you together?

Years. Many years.

Someone was able to tolerate you for that long?

Yes.

I find that hard to believe.

I'm not so bad. I'm just getting impatient. Not with you, but with age and life. I joined this app two months ago. I've had one date per week since. No matches. It's exhausting.

I'm sorry, what? You've been on eight dates, and you're tired? I've been on 800, and I'm still in the game. Listen, this whole thing is just supposed to be not terrible, and sometimes fun. If you're lucky, sometimes great. But it feels like you're looking for a punching bag, not someone to date.

I can see why you'd think that, but I—You probably won't believe me, but this relationship business is easier when you start young. You learn about yourselves and the world as you go along. Your growth is tangled up. Trying to do this now, more than 20 years into adulthood, is near impossible. I don't have the energy. I don't want to push people. Being on the same page isn't enough. It has to be the same paragraph. Or sentence. Make sense?

Sorta. Not really. No shade, but I'm ten years behind you. Maybe I'll feel the same when I'm in my forties. I hope not, though. I hope I'm still willing to give people a chance. I hope I'm not looking for a carbon copy of myself.

It's not like that.

If you say so. Well, I guess this was a waste of time.

Wait.

What?

Why did you respond to me? Why are you on a dating app designed for lefties?

I like having options. Besides, I just look at the pics and the distance. I skim the rest. You didn't seem creepy or scary. And you have a nice cock. And I'm a sucker for Latinos.

Oh, for the love of Pete.

What?

Nothing.

Well, same question for you. My profile isn't, like, political at all. Why did you agree to meet with me?

Honest?

Yeah.

I figured since you were on that app, there was a baseline. Besides, I was feeling kinda top-y this morning when you messaged, and I liked your pics. Your ass is truly amazing.

Thanks.

So maybe there's something to salvage from tonight?

You called me a fucking third grader.

But then I explained myself, so doesn't that work in my favor? You won't be disappointed. I promise.

VICARINATUTU
40 y/o, 5'8", 148lbs, single
Fact checker at literary mag
FUN FACT: I can list all the US Presidents, chronologically, in under a minute.
PAST: :-(
FUTURE: ???
FREE TIME: Museums and galleries, weekend hikes, WFP
IN BED: Sub bottom, pig play
SAFETY: PrEP, condoms
PREFERENCES: Silicon-based lube, Rhythm Nation, term limits for all elected officials
POLITICS: Bernie ho
CLAIM TO FAME: n/a

You weren't kidding when you said, "drinks and questions." Lots of questions.

I hope it hasn't been too unpleasant so far.

Not terribly. It helps that you remind me of my high school crush.

Thanks, I guess.

What's next? We've already covered electoral reform, reparations, Middle East politics, a national health service, and the minimum wage. I hope you don't intend to question me about housing policy because I know next to nothing on the matter.

Actually, I was thinking of something a bit more personal.

What?

Do you want to have children?

Yes, I think I do.

Cool.

You?

Yeah.

Cool. And sooner than later, I think.

Agreed. I'm nervous about being an older parent.

Me too. Also, my mom is eager to be a grandmother.

Same.

Mine was a teacher for forty years, and I think she misses being around children. I can tell by the way she talks to her plants: indirect conversations, as if she wants them to draw their own conclusions.

Public school?

Yes.

You probably grew up with an appreciation for public education.

Yes, of course.

Not me.

Private school?

I was in Catholic school till college. My parents worried about drugs and violence.

I mean, your parents weren't totally wrong. Some schools are rough.

In college, I met a kid whose high school's theater budget was one hundred thousand dollars. There were many kids with similar public school pedigrees. Before then, it had never occurred to me that something could be good *and* publicly funded.

There's a range, for sure. Some public schools are better than others. It can get competitive.

I've never understood this. Aren't you zoned for public schools? Don't you just go to the kindergarten down the street?

You're thinking of Finland.

Even kindergarten?

Yes.

That's absurd. Promise me, please, that if this date leads to marriage and children, we'll send them to the neighborhood school, no matter the perceived condition.

Okay.

Can we add that to our wedding vows?

Yes, so long as there's an escape clause if the school is dangerous.

What sort of danger?

Guns, knives, fists?

Like *West Side Story*?

Funny.

None of this is going to happen where you and I would send our kids.

Maybe. Maybe not. We should have a plan B just in case.

As long as plan B isn't using the pretext of safety as an excuse for not participating in our community.

What do you call it when you knowingly send your kids to a poorly performing school? Bad parenting.

You're underestimating how influential we'll be in our children's lives. And you're overestimating how important gardening or Latin classes are.

So you don't think there'll be consequences to our children being in classrooms with underprivileged kids?

If I hear one more person say *underprivileged* . . .

Oh my god. This is your idea of wooing someone?

It's just that a decent education isn't a privilege. It's basic, and if you deny it, you're effectively oppressing people. We should call them what they are: oppressed children.

Fine. There'll be consequences to our children being in classrooms with *oppressed* children—This is pointless.

Public education?

No. A first date is supposed to be about flirting. Not dissecting the world's problems. You haven't asked, but I am good at giving head.

I've heard that before. The guy I took home a few weeks ago thought Africa was a country, and he was all gums and teeth. Plus he kept scraping my shaft with his stubble. I had to spend the entire time rimming him because I was afraid he'd bruise me. Then I got E. coli.

That sounds traumatic and unlucky. I'm sorry. But I am actually good at it. Not only that, I'll let you fuck me raw all you want; then, I'll suck you clean. How about we spend some time talking about that? Would you like me to ride your cock before you come in my mouth?

Definitely. Down the road. When we've both had full STI screenings and are in a committed, monogamous relationship. Until then, condoms.

I've got plenty of PrEP if you want some.

No, thanks.

There's always PEP, after the fact.

I'm not afraid of HIV. I'm afraid of the next super virus that incubates silently for ten years before completely wiping out our immune systems and communities.

Jesus Christ! How do you function in this world with that type of neurosis?

I drink. Now, can we return to the oppressed children?

Did you hear what I said? I'm a first-rate bottom. Have you seen my ass?

Yes, I saw the pictures. I see the tight pants. It's an incredible ass. I look forward to it. But I can't get waylaid by porn sex. I'm 42. Life expectancy in this country is 79 and dropping. If you factor illness, I don't have much time to accomplish anything worthwhile on this planet. I need a partner who's ready to spin the world with me. We don't have time for negotiation.

That's noble, in a way, but being sexually compatible is essential.

I don't foresee that being a problem.

But I'm strictly a bottom, and your profile said you're *vers*. I see potential for unmet needs.

If I get topped once or twice a year, I'll be fine. We can invite a friend over. Or hire someone. I'm not worried. I'm prone to hemorrhoids anyway. I'm more concerned with our participation in the public school system. If you don't want to engage—

Fine.

Fine what?

Keep preaching, but when I get to the cherry at the bottom of this Manhattan, I'm leaving.

Thank you. Well, those oppressed children in our nonoppressed child's classroom might benefit from being around non-oppressed children whose bougie parents bring their privileges to the common space, consequently making it *better* so that, one day, these oppressed children won't be oppressed adults with whom we have to ride the subway and of whom we don't have to live somewhat in fear, which isn't to say that all oppressed children become asocial types who wreak havoc on society or who can't manage to extend their arms six inches in order to discard their trash into the appropriate receptacles instead of dropping their refuse directly onto the side-walk, but more resources devoted to early childhood education never hurt anyone.

I'm not using my children as tools to repair a faltering system.

The absence of participation is also political.

Gimme a—

What do you think happens when all the folks with power isolate themselves from the disempowered folks? They aren't only protecting their own power, they're growing it.

Whatever you say.

Do me a favor: close your eyes.

No.

C'mon. Please.

Fine.

Pretend for a moment that this date leads to another and we end up together and suddenly the aggregate of our lower middle-class incomes is enough for a down payment in one of the third-wave gentrification neighborhoods where we feel safe enough to hold hands on its streets, sunbathe half-naked in its parks, and sit at its sidewalk cafes, but somehow still fear its public schools. Do you see it?

Yes. Whatever.

Now, envision the people who've been living there for decades. Our future neighbors. Now imagine all their children and grandchildren. Do you see them?

Sure.

Well, if our kids go to the local school, we'll know all those kids. And we'll know their parents. They won't be strangers. We'll learn from them; they'll learn from us. Etc. Etc. Aren't we then more likely to see our society's distant, intractable problems as urgent matters of human justice?

I don't know. That's a stretch.

Well—

No, now it's my turn. Close your eyes.

Okay.

No, really, close them. Just like I did.

Okay, okay.

Imagine our first born: Sandy. Imagine raising him to be free and body positive and as femme as he wants. Then imagine little Nicky calling him a fag. In the cafeteria. During recess. During PE. Now imagine Nicky and her friends poking fun at our Sandy because he has two dads or because of his proclivity to sashay and shante down the halls. Imagine, too, that Nicky is broke and her parents beat her and berate her and, hard as they try, don't give her the love that she needs to be a happy and healthy child, which of course she's unloading on our kid because, well, hurt people hurt people. And let's imagine further that we talk to Sandy's teacher, who then convenes a meeting between us and Nicky's parents, who is really just her mom because dad is incarcerated—and yes, prisons are bullshit and should be dismantled, but that doesn't change the fact that Nicky grew up with only one parent who had very little support and who was herself a survivor of physical and possibly sexual violence—and as a result, Nicky's mom simply rolls her eyes at us when we try to talk to her about her daughter's bullying of our son. Worse, she whispers "maricones" under her breath when the teacher and principal aren't within earshot, which is just for effect because little Nicky's mom probably isn't even homophobic; in fact, she's probably herself a lesbian or bi, but she's angry and feels powerless in the face of our bourgeois affect. Or let's say she slaps Nicky around in front of us. What do we do then?

I don't know.

Do we still take a chance that Sandy won't be forever damaged by twelve years of this?

I don't know.

Do we just tell Sandy to tough it out? Do we put him in martial arts classes, knowing full well that there's a better, gender-affirming charter school seven blocks away whose nonbinary faculty all have chic undercuts and are quite proud of following Roxane Gay on Twitter?

I don't know. But can't we keep trying? Can't we check in with Sandy and help them to understand, as you say, that hurt people hurt people? Can't we share with Sandy all the times that we've been bullied? Can't we watch coming-of-age films that help give Sandy perspective? Can't we lobby our elected officials for more school funding? For more social workers? Or—I don't know—maybe we terrorize little Nicky. Maybe I whisper sinister things into her ear at morning drop off. Maybe I tell her that Freddy Krueger is going to get her and her mom if she doesn't leave our kid alone. I really don't know what the answer is, but running away from situations where one might encounter a conflict isn't a healthy way to live either. Besides, we could send Sandy to the most elite school in the city, and they might still face bullies. And trust me, in rich-people settings, the reasons for bullying are always more layered and nefarious. Rich folk can't fault the simplicity of poverty for their problems.

Kids today won't know who Freddy Krueger is.

Fine. Candyman.

I dated a guy like you once, who talks like this. Always planning for the utopia, trying to live his values all the freaking time. Not as bad as you, but annoying just the same. In addition to impractical. I don't mind growing; I just don't want to be educated all day long. I can't live my life fearing the future or obsessed with the past. And you shouldn't either. That's not a life worth living. Try the present.

Can I have his number then?

Who?

Your ex.

Fuck off.

I'm kidding.

RICKY MARTIN'S DAD

46 y/o, 6'1″, 174lbs, single

Social worker

FUN FACT: O.J.'s car chase was playing in the background while I was giving my college best friend a blow job.

PAST: Capitalism

FUTURE: Anarcho-syndicalism

FREE TIME: n/a

IN BED: I aim to please

SAFETY: Condoms and PrEP

PREFERENCES: 420 friendly

POLITICS: My dad was a Young Lord

CLAIM TO FAME: Gabriel García Márquez once ate at the
French restaurant where I worked. I cleared his table.

You do look like him a bit.

Who?

Ricky Martin.

Except for the grays.

True, a few more grays.

And I'm a little darker.

A little bit darker, yes.

I don't know if you're keeping score, but I believe I've answered
all your questions satisfactorily.

Yes, I think you have. You're officially the best date I've had in
three months of this.

And thank you for being so respectful. This felt like a conversation and not an inquisition.

I'm learning.

I'll be honest with you, papi, if you weren't so cute, I wouldn't have
come. The idea of something so businesslike was a little—

Daunting?

Demeaning. Lucky for you, I'm tired of meeting Mr. Almost
Right only to find out that he's Mr. Center Right. I also want to hit
the ground running. Two wheels instead of one.

Like a sturdy bicycle.

Exactly!

Until, that is, we upgrade to a four-wheeler.

You said two kids, right?

Yup.

Maybe we can get one of those old-timey pentacycles with the
basket on the side. Space for the dogs too.

Dogs?

Well, Fidel and Hugo—my babies—are both fourteen. They don't have much longer. When their time comes, I'm adopting two more.

But I—

Let me guess, you're a cat person. That's fine. I'm open. We can have both.

What? Didn't you see "no pets" in my profile?

Really?

Yes, really!

I thought you were kidding. Like "no pets" should reply to you.

Why would a pet reply to me?

Like a joke.

That's not funny.

I didn't think it was funny. I just thought it was a joke.

Fuck. I can't believe this. I really don't want a dog in my life. All the cleaning and grooming and slobbering and shedding.

What do you think kids are like?

Kids grow up. Dogs continue to shit in public and drool on your pillows—my pillows!

Some dogs are worse than others. You just haven't met the right one.

No. I've met all of them. I live in Brooklyn.

Damn, girl.

There are already eight and a half million humans in New York City to navigate, plus all the squirrels, pigeons, and cops. Do you have any inkling of the dog-shit epidemic slowly taking hold? It's like *The English Patient* out here. A veritable minefield. Every day. To and from the subway. To and from the park. To and from the bodega. Don't get me wrong: I don't blame the dogs. In fact, I think most dogs are interesting; some are even cute. But it's incredibly selfish to have a dog in a dense environment populated by humans. What, then, was the point of the suburbs? Isn't that where everyone moved for space and yards and away from poverty and us? That's where the dogs belong!

Mi'jo, do you have any idea how many people, including me, depend on their dogs for love and comfort and sanity?

Because we have to. What if we humans tried depending on each other instead? Our country is designed to keep us apart. That's why we turn to solutions that make everything worse.

Do you hear yourself?

I'm not suggesting anything extraordinary. We simply develop a permitting system. Show us you need a dog for your survival and you can have one. The current situation is unsustainable. The other day, I saw someone riding their massive greyhound sidesaddle. So please, spare me the love-and-support pets.

You're a damaged soul. You're spinning intolerance and ignorance into worthy values. Actually you're conflating them. That's a disservice to everyone.

I can't force myself to like something that I don't.

I know what you mean.

I assume that going back to your place is out of the question?

What?

Have sex. Do you still want to have sex with me?

Maybe, mi'jo. Maybe.

FOX IN YOUR HENHOUSE
44 y/o, 5'11", 169lbs, single
Political campaign manager
FUN FACT: n/a
PAST: Summer high school job was selling Häagen-Dazs at
     the US Open
FUTURE: Run for office; write a screenplay
FREE TIME: n/a
IN BED: Top, mostly; will try anything once; eating ass +++

SAFETY: n/a
PREFERENCES: n/a
POLITICS: Left of center
CLAIM TO FAME: n/a

Defund or reform police?

I'm all for cutting excess budgets, but I don't think we should do away with the police or even most of the police. We still need them.

I'll spare you my ranting. Goodnight.

WORK 'N' WERK
36 y/o, 5'10", 172lbs, single
Community organizer
FUN FACT: My brother and sister are also queer
PAST: n/a
FUTURE: n/a
FREE TIME: Bike rides, beach time, gym, gay bars, the streets, Twitter
IN BED: Vers, tantric play, cuckolding
SAFETY: PrEP
PREFERENCES: n/a
POLITICS: Marxist
CLAIM TO FAME: My dad is friends with Danny Glover.

Danny Glover is the man!

Super sweet person. About as rad as you imagine him to be.

I've always wondered how he squares his friendship with Mel Gibson.

Yeah, that's weird.

Maybe they're not friends. It's been a long time, after all, since the *Lethal Weapon* movies.

Possible. I've never asked Danny. By the way, you didn't have a mustache in your profile pic, right?

Nope.

This new?

Your profile said that you had a preference for them.

You did that to impress me?

Or to turn you on.

Mission accomplished.

Wait. Is that why you postponed last week?

My facial hair grows rather slowly. I accidentally shaved a few days ago, and I had to start from scratch.

I appreciate the effort.

Let's just say, I'm trying to be . . . Nicer or more romantic, I guess. I've been in the dating game for a few months now, and I haven't had much success. It's possible that I've been too regimented.

Flexible and open to growing: I like that.

So . . . Can I get you another drink? Or do you want to head back to my place?

Well, I know it's kinda soon, but do you want to meet my friends?

What? Tonight?

It's not like that. It's just that *Drag Race* starts in an hour, and we always watch it together.

Can we meet up after?

Not a fan of drag?

It's not that.

What then?

Nothing.

C'mon, what is it?

I just can't get into that show. It's minstrel-y.

Excuse me?

It feels like a free pass for men to laugh at women and for white people to ridicule Black people.

I think you're missing the point.

There's a point?

It's hella uplifting, in addition to entertaining. It showcases super talented people who would otherwise go ignored or ridiculed. It's a platform. It's also a refuge. And it's an art form.

Trust me, I don't like being the guy at odds with RuPaul, but it's not my thing. Is this a deal breaker?

I don't know. Not liking *Drag Race* is one thing, but being closed minded is another. My friends and I have been watching it together for years. It's kind of important. Also, it's fun. It'd be a great way for you to meet my inner circle.

Do you have a non-*Drag Race* community, too? Maybe I could hang with you when you're with those folks?

You're a dick.

Sorry.

No, you're not.

P-VALUE
41 y/o, 5'10", 159lbs, single
Biostatistician
FUN FACT: The degree of inequality between top 20% & bottom 20% of a given society accurately predicts health of that population, i.e., the bigger the gap, the worse the health outcomes.
PAST: Backyards and attics
FUTURE: Fire escapes and rooftops
FREE TIME: Crossword puzzles, basketball, LEGO-building
IN BED: Kisser; cuddler; vers top
SAFETY: PrEP and condoms

PREFERENCES: Honesty, humor, intellectual curiosity,
    radical politics
POLITICS: Far left of center
CLAIM TO FAME: I interned for Dr. Fauci after college.

Do you always bring your dates to this bar?

The last dozen, yes.

Why this place?

It's a constant variable. Plus, you can't beat the happy hour. And the jukebox has the Smiths and Luther Vandross.

You know Morrissey is a fascist, right?

I'd heard something, but I guess I haven't allowed myself to investigate further.

I see.

What?

Why not ask yourself difficult questions?

Hold on a second, aren't I the one who's supposed to be asking the questions?

Well, I might as well maximize my time too, no?

Fair enough.

I looked you up after we chatted the other day. We did, in fact, attend the same graduate school, at the same time. But somehow, we never crossed paths?

That was a long time ago. I don't recall for sure.

Were you part of any of the queer groups on campus? Did you go to the gay bars in town?

Not really. I was in a new relationship then—the one that ended last year. We were playing house in the beginning. It wasn't till we moved back to New York that we started going out.

So you're the type who gets lost in his relationship and abstains from community?

That's a type?

In my experience, it is.

Well, I was young. And frankly, insecure. The attention and affection that comes at the beginning of a relationship were addictive.

I've always felt it's important to build power with others. Strength in numbers, and community as a—

Buffer.

Exactly! Ecological model of health!

So you've never been in a relationship before?

You mean a romantic relationship? Yes, I have. Mostly short-term. One lasted a year. But truthfully, they've always felt rather selfish. Self-involved. I couldn't go very long without wondering what the utility was.

What's changed then? Why are we here?

A confluence of factors. Experience. Shifting priorities. I want to start a family. I want an actual partner. Like you said when we were chatting: someone who can move in sync with me.

Very romantic.

They're your words.

I know, I just haven't had much luck meeting guys who fully agree with me.

For me, it's become an inescapable truth: there is value in continuing with someone by your side. Capitalism doesn't allow for the sort of communal living that would de-prioritize—

Traditional partnerships!

Exactly! And sometimes you need someone to scratch your back. More importantly, someone to let you know if the mole on your back should be checked out. Once I realized that, I didn't want to waste more time. In fact, I'm here today specifically because of your post, *Mr. To the Pointdexter*. I, too, am done educating people about things they should already know. I mean, pick up a book. Look at history. Look upstream. Pay attention. Who has the time to suffer fools?

I guess I can't argue with that.

My worst fear is a co-parent who doesn't see the world as I see it. I don't want to find out that we're incompatible when the kid is five years old or, worse, in high school. I want to know now. Child-rearing is a revolutionary act, and both parents must be revolutionaries, in a way.

Wow.

Something wrong?

No. I couldn't have said it better. I just wonder if this is how I sound to others.

If you ask me, it's refreshing to be clear and direct.

That's what I thought, but that hasn't proven to be the case.

Well, you have my attention.

Can I play devil's advocate for a moment?

By all means.

Parenting must lead to unexpected situations, feelings, emotions, etc. We can't possibly know who our partner will be in the future.

Raising children is as old as time. If you're committed to making it work, it'll work.

I see that.

I figured you would. Now what do we do?

Sex?

Well—

I'm kid—

How about a bite to eat first?

Sure. There's a vegan place with the most amazing bulgogi. Just a few blocks from here.

Hmmm.

You don't like Korean food?

In fact, I like it very much. But a lot of these vegan places with fake meats are so overly processed. You're better off eating the chicken at a farm-to-table place.

Good point. How about the sustainable sushi spot that just opened on Avenue A? It's—

The fish are probably traveling from a conscientious farm in Alaska. Truly sustainable sushi would have to come from somewhere nearby. The Rockaways or Long Island. Otherwise, we're just playing faux conservation games.

I guess you're right. Well, then, how about another drink here; then we can see how we feel?

Three drinks in one night is a bit excessive, no? More than fourteen alcoholic beverages in a week is a steep tax on the liver.

How about a mocktail?

COLLECTIVE[G]LIB
37 y/o, 5'10", 150lbs, single
RN
FUN FACT: n/a
PAST: Still recovering from my suburban adolescence
FUTURE: n/a
FREE TIME: Enjoy tennis and swimming
IN BED: Flexible, open-minded, sometimes rough
SAFETY: PrEP, condoms
PREFERENCES: Not interested in "preferences" or agendas
   or tirades
POLITICS: Well left of center
CLAIM TO FAME: I went to school with Jared Kushner and
   hated him then too.

I'm surprised you reached out.

I figured six months was a sufficient amount of distance.

You're not far off. Anything sooner, and I probably wouldn't have responded. Why'd you reach out anyway? Are you anti-Palestine now?

Ha. I guess I deserve that.

And more. A hell of a lot more.

I felt bad about how things went between us. Admittedly, my approach could use some tweaking.

Some?

Why did you respond?

Your apology seemed sincere. And before you had your geopolitical tantrum, I liked you. I even found your lecturing kind of cute. You're still kind of cute—have you been working out?

I gave up on trying to find someone six weeks ago and joined a gym instead.

Bravo.

All my dates had been with people who were in much better shape than me. Plus I had my annual physical, and my doctor explained that in our forties, we begin to lose muscle mass. Apparently I have to work out just to maintain my low-level fitness—Wait! You thought my madness was endearing?

Let's not get carried away. You're insufferable, but you have potential.

As the man of your dreams?

As a friend.

Fair enough.

Do you test your friends too?

No. But I am curious about a few things.

Here we go.

Friendly inquiries.

Let's see . . .

You have pets?

Eww. No.

Cool.

I also have a question.

Shoot.

Could we talk about something lighter this time? You have a favorite movie?

Favorite? Not really. But I have a list of ones I really like. You like Frederick Wiseman? The documentarist?

Who?

How about Apichatpong Weerasethakul?

You know what? You'd be ideal for my friend Matt. He's kind of a film snob and very patient. He's a software engineer.

Oh.

Trust me, he's a good guy. Our age. Also just got out of long term relationship. I'll give you his number. Just tell him Tomás sent you.

Tell me more.

Maybe a drink first?

Yes.

Slightly dirty gin martini?

Please.

Olives?

Three.

MATT

Early forties

Software engineer

Friend of Tomás

Patient

Film buff

. . .

GRAND OPENINGS*

I

Eduardo and Gus meet in college. They fall in love, move to Seattle, marry in Vancouver because their relationship isn't recognized in the United States, adopt children, remain monogamous until their children leave for college, at which point they open up their relationship. Eduardo leaves Gus for Richard. Gus meets Antonio. All of them get along and take vacations together. When Antonio and Richard die, Gus and Eduardo reunite, at first because of loneliness and convenience, but soon for love. They live out their last days together.

---

*After Margaret Atwood ("Happy Endings")

II

Eduardo and Gus meet in college. They fall in love, move to NYC, and open up their relationship after two years. Gus meets Antonio, leaves Eduardo, and moves with Antonio to Seattle. Eduardo, left distraught by a breakup that dredges up the fears of rejection and abandonment sown in his high-stress, near-poverty upbringing, kills himself. Gus is overcome with guilt. Antonio eventually leaves Gus because he refuses to compete with the ghost of Eduardo.

III

Eduardo and Gus meet in college. They fall in love, move to Seattle, marry in Vancouver because their relationship isn't recognized in the United States. Eduardo works on a reparations campaign for the long-term socioeconomic effects of slavery on Black Americans. Gus designs semiconductor chips for data-center computers. They open up their relationship after ten years. Eduardo falls in love with Richard and proposes that he come to live with him and Gus. Gus accepts because he doesn't want to lose Eduardo, but he isn't particularly fond of Richard, not enough to share a home with him. After a few years of living together as a trio, Gus and Richard fall in love too. They move back to the East Coast and buy a co-op apartment (2br, 2b) in Jackson Heights. They also buy a king-sized bed. Eduardo, Gus, and Richard live happily but never come out as a throuple to their respective parents. Whenever family comes to visit one of them, the other two find excuses to stay out of the apartment.

IV

Eduardo and Gus meet in college. They fall in love, but Eduardo has already accepted a Peace Corps assignment in the Ivory Coast. Gus promises to wait, but after a year meets Antonio. When Eduardo returns, he meets Gus for dinner. Antonio comes home and finds them in bed together. Antonio becomes enraged and stabs them both repeatedly before jumping from the roof of their apartment in Fort Greene. Gus and Eduardo survive the attack, move to Seattle, marry in San Francisco, and adopt two children. Gus dies young from a heart attack precipitated by aortic damage from the stabbing. Eduardo moves to New York, where he meets Richard. Eduardo's oldest son, Felix, is incensed because he never recovered from Gus's death. The younger child, Jules, is relieved that their father isn't alone and eventually convinces her brother to be reasonable. After ten years of marriage, Eduardo and Richard open up their relationship.

V

Eduardo and Gus meet in college. They move to Boston. On a trip to Los Angeles to meet up with a couple with whom they'd had a foursome in New York during Pride weekend, their plane is hijacked and flown into the World Trade Center.

VI

At a weekly meeting of LGBT college students, Eduardo sits next to Gus, but when Gus gets up to use the bathroom, Eric takes his seat. Eduardo and Eric go home together. They date on and off for four years. At their five-year reunion, Gus and Eduardo officially meet for the first time. They both live in Brooklyn, seven stations apart on the G train. After six months, they move in together. After six years, they adopt one child. Three years later, they adopt another. Seven years later, Eduardo begins an affair with Richard despite Richard's belief that reparations should only go to the descendants of enslaved people and not to all Black people. Eduardo convinces him that the effects of modern-day racism are inextricable from the socioeconomic impacts of slavery. Their affair goes on for ten months before Gus confronts Eduardo. At first, Gus asks for a divorce, but after some consideration, they determine that divorce would be too disruptive for the children. Instead, they buy the apartment downstairs and live loosely as a family. Gus and Eduardo occasionally have sex, but their relationship transitions into friendship. The children refer to Richard as Uncle Richie. Gus and Richard sleep together once, while Eduardo is at a conference in Greensboro. Neither of them ever tells Eduardo because they know he won't take it well, and besides, it was just an itch they needed to scratch. They aren't truly interested in one another.

VII

Eduardo and Gus's youngest child, Jules, comes home for Thanksgiving with their partner, Nellie, and newborn (Raven), and after everyone else has gone to bed, they—Jules is nonbinary and uses all pronouns—confide in Eduardo and Gus that they and their partner have met someone (Lily, the doula who helped with Raven's homebirth) and would like to live ensemble in a homestead community for radical queers near Burlington. Jules is afraid of telling his older brother, Felix, because Felix, to the chagrin of everyone, is a bit conservative when it comes to the social order of things. Eduardo and Gus assure Jules that Felix will be supportive and promise to talk to him if necessary. Then they set up a time to have all of them, including Lily, who they met briefly at the baby shower and soon after the birth, over for dinner. Felix, who was already uncomfortable with his fathers' unorthodox relationship, doesn't take the news well. I am the adopted son of a gay, transracial, and polyamorous couple, and I have a sibling who doesn't in any way resemble me, he shouts in the courtyard of their co-op. Isn't that enough?

VIII

In the first year of opening up their relationship, Eduardo falls in love various times. He becomes obsessive about each man he has sex with, in part because he was used to being a bottom for Gus, and is now exclusively a top. He can't believe what he was missing. The ecstasy of providing pleasure in a more active fashion becomes addictive. At first, Gus is turned on by Eduardo's escapades, but soon he becomes concerned with Eduardo's mental health. On a flight to Austin, an anxious white woman signals to a flight attendant that Eduardo looks like a terrorist. An undercover US Marshall approaches him, precipitating Eduardo's first full-fledged panic attack. The flight is grounded in Atlanta. Soon after, Eduardo begins taking anti-anxiety medications. The pills cause chronic bloody noses and numbness of the jaw. After some trial and error, Eduardo finds a treatment plan free of side effects that reduces his anxiety and makes the extramarital dating easier. From time to time, Eduardo brings home his dates and Gus participates. Gus is often content to merely watch. In their third year of an open relationship, Gus meets Antonio. When their dalliance becomes serious, Eduardo adjusts his treatment plan. Eventually things fizzle out with Antonio. After the birth of their fourth grandchild, Eduardo is diagnosed with anal cancer. The stigma and internalized Catholicism send Eduardo into a depressive spiral. He becomes especially frustrated when he finds out this could have been prevented if he'd had more frequent anal pap smears. He considers suing his primary care provider for negligence, but soon realizes that the stress of it all will only make the recovery more difficult. His remission lasts three years. Life was primarily good, he says to Gus from the hospital bed. Gus dies in a car accident on the way home from the funeral. Felix and Jules are quietly relieved that Gus won't have to live out the pains of being a lonely widower. The grandchildren are devastated, but they recover quickly.

IX

Moral? There is no moral, but some observations about pleasure and monotony: they are powerful. They will make one do things they promised they would never do, and they will accelerate a train already in motion. At times they work in conjunction; sometimes they're free agents. Pleasure will disrupt monotony, sure, but only momentarily. And the effort to maintain that disruption will, in most cases, lead to irreversible effects. Life continues. Until it doesn't.

THE PEOPLE
WHO REPORT MORE
STRESS

THE EVENING IS TEPID AND sunlit, typical of August in New York City, but the cold in my bones is late winter. I'm on my way to buy a new phone, too weak from weeks of radiation treatment to walk the remaining twelve blocks. Three empty taxis zoom past, their on-duty lights taunting me. I wait for a familiar, neurochemical heat in my chest and face that doesn't come. Even the audience of restaurant-goers dawdling across the street does nothing to me. Some of my composure is an unintended side effect of being an enervate survivor; some of it is calculated: cancer reoccurrences are likelier in people who report more stress. I force a smile that I hope will dupe my body into thinking I'm happy, or at least keep the cortisol at bay. I don't give up. I step further into the street and throw both arms in the air—a dare.

A taxi stops.

"Straight ahead. I'll tell you when."

The driver is a chatty, mustachioed man who keeps a neat carriage, and immediately discloses that he's from Kerala. He praises the weather and laments cops who U-turn. He wonders aloud if I, too, am Indian, then Pakistani, then Palestinian, then Mexican. The conversation doesn't rankle; instead, I'm intrigued. No one ever mentions Palestine casually. The driver's passing remark takes on an air of protest. I explain that my mother is from El Salvador and my father from Colombia—after all, it's true. From the latter, he references a famous drug dealer, a pop singer, and a soccer player, but he says little of the small Central American nation: "Pupusas, right?" At a red light, he broaches the topic of children.

"I have two," he says.

"Me too."

"Very lucky we are. They are home with your wife?"

"With my husband, actually."

"Oh," says the driver.

The car's hum is louder in the ensuing quiet.

Months ago, I might have changed the subject or pretended to take a call instead of outing myself. But evading the truth requires energy and leaves a pernicious mark. The fear of honesty, however, is momentary, like a steep rollercoaster drop. This freedom is becoming addictive and makes me wonder about all of my inhibitions, past and present. Has this sense of liberation always been so readily accessible? Have I given my fears too much weight? Surely society shares the blame. Wait, I'm doing it again. I'm overthinking instead of—

"Every day, different people in my taxi. That's what I love about this country," the driver says, like a paid advertisement, and double-parks outside my destination.

The storefront is blue glass, including the heavy door, which requires both hands and a wide stance to open. The air conditioning is gale force. The smells of new plastic and carpet freshener invade my senses. A man with a frosted beard and a lumbering gait arrives like an aged tree. He's wearing standard khakis and large eyeglasses, the kind I've come to associate with the 1970s. He reminds me of my father, but not in appearance—my father is short, stout, and still has perfect vision. Every man who should be resting instead of working reminds me of my father.

"Welcome to Cell Phone Warehouse, Sir. My name is Jerry. How can I help you today?" he says in one breath, as if his time is also precious, as if he weren't many years my senior.

Jerry helps me leave the store with a phone and a hard-plastic sleeve for its protection. I slip him a twenty—I've been tipping extravagantly since the diagnosis. After a brief silence, he nods at me with a mix of gratitude and umbrage. I fear I've been condescending.

My walk home is unhurried but alert. Everyone around me is glowing effortlessly. Sunlight and evening are tangled in a vibrant pink-orange sky, a cocktail. I pull out the new phone and glide my fingertips across the screen. I refrain from calling Gus because he'll hear I'm out of breath and worry. My mother doesn't answer. It is nearly eight. She is probably putting my kids to sleep, and a missed call from me will certainly trigger a panic loop. I begin to regret but take long calming breaths. I feel repetitive and temporary, like a pop song or a yoga class. The intersection ahead is hazy—a combination of steam spewing up from beneath the city and the dizzying effect of everyone's economic ambitions. An equitable redistribution of wealth in my lifetime is beginning to seem unlikely. I see a pharmacy on the corner; I'll pick up the sunscreen for Gus there. I'm worried about his skin. We're both getting older, but he seems to be getting their faster. I slip the phone back into my pocket.

Before I reach the corner, it is again in my hands. The urge to talk to someone won't loosen its grip. If my memory bank is a Rolodex, it contains only a few worn cards. One is my sister Carmen—somehow, she secured a phone number that is exactly her birthday: month, day, and year. But it's Friday, and she's probably napping before going out. My breathing has steadied. I dial Gus. When the ringing begins, it dawns on me that he was the last person I called before this all began five months ago.

〰

Despite the imposing sun, a chill persisted. The air was thick with pollen and construction dust: everywhere a bloom and a brownstone renovation. In the background, late lunchers wrapped in scarves hid behind sunglasses, each with an aura of anonymity, like film extras who'd been directed to play their roles with a disengaged and morally ambiguous affect—years of this. I was on my way to pick up my older son from school. I had just crossed from one café-strewn street corner to another, when my younger child, hanging marsupial-like from my chest, let out an important sneeze.

"Hold on a sec, hon," I said to Gus, who'd stepped out of a meeting only moments before to answer my call. But in the process of wrangling the tiny, intransigent nose, the phone slipped out from between my ear and shoulder and onto the pavement. Gus continued talking because he had no idea he was lying on a slab of cracked bluestone that was being colonized by tree roots and untamed weeds.

"I broke it."

"What?"

"My phone. I just dropped it on the street. The screen is completely shattered."

I held the wreckage a centimeter from my ear, then, a few inches from my face, then, back to my ear. I was quickly coming to terms with its essential nature. What if I got to the school and our son had a fever or a lacerated cornea? How would I contact his pediatrician? How would I get to a hospital?

"Can you stay on the line until I pick him up? Just to be safe. I'm afraid I won't be able to call you back if I hang up."

"Okay," he said, like a man whose day couldn't be ruined. He simply walked away from the room full of casually dressed male engineers without saying a word and made his way to a common area or kitchen or brightly colored conference room where he could continue listening to me wail about my broken phone, never once telling me to hold on or wait a minute. Just *Okay*.

Our son was fine. My right index finger, however, was full of tiny cuts from swiping at the screen.

I lay rigid on the living room floor, doing my best to smile and balance my children's bodies, while trying to forgive myself for being so clumsy and stupid. But even with one child perched on my knees and the other sitting cross-legged on my chest, the isolation and despair became something like relief. My phone, after all, hadn't been only a multipurpose tool—dictionary, map, personal assistant, bridge. It had also been a years-long addiction (screen on, screen off, screen on, off, on, email, refresh, email, refresh, *New York Times*, refresh, tennis scores, refresh, porn, email, screen off, screen on). And just like that, I was free of it.

"I'm not going to replace it."

"Really?" Gus set down his can of pale ale and burped quietly. We had just put the kids to sleep, and we were in the kitchen, acclimating to the calm. "How am I going to call you in the middle of the day?"

"We can email."

"What about family and friends?"

"We can get a landline."

"But you're always worried about an emergency with the kids."

"And you're always telling me not to."

"Let's see how you feel tomorrow."

. . .

The moments of concentration were ephemeral. In a café a few blocks from home, I stirred a bowl of eight-dollar oatmeal festooned with dried berries and pecans, trying, unsuccessfully, to grade my students' papers ("Racism, a System of Social Hierarchy, as a Risk Factor for Low Birth Weight"). It was my first day without a phone in nearly fifteen years, and I couldn't submerge the fear that everyone in my life was in the midst of a crisis and desperate to reach me. I emailed Gus and reminded him to keep his phone handy in case the daycare or school needed us. Then I pressed the headphones into my ears and turned up Yaz, followed by Tears for Fears, and finally Anita Baker, but none of them comforted me like they usually do.

On the second day, I expected more of the same internal frenzy, but to my surprise, the withdrawal symptoms were more bluster than tropical cyclone. To fill the time, I stuffed Frantz Fanon's *The Wretched of the Earth* into my backpack for the subway trips—more than a decade of stalling after the first chapter. On the walks to and from the train, instead of calling anyone or reading about Roger Federer's hopeless French Open run, I did my best to notice tree beds and stoops and mail carriers and the minutiae of race relations. I also found myself ogling at every even mildly attractive man who crossed my path: skinny-legged jeans and fanciful haircuts; bright sneakers and baggy pants; standard business casual, jacket, no tie. A few called my bluff, but I balked when it was my turn to glance back.

On the third day, with a thin scarf wrapped around my nose and mouth as a guard against the pollen, I walked slowly, on the balls of my feet, and took mindful, yogic breaths. But after only a few blocks, my mind coiled itself around the possibility that everyone thought I was a terrorist because of my makeshift balaclava. I stuffed my hand into my pocket in search of the phantom phone, but I found only a tiny opening in the threadbare depths. I pinched tightly the skin of my thigh, hoping it might recondition me. In the afternoon, I stopped at the bank by the university and deposited money into my father's account—money he's never requested but that assuages my class guilt. Afterward, I calculated my students' final grades. My mother emailed to say hello. A short time later, she sent another email expressing concern about the lack of response to her first email.

"Try the Internet," said the man at the fourth phone repair shop I visited—tiny and decorated in old calendars and foreign currency. Five phone-free days had passed before I succumbed to the search for a replacement screen. "This," I said, pointing to my phone, "is my Internet." The man nodded but didn't glance up from his screen.

By the seventh day, I was free. The urge to call someone or to browse the Web had vanished; I was no longer reaching, digging, or pinching. Instead, I found myself massaging the bottom left side of my abdomen. I assumed the unfamiliar pressure was gas, so I stretched and lay on my back and tried diamond pose, but the relief was only ever short-lived. I thought it might be appendicitis, but Gus pulled down the loose waist of his jogging pants to reveal the reddish-pink scar where they'd cut him open. "Appendicitis would be on the right side," he said.

Gus mentioned the discomfort to my mother when she called looking for me a few evenings later—he shouldn't have. She asked him to ask me if I'd noticed changes in my bowel movements—yes, more constipated than usual. The next day, she told Gus to tell me to stop drinking kombucha—I did. I also increased the fiber content in my diet and cut out alcohol and caffeine. The pressure didn't care.

My doctor was on vacation, so I made an appointment with the physician's assistant, Kelly—a bubbly, bow-tied Texan who wore short-sleeve dress shirts that brandished her biceps. The redhead with curls who walked into the cramped, L-shaped examination room was neither Kelly nor familiar. He smiled often, and gave curt commands. His name was Kenny, and he wore a dark tie. Kenny had me lie on my back and pressed his hands onto my belly, gently at first. His thin necklace with a crucifix charm dangled over me. He asked if I was in a monogamous relationship, but never made eye contact. Kenny then handed me a cup and asked me to pee in it. "I see here you've lost eleven pounds since your last physical. Are you getting more exercise?"

In the weeks that followed, there was a fecal exam, a sonogram, a CT scan, and a colonoscopy that required a foul laxative far worse than the abdominal discomfort. I suspected the entire time that it was cancer, but I said nothing because when the time came for them to tell me I had cancer, I wanted them—all of them—to focus specifically on the cancer and my treatment and not on any ego-induced awkwardness for having previously reassured me it was not cancer.

My mother cried quietly when the news came. She was nowhere near the doctor's office, but I heard her sobbing into my father's chest. She knew what I was being told. She'd known for weeks. "Discomfort in that part of the body, with no other symptoms, worries me," she'd said to Gus. "It could be pancreatic cancer—como mi mamá," she trailed off, before catching herself, "but don't let him be nervous!"

I'd been nervous from the beginning. It wasn't only the thought of something unwanted growing inside of me; I was also concerned with its severity. Years before, in East Harlem, in a Pentecostal church basement with orange carpeting, I'd interviewed a group of women as part of a breast cancer study. It hadn't taken long to determine that their primary reason for evading screening exams was fear (of death and doctors). "Principalmente los americanos y los hombres," called out a petite grandmother with a thick braid of gray hair draped, like an elegant stole, over one shoulder. The others nodded along. As the meeting progressed, I learned that they had each known other women (usually relatives, sometimes neighbors) with breast pain who'd died shortly after being diagnosed. *It only gets worse when they open you up* was the popular sentiment in the room. Stuck with the limited script in my hand, I focused on the importance of early detection, but the room stared skeptically, nibbling complimentary Melba toast and sipping instant coffee, as if I were a double agent.

"I have your results," said the gastroenterologist. Gus and I were holding hands across the space between our seats—plump, maroon leather in Queen Anne mahogany frames. The office resembled a small Ivy League library. It was a Tuesday. "The polyps are malignant. Colon cancer, stage II," he said. The low-budget horror movie sequel of cancers.

My first thought was, *Fuck, a lot of people are going to assume this has something to do with anal sex.* Then, something else occurred to me. Years before, when the second Bush was reelected, I joked that if I were ever terminally ill, I would find a way to take out the conservative wing of the Supreme Court. Nothing excessively violent, but murder nonetheless. Now, here I was, terminally ill–adjacent, and I didn't want to harm a soul. I wanted everyone to live, even Clarence Thomas.

"The good news is, it's still early," said the doctor, his way of tying a red bow around a live grenade.

I wanted to believe him, but my mind couldn't suppress the memory of our first meeting a few weeks earlier, when he'd forgotten me in an examination room.

"I am very sorry. This has never happened before," he'd said, as I pretended not to hear, hurriedly zipping up my pants and forcing my heels into my shoes. "Please don't leave. This is important."

Thirty-four minutes I'd lain, awkward and cold, over a thin sheet of paper, naked from the waist down, like a cartoon character with pubic hair, telling myself this was a completely acceptable length of time to wait for a doctor, that this wouldn't even constitute a wait in Canada or England, that this had nothing to do with anything other than his patient load, that (at least) I could rule out homophobia because he was a gay physician highly recommended by another gay physician. But in the end, I could think only of the nodding Latinas in East Harlem, who'd relied on empirical evidence to arrive at the same conclusions as those in the research articles I'd been assigning to my students for years about how non-white patients fare worse.

In the weeks following that first meeting, the forgetful clinician with an artificial tan and a shaved head proved himself friendly and contrite—he waived my copays and gave me preferential appointment times. In fact, even on the day of the bad news, he seemed genuinely affected, alternating between comforting tones and championing eyebrows, as if the cancer were somehow his fault. If we're being honest, I felt a tinge of gratitude that he was willing to shoulder a portion of the blame.

As the doctor spoke to us about treatment options, I sized up the desk between us (nutmeg-stained cherry wood) and wondered if it had ever been the site of a post-diagnosis sexual encounter—it was quite a large desk. I wondered, too, if we might be in an Edmund White novel or an entry in Gary Fisher's diary. Everything felt possible. And unless the cancer had recalibrated my pheromone detector, I'd sensed subtle, triangulated longing originating from the doctor— extended stares and exaggerated laughter amid the textbooks and framed diplomas—mostly directed at Gus, who, ironically, has seldom been spontaneous about sex and has never been attracted to older men.

My mother took to calling Gus. I was in shock and should buy a phone, she told him. She also started visiting more, even got my dad to take off work. On Fridays, she brought food, sat and watched me eat it, and took the children. On Sundays, she brought the children back, brought more food, and watched me eat that too. I knew she was on edge, and I found myself surprised at her composure, which was probably why I didn't react when she blurted out, "You had all the opportunities! You speak the language! This is your country! Why do you live like this? Anxious, like me?" These must have been rhetorical questions because immediately after asking them, she left the room.

Whatever Gus might have thought, he kept it to himself. He resorted, instead, to being attentive and caring, while I sat in bed with my laptop, telling myself I was on vacation, researching odds ratios and advances in treatment.

As for my kids, I made an effort to be more engaged, fearing that they were too young to retain clear or definitive memories of me. I built elaborate LEGO structures with weak foundations, I read stories while affecting accents and playing with the register of my voice, I gave longer hugs, I made more eye contact. With my older child, I had a small chance of being indelible, but I knew there was no hope for the baby.

"Your five-year survival rate is eighty-three percent. That's good news," said the oncologist, an Argentine man with a pronounced overbite and the British diction of an expensive education. "The first round of radiation begins next week," he continued. "We want to be certain we got it all."

Radiation. For fifteen years, I'd walked around with it in my pocket. A couple of Scandinavian studies from the early cell phone days suggested that consistent exposure to mobile phones might increase the risk of brain tumors. They said nothing about the colon, but was this a coincidence? Often I kept my phone in my coat pocket, which rested somewhere near the height of my intestines. Radiation was the cure, but could it also have been the cause?

I created an email account—curiousaboutcancer1848—and sent out inquiries.

"Dear Swedish Cancer Researcher, Is it possible that my phone caused the cancer? And beyond that, did my phone keep the cancer at bay? Was I symptomless all this time because I'd been self-medicating with a DIY course of radiation in my pocket?"

"Dear Crazy American, That seems impossible."

I sent more emails. Most went unreturned. A researcher at the University of Pretoria found my hypothesis implausible but entertaining. She wished me luck.

After a week, I came to my senses. I was embarrassed but still wanted answers. I contacted a few people who researched stress. A famed epidemiologist at Harvard responded:

"There is no evidence of a relationship between stress and the onset of cancer, unless stress leads to unhealthful habits, e.g., excessive drug or alcohol use or a poor diet. But chronic cortisol, consistent with the reported stress levels in Blacks, Latinxs, American Indians, some Southeast Asians, and all people with low socioeconomic status, has been found to make a cancer grow, spread, and return faster. It must be said, however, this area of research isn't as robust as it could be, not least of all because of whom it affects."

After a short-lived back and forth, he wrote: "Are you familiar with the extensive canon of social support research? An ounce goes a long way. Godspeed."

I was familiar. In brief, feeling cared for and caring for others activates safety-related neural regions and inhibits threat-related ones. It does the opposite of what stress does. This is why tighter-knit societies are healthier. It's why tighter-knit communities within uneven societies survive for as long as they do.

Yoga, it turns out, cannot undo the deluge of cortisol that is unleashed while trying to catch a cab to yoga.

The air conditioning was set to low as a compromise. Gus was in his underwear enjoying a beer on a couch that cost us the equivalent of a year of community college tuition—the last expensive purchase before we had children. He was reading the newest N.K. Jemisin book—he reads only Black women's work in the hopes it'll autocorrect his whiteness. I was beside him, dressed for a colder climate, trying to make my way through *Before Night Falls* in Spanish—Arenas was up a tree, hiding from the police, famished and delusional. My mom had come by earlier to take the kids. My sister, too, had been babysitting, but never on the weekends. "Your cancer is not going to keep me from meeting Mr. Right," she'd said after the diagnosis. We'd both laughed, but it gave me perspective.

Gus continued doting. Every morning, he awoke earlier than usual, in the hopes of keeping the kids quiet while I slept in. He brought me breakfast in bed—blended soups and chamomile—on a sturdy tray he'd ordered from a home health attendant website. He massaged my shoulders unprompted, and he replaced all the batteries in our remote controls; faltering remote controls frustrate me easily. He also surprised me with fourth-round tickets to the US Open—my favorite round. But most importantly, Gus served as my intermediary to the world. There were weeks of fatigue and nausea, when I didn't want to expend energy explaining my condition or listening to people's heartfelt words. I wanted only to watch reruns of *227* and *Frasier* and eat gummy worms. I wanted nothing more than this. Gus was okay with that.

"Honey, I want to go to Bolivia and Russia and Cuba. Soon."

"Okay," he said.

"I don't care if Russia hates us, I want to visit anyway. Too much has happened there for me not to. And one day it won't hate us, but I may not be around to see it."

"You'll be around."

"But just to be safe . . ."

At this, Gus leaned forward, disrupting the thin layer of sweat between our thighs and the cushions, and set his beer down on the braided jute rug. His head dropped low, like a person in a church pew.

He was crying, and the more he sobbed, the heavier his head grew, until finally, it looked as if he were bracing for an impact. I'd never seen him like this. I'd never seen him afraid.

But it wasn't fear alone. No, that's not Gus's way. It was the loneliness. Everything, after all, had fallen on him—the kids, our home, the doctors, my sarcasm. He'd been left behind. I'd left him behind.

I rested my chin on his bare shoulder. "No need to get upset. Russia doesn't really hate us. They're just reacting to our military presence," I said. He continued crying, but now laughter had found its way into the room. When both subsided, he stretched out and rested his head on my lap. "Putin is certifiable," he said. I didn't respond. Instead, with the tip of my finger, I drew small circles against the grain of his cowlick. He dozed off quickly, but I continued to stare at his profile. The lines around his eyes were no longer few or impermanent, and the faint freckles on the bridge of his nose had multiplied. For years, I'd been telling him to use sunscreen. White skin does not hold up well. Many times, I'd said that. But Gus has never prioritized those sorts of vanities. And he probably never would.

A fierce urge to protect him gripped me, different from the sadness and dread I'd been feeling whenever I imagined leaving the kids. Gus hated long silences, as well as eating or sleeping alone. But neither was he the sort of person who made dinner plans with friends or who bought tickets for the theater. What would he do without me?

I remained there beneath his weight for a while longer, crafting a mental list of tasks: I needed to send my syllabi to the new administrative assistant in our department. We also needed to make doctor appointments for the kids: another round of vaccines and an overdue visit to the dentist. And I had dozens of calls to return to family and friends. I looked around for Gus's phone, hoping I could take care of some of these tasks or at least set a few reminders, but it was across the room, on the mantel, between two candles that we'd owned for years but had never lit.

"I need to go."

"Huh?" Gus shot up ninety degrees. "What? Is everything okay?"

I kissed his cheek and lips and tugged gently at his chest hair. "Everything is fine."

"Where are you going?"

"Down the street."

"For what?"

"I'll be right back."

"But I already bought kombucha!" I heard through the door, as I hurried down the stairs.

By the time I reached the end of our block, I was winded. A burning seized the area where the radiation had been aimed. I doubled over and placed my hands on my knees, like I might have after a longer, more strenuous run. A handful of intrepid leaves had already begun the process of separating from their trees. They dotted the bluestone, masking some of the cracks and their untamed weeds. Across the street, a breezy, cosmopolitan crowd spilled out from the restaurant onto the sidewalk—people in summer dresses, tank tops, and wrinkled linen shirts, waiting for their names to be called. All of them enjoying life in the precious hours of a precious season. They didn't see me, but I found myself straightening up, brushing off my creases, and stretching my lips into a smile anyway.

Why did I do that, I wondered. Certainly, if the streets had been devoid of life, I wouldn't have been concerned by my appearance.

There it was: the overthinking I'd been told to avoid. "Reduce your stress," said the oncologist.

No directive has ever been easier to say than do.

The last time, I thought. That was the last time I would give currency to what others thought of me. I had no other choice but to care less. Not careless or carefree, just not so much. *Care less* would be my new mantra. I'd need help: buffers, coping mechanisms, social support. I'd need people. Touch. Laughter. More family visits.

Friends. Sunday dinners. Movie nights. Community. Isolation would solve nothing.

First, a new phone.

I resumed my journey. I wasn't traveling far, but walking, I realized, was an unnecessary expenditure of energy. In the distance, a few yellow cabs were approaching. I scanned the intersection to size up my competition. Immediately, I felt something familiar shift inside of me. A minor surge of electricity. It was the old me. The one from thirty or forty seconds ago. The one I'd just banished from existence. No problem, I thought. It was merely a false start. I could try again. I would try again. Beginning . . . now.

I stepped into the street and threw both arms up.

ACKNOWLEDGMENTS

Robert Guinsler, for making a way out of no way, and for the martinis. Danny Vazquez, for the regular reminders that we're seeking entry into the very institutions we're trying to tear down. Rachael Small and Tiffany Gonzalez, for teaching me that being cheesy doesn't make me less human, possibly more. Rola Harb, for keeping us on track. Sarah Christensen Fu, for the backstage magic. Ben and Alessandra, for their impeccable taste. And everyone else at Astra House who has made this book possible.

León and Camilo, for providing endless growth and entertainment, and for being more excited than I am. My siblings—Ernesto, Maria, and Nathalia—for telling me what they see that I don't; their spouses, for the support; and all the nibblings—Aidan, Ethan, Penelope, Caleb, Luca, Jasper, and Ignacio—who will continue this in some shape.

Jeffrey Masters, for choosing restaurants that accommodate my dietary restrictions—one of the many things I love about him.

Lisa Chen and Hugh Ryan, for reading everything, always, and rather quickly.

Adam McGee, Allyson Paty, Ana Melo, Catie Napjus, Chris Gonzalez, Deborah Treisman, Denne Michele Norris, Elias Rodriquez,

Ellen Rosenbush, Gerald Maa, Jael Humphrey, Josh Glaser, Katie Kendall, Maggie Su, Melissa Lozada-Oliva, Melody Nixon, Michele Hoos, Michele Johnson, Radhika Singh, Robin Moore, Sara Nović, Stacy DeLong, and Traci Arnold for their feedback on these stories. Mark Galarrita, for his eleventh-hour notes.

Akil Spooner, Alexandra Watson, Alexis Lin, Amy Hagopian, Andrew Bryant, Andrew Lin, Angela Mignone, *Apogee* journal fam, Brett Goldberg, Carrie Sopher, Catherine Cole, Cherry Grove family, Chris Gual, Clarice Wirkala, Claudia Vélez, David Johnson, David Kaplan, Devin Smith, Ed Murray, Elena Jones, Elizabeth Weinstein, Gretchen Strauch, Heera Singh, HESS Committee pals, Ian Douglas, Ileana Méndez-Peñate, Irene Pangilinan, Janko Williams, Jason Barrett, Jason Weinstein, Jeffery Kissinger, Jenna Lanterman, Jennifer Friedman, Jennifer Kidwell, Johanna Freeman, John Nyberg, Justin Rich, Kara Niland, Kitsy Roberts, Kyung-Ji Kate Rhee, Lauren Karchmer, Lauren Ray, Lenna Liu, Lindsay Lyman-Clarke, Loren Merrill, Lorena DeMarco, Lucas Shapiro, Malcolm Sacks, Malika Edden Hill, Margie Mercado, Maricela Ponce, Martín Pelenur, Mary Anne Mercer, Martin Backer, Miguel Gutierrez, Mike Clemow, Mindy Huffman, the Moores (Robin, Mary Margaret, Russell, and Brenda), Naomi Gordon-Loebl, Naybi Sansores Luna, Ora Wise, Paola Morales, Paula Orentraij, People I've Forgotten, Peter Rider, Polly Jirkhovsky, Ramon Davon Coe Kissinger-Johnson, Rebecca Wender, RJ Maccani, Ron Ragin, Saran Simmons, Sharon Cromwell, Sofia Santana, Stephanie Douglass, Stephen Bezruchka, Suzanne Fishel, Tadashi Dozono, Toi Sennhauser, Travis DesAutels, Veena Chintam, Victoria Cho, Victoria Varela, and zavé martohardjono, for cheering me on, for showing up, and for telling other people to show up. Extra love for Akil, David J., Elena, Heera, Ily, Jeffery, Lucas,

Martín, Poli, Radhika, RJ, Saran, and my parents, who are always willing to keep an eye on the kids.

Jerome Foundation, Lower Manhattan Cultural Council, New York Foundation for the Arts, and New York State Council on the Arts, for their early support. The National Book Foundation, for recognizing my work. All the book evangelists, readers, and book-sellers, including Reggie, Minnie, and Lynn, for giving it a platform. Aisha Tandiwe Bell, whose early sketch served as an inspiration for the book cover. Jazmine Sullivan and Bad Bunny, for the hell of it.

Alexander Chee, Danielle Evans, Isle McElroy, Justin Torres, Mat-tilda Bernstein Sycamore, Rosa Hernandez, and Zain Khalid, for saying nice things convincingly. Alex (again), Cleyvis Natera, Dee-sha Philyaw, Kiese Laymon, Nicole Chung, and Robert Jones Jr. for creating platforms for many of us.

And again, Robert Guinsler and Danny Vazquez, for liking these stories from the beginning.

Lastly, I am inspired—consequently my writing is too—by the various people who fight for a collective liberation and who live by the princi-ples of transformative justice. In particular, prison abolitionists; the people who research the effects of chronic stress and hierarchies on societal health; the advocates for reparations for all Black people for the socioeconomic effects of slavery; the people who fight for land back for Indigenous Nations; the organizers and activists who make the case for a $30 minimum wage because that's what it would be if it had increased with inflation, corporate profits, and productivity levels; and the people who agitate for a national health service where all health care workers are government employees. Their work feeds mine.

PHOTO BY ALLISON MICHAEL ORENSTEIN

ABOUT THE AUTHOR

Alejandro Varela (he/him) is a writer based in New York. His writing has appeared in *The Point Magazine, Boston Review, Harper's Magazine, Split Lip Magazine, The Georgia Review, The Rumpus, The Brooklyn Rail, The Offing,* and *The New Republic,* among other publications.

Varela is a 2019 Jerome Fellow in Literature. He was a resident in the Lower Manhattan Cultural Council's 2017–2018 Workspace program and a 2017 NYSCA/NYFA Artist Fellow in Nonfiction and an associate editor at *Apogee Journal.* His graduate studies were in public health. His debut novel, *The Town of Babylon* (2022) was published by Astra House and was a finalist for the 73rd National Book Awards.

Varela believes strongly in reparations, land back, a national health service, and a thirty dollar minimum wage pegged to inflation as interventions essential for the collective liberation of our society. Access his work at alejandrovarela.work. You can also find him on Twitter and IG: @drovarela.